Also by Brenda Hasse

Books for young adults

Wilkinshire

Books for children

Yes, I Am Loved
My Horsy And Me, What Can We Be?
A Unicorn For My Birhday

THE FREELANCER

~

Brenda Hasse

The Freelancer

Copyright © 2014 Brenda Hasse
Cover design and image © 2014 Alison Hatter

This is a work of fiction. All of the characters, names, incidents, organizations, and dialogue in this novel are either the products of the author's imagination or are used fictitiously.

Because of the dynamic nature of the Internet, any Web addresses or links contained in this book may have changed since publication and may no longer be valid. The views expressed in this work are solely those of the author and do not necessarily reflect the views of the publisher, and the publisher hereby disclaims any responsibility for them.

ISBN: 978-0-9906312-0-0 (pbk)

ISBN: 978-0-9906312-1-7 (ebk)

Printed in the United States of America

To Evan, who brings joy and love to my life.

To Jackson, a stray feline who chose me as his keeper.

Chapter 1

Lord William's vision clouded with darkness. His chin sank toward his chest. Teetering on the edge of unconsciousness, he jerked his head upward causing his pet raven, Corvus, to flap his wings and reposition himself upon his master's shoulder. Lord William opened his eyes wide in an attempt to clear his blurred vision, but strands of his untamed, long black hair hung in his face. He tilted his head to the right, shifting his hair away from his eyes, and swayed in his saddle as a wave of lightheadedness threatened to topple him from his horse, Adair. He straightened his right leg in the stirrup and centered his weight upon his steed.

As the trio made their way through the moonlit summer night, they traveled on the dusty road that led them home. Lord William's head rocked from side to side with each step of his ebony war horse. He watched suspicious shadows dance between the trees along the roadside knowing highwaymen preyed on those who traveled at night. As a shadow seemed to lunge toward him, he reached for his sword tilting dangerously in the saddle as he tried to pull it from its sheath, but he was too weak to draw his weapon and collapsed onto Adair's neck.

Corvus flapped his wings, momentarily hovering in the air before landing on his master's back.

Lord William unfolded his fingers, letting the reins slip from his hand and relaxed, for the destrier knew the way home without his guidance. He tangled his fingers into Adair's mane and tried to fight the fuzziness in his head. *So this is what it feels like to die*, he thought as he closed his eyes.

His left arm dangled lifelessly from his shoulder as blood seeped from the saturated bandage, trickled down his arm, and dripped from his fingertip. Lord William prided himself in leading a life of secrecy, but the bloody trail he was leaving was beyond his control.

As he was rocked by the even gait of his horse, the battle with Lord Redmond of Langston replayed in his mind. He had planned his attack carefully and stood behind Lord Redmond's bedchamber door with his sword drawn. As the evening in Langston came to a close, its lord entered his room and closed the door. As Lord William charged, Lord Redmond unsheathed his sword and responded to the challenge bravely. All was in Lord William's favor until a woman entered through the unbolted door and gasped, causing him to look away from his target. His mistake had given Lord Redmond the opportunity to slice his left arm deeply. Angry with himself and his stupidity, Lord William turned in a circle with his sword held chest high. He sliced the woman's throat, pivoted, and thrust his sword into Lord Redmond's heart. He made his way to the castle's sally port, exited, and climbed atop his waiting horse to make his escape into the night. After distancing himself from Langston, he stopped briefly, tore strips of cloth from the bottom of his tunic, and dressed his wound.

The injury would lay him up for some time, that is, if he survived it. Word of Lord Redmond's death would spread quickly, and requests for Lord William's service would come sooner than he would be able to accommodate them. After all, he was of royal blood, a lord without a kingdom, hired to kill. He was a freelancer.

Lord William opened his eyes as he realized Adair had stopped walking. He lifted his head and looked at his surroundings. He recognized the large maple tree at the side of the road and exhaled with relief. *Did I black out or just become lost in thought,* he wondered at their sudden arrival. He straightened himself upright in the saddle and picked up the reins from where they lay upon Adair's neck. Corvus resumed his place upon his master's shoulder as Lord William pulled the reins and nudged his stallion forward with the heel of his boots. The well trained destrier understood his master's signal, turned off of the road, and went into the thick forest.

The pathway was barely visible as they dodged trees and large rocks beneath the canopy of sheltered darkness. They went deep into the forest until they emerged into a clearing. The hut was a welcomed sight with its lit window indicating Rowena had a fire burning in the fireplace. Lord William hoped the old apothecary had leftover stew in a pot warming over the fire.

He dismounted from his horse and held onto the saddle until a wave of lightheadedness passed. Corvus flew to a nearby tree and landed on a branch as Lord William staggered to the hut, pushed open the door, and fell onto the dirt floor unconscious, but safe.

The noise woke Rowena, who rolled over in bed, opened her eyes, and saw Lord William's lifeless body on the floor.

"My goodness, what now?" she said as she pulled back the covers and rose from the cot.

The mystical apothecary examined the mercenary's arm and grew concerned over the amount of blood that continued to seep from the wound. She had treated Lord William's injuries over the years, but this cut was severe and the worst he had ever received.

"My, my, my, you have gotten yourself into trouble this time," she said as she took a ladle hanging from a hook on the mantel. She dipped it into a pot of hot water that hung over the fire, poured the steaming liquid into a wooden bowl, and began pulling jars filled with herbs from the shelves. She knew if his arm became infected, amputation would be necessary or he would die. She called upon her vast knowledge of remedies and pulled a bottle of medicinal oil from a shelf, uncorked the top, and dribbled some of it into the bowl. She stirred until the herbs absorbed the oil and water and formed a paste.

Rowena cleansed the wound, stitched it shut, and applied the poultice. She wrapped his arm with bandages, knowing she had done all she could for now and hoped it was enough to stave off infection and allow the mercenary to keep his arm.

Chapter 2

As the sun peeked over the horizon announcing the dawn of a new day, residents within the kingdom of Thornwick went about their lives as best they could. The livestock received their morning feeding. Crafters set out their wares. Pubs opened their doors and swept what littered their floors into the streets. Peasants made their way toward the fields to tend the crops.

The men of Thornwick's garrison had filled their stomachs with the morning meal and followed Sir Kenneth, who sat atop his horse, to the practice field. The knight reined his destrier and watched the men pass; noting Harlan was the last to arrive and appeared to be in his usual foul mood.

Sir Kenneth knew very little about the tall warrior. Harlan had appeared before him several months ago with a puss-filled cut on his temple and asked to become a member of the castle's defense. With an impressive physique, the knight assumed the new warrior would possess superior fighting skills but soon discovered he fought more like a drunk in a pub brawl. With his piercing chestnut eyes and auburn straw-like hair, those within the garrison believed Harlan was the spawn from the devil himself. Many of the men knew to stay out of his way or suffer the wrath of his brutality.

The men selected their equipment, paired themselves, and began to practice. Harlan grabbed a sturdy wooden practice sword with one hand and two men by the front of their tunics with his other and pulled them to stand before him. The innocent warriors looked to one another, readied their swords, and waited for the attack from their aggressor.

A wicked sneer appeared on Harlan's face. He looked down at his opponents, knowing his height gave him the leverage to deliver merciless strikes and attacked fiercely. The helpless men tried to defend themselves, but were soon lying upon the ground battered and bruised.

"Harlan!" Sir Kenneth said, having witnessed enough of the soldier's cruelty.

Panting from exertion, Harlan lowered his practice sword as he looked down upon his fallen sparring partners who writhed in pain. He gritted his teeth and rolled his eyes skyward before turning his head and glaring at Sir Kenneth.

After surviving most of his solitary life by taking what he needed from others, Harlan despised any command from a superior, especially from Sir Kenneth. He was confident his fighting skills surpassed those of the knight. As sweat beaded upon his brow, Harlan raised his arm and wiped his cheek and forehead. They were still tender and a reminder of that fateful night when the legendary man dressed in black and his companion bird thwarted his attack on his latest victim. He had recalled the sound of flapping wings before a painful scratch impaled his cheek. He touched the scar on his temple, a reminder of the thud that jarred the side of his head before his vision faded to black, and he fell from his horse. Perhaps his unconscious state had saved him, for when he woke the next morning he was lying in tall weeds at the bottom of a dry ditch. With his horse nowhere in sight, he hitched a ride on a passing wagon to Thornwick and hid within the ranks of the garrison to avoid being identified, tortured in a dungeon, and drawn and quartered for his crimes.

"That's enough. Employ yourself elsewhere," Sir Kenneth said as he turned his attention to the quintain.

I would like to employ my blade to your skull, Harlan thought as he stared at the back of Sir Kenneth's head, but redirected his line of sight to watch Farley ride by on his way to the castle. *I wonder what the old wretch is up to now,* Harlan surmised, as he threw down his practice sword and picked up a lance.

Farley, Lord Sheridan's messenger, trotted his horse over the drawbridge, through the bailey of Thornwick, and reined it before the stable. He greeted the stableboy, who was eager to relay a message.

"Lord Sheridan requests your presence at once. I have been told to warn you. He has had too much to drink." The lad reached for the horse's bridle and stroked its nose.

Being of slight build, Farley dismounted easily and looked skyward to locate the sun. *It is not yet midday and he is already drunk,* he thought as he headed toward the Keep as the stableboy led the tired horse away for water and a bucket of oats.

Even though he dreaded the encounter with his lord, Farley quickened his steps with the hope of conveying his loyalty as he entered the empty Great Hall. His eyes were drawn to the back of a carved wooden chair that sat before the fireplace. He assumed the arm that was raising a tankard belonged to Lord Sheridan. Farley approached the chair and knelt onto one knee.

Lord Sheridan lowered his tankard and peered down at his messenger with heavy-lidded bloodshot blue eyes.

"Rise," he said as he looked into his tankard and tipped it upside down. It was empty. "Wench!"

Farley stood and tried to ignore the droplets of wine that had dribbled from Lord Sheridan's mouth, down his graying beard, and rolled over his bulbous belly.

A serving wench scurried into the Great Hall, filled her lord's tankard, curtsied, and left.

Lord Sheridan tried to focus on his full tankard as he moved the mug in small circles and swirled the spiced red wine. He took a long swig and forced it down his throat as if it was painful for him to swallow. He ran his hand over his stomach and attempted to pull a coherent thought through the distorted fog within his mind. He reached into his shirt and withdrew a sealed missive.

"Please deliver this immediately," he said, slurring his words.

Farley took it and bowed.

Lord Sheridan waved his hand indicating the messenger should leave his presence.

Farley left quickly. Once out of Lord Sheridan's sight, he glanced at the missive and rolled his eyes skyward. It was addressed to Lady Christine of Wildenham. *What a waste of my time*, he thought as he looked back at his intoxicated lord before exiting the Great Hall.

The logs in the fireplace snapped and crackled, drawing Lord Sheridan's attention from his mug. He became lost in thought as he stared as if hypnotized by the mesmerizing flames. He drank another gulp of his wine and allowed his eyes to scan the decrepit, dirty walls of the Great Hall. The baron had granted him the lesser kingdom of Thornwick and cast him into a life of wanting and loneliness. How he resented the baron's decision and wished he had obtained the glorious kingdom of Wildenham instead.

A smug smile donned his face as he recalled the day he received word that Lord Bradford's son, William, the only heir to Wildenham, had disappeared. Search parties scanned the kingdom and beyond, but the young lord was never found. With Lord Bradford consumed by grief over the loss of his son, Lord Sheridan sensed an opportunity and devised a plan to overthrow Wildenham, kill Lord Bradford, and take the kingdom as his own. Before his plan could come to fruition, he was informed by Farley that Lord Clayborn had overthrown Wildenham, killed Lord Bradford, and become the new Lord of Wildenham. Once learning Lord Clayborn's only heir was female, Lord Sheridan's easiest recourse to obtain Wildenham was to pursue Lord Clayborn's daughter, Lady Christine, who was of proper age for marriage. He sent a missive requesting an audience with Lord Clayborn and the offer of his hand in marriage to his daughter. His messenger returned with a reply that conveyed his visit and offer were both refused. Believing he could convince the young and naive Lady Christine into marriage, he sent his messenger with his offer to her directly, but she refused as well. He continued to send a missive every year offering his hand in marriage, but her reply remained steadfast and unchanging.

Lord Sheridan tapped his left hand's fingertips on the arm of the chair as he raised his mug, took another sip of wine, and drained the tankard dry.

"Wench, more wine!" He held his tankard over the arm of his chair and could hear the servant's shuffling feet as she hurried toward him. He waited as she filled his tankard and left.

He took a long drink and sighed. *If you refuse me again, Lady Christine, you will regret your decision.* His head tilted toward his shoulder as his eyes fell shut. His tankard tipped to the side, and its contents spilled to the floor as a deafening snore resonated throughout the room.

Chapter 3

Farley went to the kitchen and enjoyed a delicious meal before requesting a fresh horse at the stable to begin his journey to Wildenham. He breathed a sigh of relief as he climbed atop his stallion and rode away from the demands of Lord Sheridan. He traveled at a leisurely, comfortable pace, spent the night camped off the roadside and rose early to continue his journey. It was a pleasant morning as he and his horse crested a hill and Wildenham came into view. *Such a nice kingdom,* he thought as he passed some of the residents on his way to the castle. *Even the peasants seem to be happy and healthy.* He looked up at the flags and banners flapping in the wind as he crossed Wildenham's drawbridge, reined his horse, and gave his name at the gatehouse. While he waited, he estimated the sun at midday. When allowed by the guard to proceed, he touched his heel to his horse's belly encouraging it into a slow walk through the baileys. He admired the splendor of the shops and establishments and gave little concern for the rumors of Lord Bradford's spirit haunting the castle. With his stomach empty and his body weary from the ride, he was looking forward to a delicious meal and hoped to receive an invitation for a restful sleep in a cozy chamber for the night. He reined his horse before the stable and was greeted by one of the stableboys. Farley almost grinned at the eager freckled-faced redhead whose blue eyes seemed to sparkle.

"Another missive from Thornwick?" The lad reached for the horse's bridle.

"Good day, Conal. Yes, for Lady Christine," Farley said.

"She is at the practice field. Let me get my pony. I shall escort you there." Conal went into the stable and returned moments later mounted on a little fuzzy brown pony.

They rode to the practice field, dismounted, and waited patiently while they watched an impish warrior thrust a wooden sword toward a towering knight. The attempt was weak and easily batted aside by the knight causing his attacker to become off balance. With a pause in the sparring, the stableboy approached the smaller of the two warriors and bowed.

"My lady." Conal requested her attention respectfully.

Lady Christine lowered her practice sword as she removed her helmet and tossed it to the ground. Long blonde locks fell down her back. She took a moment to catch her breath as her chest heaved from the exertion of training with her father's knight, Sir Farrell. She straightened her tunic, let out a disgusted sigh, and looked toward the stableboy.

"Yes Conal, what is it?" Her narrowed brown eyes conveyed her impatience, for she despised interruptions during her practice.

"A messenger from Thornwick, my lady." Conal motioned his hand toward the blonde haired, blue eyed man standing behind him.

"Thank you, Conal." She tapped her practice sword impatiently against her leg as the stableboy bowed, dismissed himself, and returned to the castle. She shifted her eyes to look at the messenger.

Farley stepped forward and knelt onto one knee. Returning to a standing position, he said, "Lady Christine, I have been instructed by Lord Sheridan to deliver this to you." The messenger reached into the fold of his cape. Sir Farrell dropped his practice sword and grabbed the hilt of his sword. The messenger's eyes focused on the knight's hand and then his face. Farley withdrew the missive carefully before handing it to Lady Christine.

"Farley, isn't it?" She inquired pertly, trying to recall the messenger's name.

"Yes, my lady." Farley nodded his head in affirmation while still holding the missive for her to accept.

Lady Christine tossed her practice sword to Sir Farrell, whose quick reflexes allowed him to snatch the wooden sword from the air. She knew what the missive contained, but accepted it with a nod, opened, and read it. She shook her head in disbelief. Her eyes looked skyward in disgust. She pressed her lips together, making a frown. It was another request for her hand in marriage from Lord Sheridan. *Is he daft*, she wondered.

She looked down and examined the scribbled message as cruel rumors crept into her mind. She was quite aware of the whispered gossip that circulated within Wildenham's walls. They were vicious misgivings suggesting she lacked the qualities of a good wife, she was incapable of recognizing a proper husband, and her father had too high a standard for any man who would take his beloved daughter away from him. *Perhaps I am incapable of recognizing a suitable man,* she thought. Her previous relationship with a handsome gentleman came to an abrupt, heart-crushing end when she discovered his lustful affection for his cousin. The fiasco had hurt her deeply, and she vowed never to trust another man with her heart until she was confident of his worthiness and love. She knew a lifetime with Lord Sheridan would be unbearable and intolerable. She would never love him.

She looked up from the missive to Farley. *Perhaps Lord Sheridan possesses a thick head and needs a more poignant and blunt response,* she thought. She spit on the missive, folded it in half, and gave it back to the messenger.

Farley's eyes widened as he looked at the wet reply and accepted it from her hand. He knew Lord Sheridan would be angry and feared his wrath from such a response.

"My Lady." Sir Farrell protested. "Your father…"

She snapped her head toward the knight.

"Does not need to know or be troubled with another silly request. Is that clear?" She grabbed her practice sword from the knight's hand.

"Yes, my lady." Sir Farrell agreed as he watched her turn her head back to the messenger before retrieving his practice sword from the ground.

"You may go," she said as she strutted past Farley, who was too stunned to move. She attempted to toss her practice sword onto the pile with the others, but it fell short and landed on the ground with its pointed blade leaning against a rock. Disgusted with her bad throw, Lady Christine marched over to the misguided sword and stomped upon the blade causing it to break in half and spin toward her head. Her eyes clouded with blackness as the broken blade hit her squarely on the temple. She closed her eyes and tried to remain standing as she teetered from side to side.

Many of the men snickered, turned their back toward their lady, and hoped she would remain ignorant of their disrespectful display of amusement.

Lady Christine recovered her senses as the dizziness eased and her vision became clear. She touched the raised bump on her temple as she glanced toward the garrison to see if any of the men laughed, but found most had their backs toward her. She jerked the reins from the hitching post, climbed onto her waiting horse, and spurred it in the direction of the castle.

Farley stared in disbelief at the feisty young lady who rode away. He had never witnessed a woman command men with such authority.

Sir Farrell cleared his throat, bringing Farley back to reality. The messenger looked at the towering knight, nodded his head, and departed obediently. As he climbed upon his tired horse, he looked toward the Keep protectively ensconced within the castle walls and faced the reality of eating jerky for his evening meal and sleeping in the woods somewhere along the roadside on his way back to Thornwick. He imagined Lord Sheridan's livid reaction to Lady Christine's reply and wished he could delay his return.

With his lady in a sour mood, Sir Farrell threw his practice sword onto the pile, climbed atop his horse, and followed her at a distance. As a loyal servant to Lord Clayborn, he accepted the difficult responsibility as Lady Christine's guardian, but there were times he wished he had the authority to bend her over his knee and spank her backside.

Both lady and knight rode to the castle in silence and dismounted at the stable. Thomas and Conal came forward, accepted the reins, and led their horses away.

Sir Farrell avoided eye contact with his lady as they made their way to the Keep. He knew she would speak her mind, but preferred she remain silent.

As they stepped into the privacy of the Keep, Lady Christine turned her head to look over her shoulder at the knight who walked only a step behind her.

"Honestly Sir Farrell, who does Lord Sheridan think he is? The man is old and disgusting."

And it begins, he thought.

"Yes, my lady." Sir Farrell looked to the ceiling as he followed her through the hallway and into the Great Hall. He had listened to her disdainful opinion of Lord Sheridan and men in general too many times before. There was little point in disagreeing with her. He wished she would see reason. Being the only child of Lord Clayborn and a female, she must marry a husband, who would become the new Lord of Wildenham. The union would allow her to reside in the kingdom upon her father's death. Otherwise, Wildenham would be granted to a lord or knight of the baron's choosing.

"Don't you, 'yes, my lady,' me. I know what you are thinking. I should take a husband so that I can remain in Wildenham upon my father's death. I will take a husband when one worthy enough comes along! That is if one exists!" Lady Christine stomped up the staircase that led to her bedchamber.

Sir Farrell stood at the bottom of the staircase and watched her ascend.

"Sir Farrell, is my daughter giving you a difficult time?" Lord Clayborn walked toward his favored knight, stood next to him, and clasped his hands behind his back as he watched his daughter climb the staircase.

Sir Farrell looked down upon his lord's balding head.

"No, my lord, she is a bit miffed is all." Sir Farrell avoided the true reason for his lady's emotional state.

"Miffed? What has set her off this time?"

"My lord, I believe men in general."

They both chuckled.

"She turns eighteen in a few weeks." Lord Clayborn sighed at the reality.

"Yes, my lord."

"It is difficult to believe she is a young woman. It seems it was only yesterday she was a little girl. So very much like her mother, she is, in both beauty and strong mindedness."

More like bullheadedness, Sir Farrell thought.

"I wish her mother were still with us. She would be proud." Lord Clayborn smiled and turned to Sir Farrell expecting him to agree.

"Yes, my lord. If you excuse me, I have duties to attend."

"Yes, yes. Don't let me keep you." Lord Clayborn dismissed as Sir Farrell bowed and left the Great Hall.

Lord Clayborn watched his daughter cross the balcony and disappear behind the wall of the hallway. He became aware of someone in his peripheral vision standing to his left. The hair on the back of his neck stood on end. When he turned his head expecting to find a servant, he caught a glimpse of a shadowed figure disappearing into a closed doorway.

A scratching noise by the fireplace caused him to turn toward the sound. Lord Clayborn ducked quickly as an empty tankard that had been sitting on a small table next to his chair went flying through the air toward his head. It smashed into the staircase behind him and tumbled down the remaining steps.

"Wretched ghost." Lord Clayborn stated aloud to himself. "This is my kingdom! Leave me alone!" He ordered before leaving the Great Hall and going to his library, hoping the spirit would respect his request.

Chapter 4

Lady Christine stormed into her bedchamber leaving the door open in her wake. Enid and Gilda, her ladies in waiting, set aside their needlework and rose quickly from the window seat.

Roaming through the hallway, her overweight cat, Jackson, had recognized his mistress's agitated, heavy stride and headed in the direction of her bedchamber. His belly swung from side to side as he quickened his pace and paused next to the doorway trying to determine if it was safe to enter the room. He resembled a little bandit donning a mask with his blotched black and white face as he peeked into the room.

"Your bath has been prepared, my lady." Enid was quick to ascertain her lady's nasty disposition. She bent over the chair next to the tub and tidied the scented soaps and linen towels. Her blue eyes peered through her long flowing blonde hair and watched Lady Christine pace the bedchamber. Well disciplined at her youthful age, she knew to remain silent and focus on her duties.

"Let me warm it for you." Gilda smiled and tried to appear cheery as she picked up a bucket of steaming water and dumped it into the tub. Her stout build accommodated the heavy bucket with ease. Several years older than her lady, Gilda closed her hazel eyes, sighed, and decided to risk a tongue lashing. She set the bucket upon the floor, flung her brunette locks over her shoulder, and approached the impending subject.

"Did your practice with Sir Farrell go well?"

"It went very well until it was interrupted by another missive from Lord Sheridan. Is that man totally daft? As if I would ever marry him!" Lady Christine kicked off her boot and it flew across her bedchamber.

"And understandably so, my lady, he is as old as your father and pales in comparison to his handsomeness." Enid agreed as she retrieved her lady's boot, ducking as the second came flying in her direction.

Jackson waddled into the bedchamber, jumped onto the window seat, and began to give himself a bath. He struggled to reach the inside of his hind legs as he scrunched his body around his bulging belly.

Enid noticed the cat and realized the bedchamber door was still open. She picked up the second boot, walked over to the door, and closed it.

Both women managed to undress the layers of sweaty practice attire from their lady while they listened to her vent her frustration.

"Who does he think he is? Father declined his offer and I have done so several times." Lady Christine lowered herself into the hot water and leaned her head back onto the rim of the tub. Gilda placed a bucket under her lady's head and began to wash her hair.

Lady Christine noticed her feline friend and let out a sigh as if to release the tension of the day.

"Jackson, have you caught any mice today?"

The chubby feline paused in his grooming, looked at her as if she were ignorant, ignored her question, and continued with his bath.

"Fear not, my lady. I am confident providence will provide you with the perfect husband someday and then your father's prayers will be answered." Enid commented as she selected a dress from the chest for Lady Christine to wear. She laid it upon the bed and brushed the full skirt with her hands to straighten the wrinkles and make it presentable for the evening meal.

"I am beginning to doubt there is one suitable." Lady Christine conceded as she wiggled her toes in the water. "It will ultimately be my choice as to whom I marry, not one forced upon me by my father."

Lady Christine's attention was drawn to the top corner of her bedchamber where a shadowed mist lingered.

"Enid, I think it is time to get the sage and smudge the room again," she said without fear as she watched the dark mist disappear into the wall. Even though he was a resident of the Keep, the ghost of Lord Bradford was unwelcome in her bedchamber, especially during her bath.

Lady Christine emerged from the tub, toweled herself dry, and dressed in a pale blue gown trimmed with silver stitching. She went to the Great Hall and sat next to her father at the High Table for the evening meal. She kept her eyes downcast at her plate, for when she dared to take a glimpse of those in the room, there were ogling eyes staring back at her as if she was a china doll on display. After having her day ruined by the unexpected missive, it took several tankards of warm, spiced wine to settle her nerves. Once she finished her evening meal, she returned to her bedchamber and looked forward to an undisturbed, restful sleep where she dreamt of walking down the chapel aisle wearing her beautiful ivory wedding dress while staring into the loving eyes of her future husband. How unfortunate that it was only a dream.

Chapter 5

Emerging from sleep, Lord William turned his head toward the window and was greeted by midmorning beams of sunlight. As if the brightness was painful, he squeezed his eyelids together and rotated his head away from the light. He blinked his dry, gritty eyes several times until the loft where he usually slept came into focus. He tried to stretch out his legs, but they touched the end of the bed before he could fully straighten them. Reaching for the wall, he felt the cold stone and realized he was lying on Rowena's smaller cot. He ran his tongue over his cracked lips as the popping of the fire echoed within the tiny building. *How long have I been laying here,* he wondered as he recalled his last coherent thought of opening the door to the hut before all went black. Turning his head ever so slowly, he scanned the room to see if Rowena was within its walls, but all that came into view were the many shelves of bottles that contained herbs that she used for healing, a table with two chairs, and a fireplace. He was alone. His sword was propped in the corner of the room by the foot of the bed. His left arm throbbed and smelled rancid. He assumed the horrific odor emanated from the type of swamp grass or herb the old woman had used to treat his wound. He wiggled his fingers on his left hand and flexed them a few times. All seemed to be in working order.

The door of the hut opened. Rowena's shadowed figure stood within the doorway. Corvus flew around the old woman, into the hut, and perched on the back of a chair. The elderly apothecary carried a large basket filled with various herbs she had gathered. She entered the hut and shut the door. Her hunched shoulders seemed to lower as she focused her grayish-blue eyes and looked toward the cot to inspect her patient.

"Ah, I sensed you had awakened." Rowena set her basket upon the table, went to the fireplace, and picked up the poker to stir the charred logs. "Are you hungry?" She reached for another log and set it upon the fire.

"No, but I need something to quench my thirst." Lord William tried to moisten his cracked lips with his dry tongue again as he looked to the pitcher and pair of mugs upon the table.

Rowena filled a mug with cool water.

"How did I get on the cot?" He inquired as he eased himself along the wall to an upright position. Black spots appeared before his hazel eyes and his head seemed to float from his body.

"You do not remember?" She made her way to the cot.

"No." He replied in a raspy whisper. He closed his eyes, hoping to make the room stop spinning. Unsure if his body was tipping to one side, he opened his eyes for verification as Rowena knelt upon the bed and helped steady Lord William upright against the wall. She held the mug to his lips for him to drink.

"I helped you rise from the floor and get into bed. That was several days ago. Since that time, you had run a good fever and slept." Rowena brushed Lord William's black hair away from his face and felt his forehead. It was still warm. "Just rest there a bit and let me take a look at your arm." Rowena placed the mug into his right hand and began to untie the bandages gently. She looked at Lord William's face and noted his white complexion.

Lord William closed his eyes again and leaned his head back against the wall. He gave into the blackness and let his body fall into the dark abyss. Downward he fell as the pain from his cut brought to the forefront a childhood memory. He saw Wilfred, his former steward, standing before him.

"Your father requests your presence in the Great Hall. Be brave, young Lord William."

He entered the silent Great Hall, walked by those in attendance, and stood before his father whose breath reeked of alcohol. Knowing he would soon become the evening's entertainment, he refused to look his father in the eye.

The Lord of Wildenham whipped his arm through the air like a sword slicing soft butter, backhanded his son across the face, and watched as the child fell to the floor.

"Where did you get that black hair, boy? Neither your mother nor I possess such a color of hair. Perhaps she was unfaithful. You look like a weak misfit, an abnormal piece of humanity, a monster of evil." Lord Bradford ridiculed, but no one laughed.

Little Lord William used the sleeve of his tunic to wipe away the blood from the corner of his mouth. Unsure of what expectation he failed to achieve, he assumed his father intended to send him to the dungeon to have his back stripped bare and beaten again. But as he looked up, a wench had intervened and handed his father another tankard of ale and whispered into his ear. His father took a large gulp from the mug, smiled as he hugged the wench closely, and jerked his head toward the doorway indicating he could leave the Great Hall.

He climbed the staircase and entered his mother's bedchamber. He crawled onto her bed, curled into a fetal position, and cried. *How I wish you were still here mother*, he thought. The fragrance of lilac still lingered on her pillow. It made her seem near as if she may be watching over him. He remembered the last time he had lain next to her. She had been very hot to the touch. Within a few days, she took her last breath leaving him in the care of his father at the very young age of four. Opening his eyes, he wiped the tears from his cheeks and spotted the heart he had carved into the wooden mantel of the fireplace. It had been a gift for her.

After his embarrassment had turned to anger, he sat upright, wiped the tears from his face again as he got out of her bed and walked to the secret door. He pushed a sequence of hand-carved wooden rosettes within each panel until he heard a click. He opened the panel door, walked through the small passage, and opened the panel door to his father's bedchamber. He saw his father's sword lying on a bench by the window. He looked down at it in disgust. He had planned this for a long time and had thought of taking his father's sword for revenge, but decided he wanted no part of his father or his kingdom, ever. He returned to the passage, closed both paneled doors enclosing himself within the passageway. He began pushing several carved wooden rosettes on the wall between the portals until he heard a click. He opened the door, entered his father's secret treasury room, and pushed the door shut. There was a fancy cot, desk, night stand, and several chests of coins stacked against the wall. The long and narrow room had a window on the opposite wall. There was also a narrow stairway next to the window that led downstairs. Since the room is behind the fireplaces of both bedchambers, it usually stayed warm even in the coldest of winter nights.

He opened one of the chests, took large handfuls of coins, and put them into his belt bag until it was full. He shut the chest and stepped to his father's desk. He opened the top right drawer and found a small wooden box under the false bottom. Opening the box, he took his mother's amethyst and diamond wedding ring and put it in his belt bag as well. He closed the box and drawer, went to the stairway where he took one last look at his father's room, and wondered if he would notice the missing coins and ring. In truth, he was beyond caring. He descended the stairs into darkness and felt for the latch on the wooden door. He pulled the portal open, entered the closet where he slept within the kitchen, and closed the secret door. He took his sword and slingshot from pegs on the wall and opened the door to the kitchen where the serving peasants were cleaning up from the evening meal. He spotted Libby, the head cook, who always made sure he was fed and cared for properly.

"Libby, could you pack a pouch of food and wine for me. I believe I will go hunting this evening." Lord William lied as he leaned against the table to look into a crock for a bit to eat. His belt bag bumped against the table's edge causing the coins to jingle. Libby looked at the bulging belt bag and then to Lord William's face.

"Hunting, you say. Very few creatures are hunted in the night," she said as she noticed the young lord held within his hands his sword and slingshot. "And what might you be hunting?" She spit on the corner of her apron and wiped the blood from the edge of his mouth.

"I'm not sure."

"Come with me," she said as she took the young lad by his hand, led him into a storage room, and shut the door. She took a leather bag from a hook on the wall and filled it with cheese, jerky, a few apples, and bread. She set the bag of food on the floor and held out her hand.

"Give me your belt bag."

He hesitated, but then unfastened the heavy small pouch and handed it to her.

Taking two pieces of cloth from the shelf, she took the belt bag from Lord William's hand, dumped half of the coins onto one piece of cloth and the remainder of the coins onto the other. She noted the ring, but kept her comment to herself. Libby took a few coins from each pile and put them back into the belt bag.

"Put this back on and tie it tightly," she said as she handed the belt bag to him, and he attached it to his belt. She tied each of the cloths closed, stooped down, and put a cloth in each of his boots.

The young lord had endured his abuse for nearly seven years. Perhaps Lord Bradford thought his brutal parenting would toughen his son and make a man of him. As a servant, Libby disagreed with his parenting technique, but had to remain silent or lose her position on the kitchen staff. She knew of other children who survived on their own and some of them were younger than little Lord William's age. The young lord had led a sheltered life, but she realized his determination to leave Wildenham was unstoppable.

"Now, please take care and when darkness falls, take to the woods." She selected a flask of wine, picked up the leather bag of food, draped them over his shoulder, and hugged him before opening the door.

"Thank you, Libby." He made his way to the stable and had Adair, his two year old war horse, saddled by a stableboy. He mounted his steed, rode through the baileys, crossed the drawbridge before it was raised at dusk, and disappeared into the impending night. He could only imagine his father's rage when he discovered his only son, the heir to Wildenham, had left the castle without his permission.

Lord William reined his destrier and looked back at Wildenham from the crest of a distant hill. He recalled the countless beatings from his father, the orders he gave to have him dragged kicking and screaming to the dungeon to have his shirt ripped from his body, his arms chained to a wall, and his back whipped until he bled. Never again would he have to endure such beatings. He breathed a sigh as a heavy burden lifted from his shoulders. He vowed never to return as he reined Adair away from Wildenham and kicked his horse into a gallop.

In order to increase his distance from Wildenham and his father, he ignored Libby's advice and traveled through the night instead of camping safely in the woods away from the roadside. He had lived his entire life within the protection of Wildenham's walls and was unaware of the robbers who preyed on others for survival. In the dead of the night as he struggled to keep his eyes open while Adair walked down the road at a leisurely pace, a group of men had surrounded him quickly and spooked his horse. Adair reared and kicked his front legs in the air throwing him to the ground before running away in fear. As the young lord looked into the eyes of the men who surrounded him, he realized his sword was strapped to Adair's saddle. He was defenseless. The robbers punched and hit him until he saw only darkness.

An elderly hand shook his body, forcing him to open his swollen eyes and stare into the face of a wrinkled, little old lady with unruly gray hair. He realized it was daylight and he was lying on the side of the road. Little Lord William felt for his belt bag, but it was gone. He looked to his boots. He was still fully dressed. As he lifted himself from the ground, his vision blurred and his head ached. He saw Adair grazing by the side of the road, limped to his horse, and took hold of his bridle.

"I am an apothecary and can tend to your bumps and bruises, but you will need to come with me to my hut so that I may remedy your ailments," Rowena said as she pointed in the direction of her home.

He touched his swollen eye and had to admit, she made him feel uneasy as she stared at him with eyes nearly the same color as her hair. Her ragged clothes reminded him of cleaning rags strung onto a drying line and wrapped around her body. Going back to Wildenham was out of the question. His father would only add more bumps and bruises to the ones he already had.

"I accept your offer. Thank you." He led Adair and followed the apothecary, matching her slow, leisurely pace.

They walked in silence down the road until they came to a mighty maple tree. She turned into the dense woods. He followed, leading Adair. They wove their way to a clearing that contained a hut made of stone topped with a thatched roof. He noticed a small crooked building to the left surrounded by a fence made from cut saplings. The enclosed goat looked in his direction as it chewed a mouthful of grass. Having nowhere else to tie Adair, he led him to the corral and opened a section of the fence. He encouraged his horse inside and closed the fence for safe keeping. Entering the open door of the hut cautiously, his eyes were drawn to the many shelves containing bottles and small crocks. She pointed to a chair. He sat while she applied herbs and a salve to his wounds and gave him a large mug of water and a bowl of steaming chicken stew that had been cooking in a pot over the fire. The aroma from the bowl made his stomach grumble. He ate a bite of the stew and his mouth filled with spices that burst with flavor.

"This is delicious," he said, before taking another bite.

She nodded in recognition of his compliment and watched him consume the meal ravenously while returning the bottles of herbs and salve to the shelves.

When Lord William had finished his meal, he stood and handed her the empty bowl and mug.

"Thank you," he said as he reached into one of his boots, withdrew and opened the cloth, and was relieved to find only coins. He would keep the secret of his mother's ring for he feared being labeled a thief and returned to Wildenham. He selected a few of the coins and offered them to her as payment for her services and food.

"No, thank you, but I do need some firewood gathered and split." She searched his face for an answer. He began to smile.

"I would be glad to do so." He left the hut, gathered some wood from the forest, and returned placing the timber next to the fireplace.

"May I offer you a place to stay, here with me, for as long as you like?" Rowena raised her eyebrows inquisitively.

He considered the apothecary's offer and knew he had nowhere else to go.

"I accept."

A sharp pain in his arm brought Lord William through the darkness and back to reality. He opened his eyes and raised his head from the wall.

"Your wound is healing well," Rowena said as she continued to wash away the herbal poultice and inspect the stitches.

Lord William glanced at the injury. Her stitches were neat and tidy even though he was certain her hands had shaken during the delicate task.

"I'm going to make another poultice and redress your arm. Then I will get you a bowl of rabbit stew and some bread." She patted his hand.

"That sounds good. Do we have any wine?" He hoped for something stronger than the water to dull the pain.

"Yes, but I am not telling you where I keep my stash." She chuckled as she got off the cot, grabbed a wooden bowl, took a handful of flaxseed from a crock, and dropped it into the vessel.

He smiled at her jesting for it was a standing joke between them. She had limited the amount of drink he was allowed as a young lad and continued to do so. Perhaps her husband had been one to overindulge and it brought back unpleasant memories for her. He respected her decision and had to admit, he preferred the fresh, cool water drawn from the creek behind the hut over the wine. He watched as she crushed and ground the flaxseed with a pestle and stirred while she added hot water from the kettle that was kept over the fire in the fireplace.

She uncorked a bottle that contained sweet oil, selected some clean bandages from a basket that sat on the floor below the table, and joined him on the cot. Rowena applied the sweet oil to the wound. She spread the warm poultice onto the cloth, placed it upon the injury, and wrapped it securely with strips of cloth. The poultice would draw any infection from the stitched area and surrounding tissue.

"It needs time to heal." Rowena announced as she walked across the room and set the bottle of sweet oil, bowl, and pestle onto the table.

Rowena ladled some steaming rabbit stew into the wooden bowl and shoved a crudely carved wooden spoon into its center. She took the empty mug from Lord William and set the stew in his lap. Rowena refilled the mug, moved a wooden stool next to the bed, and set the tankard on the stool so he could reach it.

Still thirsty, Lord William picked up the tankard, took a long drink, and returned it to the stool before he ate a spoonful of stew. The stew was hot. He exhaled rapidly in an attempt to prevent the heat from burning his tongue.

"It's good." He complimented before swallowing and forcing himself to eat another bite.

Rowena smiled as she turned and grabbed a ball of twine from a basket on a shelf. She selected a small bunch of freshly cut herbs, bound the stems, and hung them from the mantel to dry. The apothecary retrieved a wide-mouthed bottle from a shelf and uncorked it. She selected a dried bunch of herbs from the mantel, stripped the leaves from the stem, and placed them in the bottle. She threw the stems into the fire and the aroma of mint filled the air. She corked the bottle and returned it to the shelf.

Corvus watched her movements but was distracted by the smell of Lord William's stew. He fluttered over to the cot, perched himself on the headboard, and waited patiently for what may be left over in his master's bowl once he had finished eating.

Lord William chewed a chunk of rabbit meat and stared at a spot on the floor. *Why is it always the same dream?* He sighed and tried to shake off the haunted feeling by focusing on Rowena, who was busy harvesting another herb, but the dream seemed to continue even though he was awake.

The apothecary's age seemed suspended in time, for she looked the same as the day their lives had converged nearly a decade ago. Life with Rowena had agreed with him even though some of the aspects of his childhood within Wildenham's walls had been advantageous too. His father had insisted his military training begin at the young age of five and pushed Father Frederick to accelerate his education. Over the years when Lord William's anger overtook his good nature, he honed his fighting skills and trained while recalling all he had been taught by Wildenham's knights. With each slash and thrust of his sword, he envisioned his father and the robbers in each dead tree he encountered as he parried his way through the woods. He made a habit of patrolling the road at night and robbers soon fled in fear as they became aware of the lone swordsman dressed in black who terrorized their way of life.

Over time, Lord William earned a reputation as a nameless mercenary. Those who wished to pay for his services learned through word of mouth that Rowena was his contact and approximately where to find her along the dusty road between Wildenham and Bristolwood. After the mercenary had completed each task, his payment was given to her directly or left at the base of a tree she indicated when receiving the request. Those who hired the mercenary always followed through with their prompt payment, for they feared he would seek them out and collect his fee by spilling their blood.

A few years after Lord William had left Wildenham, Rowena received word that his father, Lord Bradford, had been killed, and Lord Clayborn was its new lord. Lord William was relieved to hear his father was dead and another had claimed the kingdom as their own. His present lifestyle suited him well. His earnings as a freelancer had filled several chests that were hidden under the stone of the hearth of the fireplace.

Lord William looked to the hearth and turned to see Corvus waiting patiently as the raven examined the bowl's contents. Having eaten all that he could, he set the bowl on the stool and picked up the tankard.

Corvus hopped down from the headboard, stood on the stool, and began to eat the leftovers in the bowl.

Lord William's arm throbbed. *Did I make a foolish mistake that nearly cost me my life? Did I misstep or stumble*, he wondered as questions entered his mind. Whatever the reason, he had turned his back to his opponent, a deadly mistake indeed.

"How long?" he asked.

"How long what?" Rowena knew what he wanted to hear, but she would answer his question honestly.

"How long before I am fit to fight again?"

"As long as it takes, but I will do my best to accelerate the healing."

"I have a feeling it will not be quick enough for those who demand my service." Lord William drank the last of the water, set the tankard on the stool, lay back upon the pillow, and closed his eyes to rest.

Chapter 6

Farley trotted his horse into the inner bailey of Thornwick. It was the middle of the afternoon as he reined it before the stable. A stableboy came running forward before the messenger could dismount.

"Lord Sheridan said to tell you he is at the practice field with the garrison."

Farley nodded his head in acknowledgment, turned his horse around, and sighed. He had risen before sunrise after enduring a sleepless night tormented by nightmares of his lord's reaction to Lady Christine's reply. He chuckled to himself in admiration of the lady's spunk as he trotted his horse through the castle and toward Lord Sheridan and Sir Kenneth, who sat upon their stallions in the distant field. The knight was pointing at a large soldier who dominated his sparring partner.

Harlan's opponent fell down upon the ground. With his lord observing, he paused to catch his breath, stood tall, and glared in the direction of the two men.

Ungrateful bastards, he thought as he spotted the arriving messenger. He watched as the Lord of Thornwick turned his head in the direction of the sound of hoof beats.

Farley reined his horse before his lord and wished he could melt into his saddle.

"Back already, Farley?" Lord Sheridan sat a little taller in anticipation of good news.

The messenger's hand shook as he took the missive out of his belt bag and handed it to Lord Sheridan.

"My lord, here is Lady Christine's reply." Farley reined his horse a few steps away from his lord and braced himself for his reaction.

"A favorable one I presume." Lord Sheridan opened the missive and confusion masked his face. He looked to the messenger for an explanation.

"What is this? I do not see a reply."

Sir Kenneth's attention was drawn from the sparring men to the damp missive.

"She did not write a reply, my lord. She spat into it and handed it back to me."

Lord Sheridan's eyes enlarged. His face turned red. He began to breathe heavily and puff up his chest as if he were a tea kettle ready to sound its whistle. He threw the missive on the ground and looked at Farley with narrowed eyes.

"Come with me." Lord Sheridan ordered as he turned his horse in the direction of the castle and spurred it into a gallop. Farley followed obediently.

They entered the outer bailey at a wicked pace as those within the castle walls scampered aside to avoid being trampled. Reining their horses before the stable, Lord Sheridan dismounted and walked with commanding strides with his bulbous belly waddling from side to side and leaving his messenger to follow in his wake. He entered his library and went to his desk. Grabbing parchment, pen and ink, he wrote a missive and sealed it with wax. He picked up the missive and cast his narrowed eyes upon the messenger who bit his lower lip and fidgeted as if he needed to use the garderobe.

"On the road south of Wildenham toward Bristolwood, there is an old woman with long white hair; a mystical apothecary of some sort. She is a friend of a mercenary, a man who is legendary, dresses in black, and has a pet raven that is known to sit upon his shoulder." Lord Sheridan handed the missive to Farley. "Deliver this to her by tomorrow morning and report to me upon your return." He instructed.

The messenger nodded in understanding, took the missive, and exited the room like a scared cat. Once in the hallway, he realized he had been holding his breath and exhaled. Farley walked toward the stable. His body ached reminding him that he needed to rest. In order to deliver the missive by morning, he would have to travel the dangerous roads through the night with a fresh horse. After instructing the stableboy to saddle a rested steed, he took the opportunity to return to the Keep and sneak into the kitchen without being seen by Lord Sheridan. Farley helped himself to a bowl of stew, sat on a stool, and ate. While he pondered his next assignment, he paused in chewing as a question entered his mind.

Is Lord Sheridan hiring a mercenary to kill Lady Christine? He took another bite of stew and chewed. *But for what purpose would he want her dead?* He swallowed and took another bite. *Revenge for her refusal to accept his hand in marriage, perhaps?*

He shrugged his shoulders and finished his meal. He set the bowl in a bucket filled with dirty dishes and entered a storage room. Taking a leather pouch from a peg on the wall, he filled it with food and grabbed a flask of wine. He closed the door to the room before leaving the kitchen.

I will travel until just after dusk and then set up camp. As far as I am concerned, Lord Sheridan's missive can wait until I have had a good night's sleep. If nothing else, my delay will lengthen Lady Christine's life, he thought as he left the Keep and returned to the stable. He looked skyward and sighed. The clouds seemed heavy with rain.

Chapter 7

A gentle rain had fallen during the night. Rowena had made a tea of chamomile and lavender for her patient to drink before they retired. With Lord William sleeping soundly in the loft, Rowena opened the door of the hut and inhaled the damp freshness of the day. She wanted to harvest a few herbs before they bloomed. She carried a basket that contained a sharp knife and ventured out into the sunshine. Rowena closed her eyes, tilted her wrinkled face skyward, and took another deep, cleansing breath. As the midmorning sun warmed her face, she smiled, recalling her mother's advice that 'sunlight is good for a person's health.'

A vision flashed within her mind. It was a man on horseback. He was coming with a missive. Lowering her head and opening her eyes, she shut the door to the hut and wove her way through the shaded woods toward the road to gather feverfew. She liked to harvest her herbs in the morning when their potency was at its peak, but the morning rain had made it necessary to gather the plants after they were able to dry in the sun. As she stepped from the woods, she looked down the road in the direction the visitor would arrive, but found it empty. She shuffled along the roadside until she found the feverfew. She selected the stalks with unopened blossoms, cut them with a clean cut, and placed her selection in the basket. She selected another cutting as she heard the sound of an approaching horse at a full gallop behind her. She put the harvested cutting and her knife in the basket and turned to face the oncoming rider.

The rain began the moment Farley had left Thornwick. His clothes became heavy with dampness, chilling him to the bone. Unwilling to bed down on the wet ground, he pushed himself and his horse beyond the point of exhaustion traveling through the night. He was in a foul mood and prayed the trip would end quickly so he could return to Thornwick, change his clothes, and warm himself by the fire.

As Farley and his horse crested the top of a small hill, he spotted an old woman who fitted the description he had been given and reined his horse before her.

"Madam, are you the friend of the freelancer, the mercenary who has a pet raven?"

"I am," Rowena said as she nodded her head to affirm her answer.

"My lord asks that I give you this missive." He bent low from his horse and handed her the wax-sealed missive.

"Tell your lord that it may be a fortnight before the mercenary receives his message. He is off on another request." She lied and accepted the missive. "When he has completed your lord's request, leave his payment within the hole at the base of that tree." She pointed to the large maple. It was her practice to refrain from specifying a fee for Lord William's service. However, most payments were generous. Perhaps those who hired the mercenary feared his revengeful punishment if their payment was insufficient.

"I will relay the information to my lord. Good day, madam." He turned his horse around and spurred it into a trot.

Rowena slipped the parchment into her basket and watched the messenger disappear over the hill. She walked to the maple tree and looked down at the triangle-shaped hole at the base of the trunk. Gone long ago were the days when she walked in the woods holding her mother's hand while listening to her tell stories of the fairy world. One tale in particular told of fairies that lived within the trunks of the trees, and if the base of the tree had an opening, it meant that the doorway to the fairy's house was welcoming. However, her mother had warned that some fairies were wicked and tricksters, so she was lucky to be too large to enter a fairy's house. Many believed in the tale and feared reaching into the little doorway, which made it an excellent spot for Lord William to receive payments for his service.

She stood still and listened to the silence of the woods. She was alone. Rowena bent down and reached into the fairy's doorway. She wiggled her fingers and rotated her hand until she discovered a small leather bag. Who had employed Lord William to kill Lord Redmond was unknown, but he or she had been prompt with their payment. As a precaution, Rowena took the long way back to the hut. She sensed she was still alone, but one was never certain who may be watching.

Upon returning to the hut, Rowena found Lord William sitting at the table eating some bread and cheese. She encouraged him to drink tea with dark treacle in order to speed his recovery and was pleased to see his injured arm remained in the cloth sling she had made for him. She reached into her basket, pulled out the bag filled with coin, and set it upon the table before Lord William.

He scowled at the bag in puzzlement. It had only been a handful of days since he had killed Lord Redmond.

"We have received payment already?" Lord William picked up the pouch to feel its weight.

"You received payment, not I." Rowena clarified as she set her basket of herbs upon the table. She selected a jar of swamp water from the shelf and opened the lid. She poured half its contents into an empty iron kettle and placed the vessel on a hook over the fire before closing the jar and returning it to the shelf. She selected a cloth-covered crock, untied the leather string that held the cover in place, and scooped a glob of dark, sticky goo with her finger. Rowena tossed the goo into the water, picked up a wooden spoon, and gave the contents a stir. She let the wooden spoon rest within the kettle as she returned to the table, selected a rag from her basket, and wiped her sticky fingers. Choosing several rusty nails from a box on a shelf, she placed them into an empty jar adjacent to the box.

Lord William went to the hearth, shifted the slate with his able hand, and opened a chest that lay beneath it. The coins jingled as he tossed the pouch into the chest. He lifted a tiny leather pouch, opened it, and took out his mother's ring. He valued the amethyst and diamond ring more than all of the coins. He slipped it on his pinky finger and admired its daintiness before returning it to the chest and replacing the slate.

"You received a request for your service today, but it can wait until you are healed," Rowena said as she lifted the missive from her basket.

He stood and faced her. He was growing tired of his sedentary lifestyle. It had been two days before he was able to rise from Rowena's cot. He was growing stronger with each day that passed, but his body needed more time to recover. He collected firewood and caught a few fish yesterday, but he grew weak from the simple tasks.

"I am getting stronger and improving every day." Lord William admitted.

"Yes, but you still need time to mend. I told the messenger you were away, and it would be a fortnight before you could honor the request." She handed the missive to him hesitantly.

He took the missive, opened it, and read it quickly. His eyes widened as he lowered the missive slowly and stared into her face.

"What is it?" Rowena noted his reaction.

"This is a request to kill Lord Clayborn."

"Oh, dear. That puts you in a precarious position, doesn't it?"

Lord William ignored her question as he reread the missive. He contemplated the haunting assignment and weighed his options silently as visions of his former home flashed in his mind. He looked to her face to convey his opinion confidently.

"Not at all, it is just another assignment." He knew what she was implying. He could become the Lord of Wildenham and assume his rightful title if he were to kill Lord Clayborn. The question at hand, did he desire the responsibility of his birthright?

"Well, you don't have to decide now. You have time to think about it." Rowena reasoned as the concoction in the pot began to bubble. She picked up the wooden spoon and stirred it again.

Lord William walked over to the fireplace while folding the missive.

"Or have you already decided?" She tilted her head to one side and scrutinized his concerned face. Her mind displayed a picture of him atop Adair. She knew what his decision would be.

He remained silent as he tried to recall how long it had been since he had turned his back on Wildenham. He wondered if it remained as he remembered. His father was dead, but what of Libby? Was she still working in the kitchen? Was Wilfred still the steward? He had little interest in becoming the Lord of Wildenham, for he had grown accustomed to his quiet lifestyle with Rowena, had plenty of money, and was happy.

He analyzed the writing addressed to 'the mercenary.' It looked as if it was written in anger. He set the folded request upon the mantel and wrinkled his nose as the kettle's contents filled the air with a pungent aroma.

"Good Lord, what are you cooking in that kettle?"

"Pine tar and swamp water. Once it boils for an hour, I will pour it in the jar with the rusty nails, seal the jar closed, and let it cure." She explained.

"Whatever for?"

"You will need it in the near future." Rowena explained, sensing the change in his pathway of life.

He ignored her mysterious reply, turned his head, and looked at his sword that now hung on a peg on the wall. He walked to his sword, pulled it from its sheath, and left the hut. Corvus managed to fly through the doorway before his master slammed it shut.

Lord William clenched his jaw and tightened his grip on the hilt. With his movements restricted by the sling, Lord William wheeled the sword over his head and brought it downward into the side of a practice post set firmly in the ground. His well-rehearsed practice routine came back to him easily, even though it had been more than a week since he had gone through the moves. His sword arm was fit, but his injured arm ached with every movement of his body. Within a few minutes, his body drained of energy and he was forced to accept his inability as he let his sword become still by his side. He hated to admit it, but Rowena was right. He would need more time to heal.

He sat on a boulder next to the stream behind the hut, rested the sword against his leg, and rubbed his hand on the back of his neck. He watched the water trickle by as he mulled over the new assignment. *Should I complicate my life by returning to Wildenham and kill my father's killer?*

Corvus flew down from a nearby tree branch with a dead rodent in his right claw and landed by the edge of the stream. He walked awkwardly toward Lord William, stopped, and turned his head as if to offer his catch.

"No thanks, Corvus."

The raven's attention turned toward the dead mouse, and he began to peck at his meal. Lord William watched the raven devour his prey as he marveled at the size the little orphaned chick had become. Now fully grown, the raven's wingspan was nearly as wide as Lord William's outstretched arms.

Lord William reached down teasingly, grabbed the dead animal's foot, and pulled it away from Corvus, who stepped on the carcass protectively and continued to eat.

*   *   *

After delivering the missive to Rowena, Farley traveled until his eyelids became heavy. He stopped by the side of the road and took a nap before continuing to Thornwick. Upon his arrival, his teeth chattered and his body shivered as he reined his horse, dismounted, and entered the Keep. His legs trembled as he walked toward Lord Sheridan, who was in his usual chair in his usual state of mind after eating his evening meal.

"My lord, I have delivered the missive to the old woman." Farley reported as he knelt before Lord Sheridan in the Great Hall. "She conveyed the mercenary is away on a prior commitment and he will return in a fortnight."

Lord Sheridan gulped another mouthful of wine and forced it down his throat.

"Well then, I have no other choice than to wait." He took another drink from his tankard and paused with the tankard at his mouth as he recalled the large soldier who had caught his attention during the garrison training. He took a gulp, lowered his mug, and displayed a malevolent grin upon his face. "That is all."

Farley nodded, rose, and left. He forced his legs to carry him to the kitchen where he asked a lad to retrieve a pallet and set it next to the fireplace. While he waited, he ladled some water from a bucket into a mug and took a long swig. When the lad set the straw mattress before the warming fire, Farley lay upon it and asked to be covered for additional warmth. The lad retrieved three blankets and spread them upon the messenger who was already fast asleep.

Chapter 8

Beads of sweat dotted Farley's forehead and face. He had lay on the pallet before the fire and shivered for three days. Those in the kitchen had tended to his needs and kept the fire burning. He knew Lord Sheridan was growing impatient, for he overheard those who worked in the Keep whisper of their lord's mood and their attempts to avoid him as he became belligerent and drank more than usual. Farley was thankful his service remained unwanted by Lord Sheridan and allowed him time to regain his strength.

A serving wench left the kitchen to notify Lord Sheridan that dinner was being served. She stood in the doorway of the library and watched him pace, lost in thought. She feared interrupting him for any reason.

Lord Sheridan turned and noticed the wench standing in the doorway.

"Have I received a missive today?" He slurred his words. He had inquired daily since requesting the service of the mercenary and hoped to receive word of Lord Clayborn's demise.

"Not that I am aware of, my lord, but dinner is served." She curtsied and left quickly.

Lord Sheridan walked to the Great Hall, paused in the doorway, and glared at those in attendance. He staggered to the High Table, kicked a bone that lay on the stone floor, and picked up a full tankard of ale.

A servant pulled his lord's chair out from the High Table and waited for him to sit. Lord Sheridan stood and peered over the top of his tankard at the Great Hall with disdain. A tattered and dusty tapestry hung at a crooked angle upon the wall. The stone of the fireplace and its blackened mantel were stained with soot. Floor candelabras used to light the room dripped wax from their burning candles creating wax stalagmites upon the floor.

The servant pushed his lord's chair forward in an attempt to catch Lord Sheridan before he sat. The Lord of Thornwick took another swig from his tankard and leaned to one side in his chair. *I should have had Lord Bradford killed long ago*, he thought with self-pity becoming his only true companion for the evening. *Lady Christine, the spoiled brat, once I take over Wildenham, I will throw her into the streets*, he thought bitterly.

Less than a week had passed since he wrote the missive to the mercenary. To Lord Sheridan, it seemed as if he had waited a lifetime to acquire Wildenham. He had grown tired of waiting and decided to take matters into his own hands. He slammed his tankard down on the High Table startling many in the room and scanned the Great Hall in search of the man who had earlier caught his attention on the practice field.

Sir Kenneth sat to the left of his lord. He lifted his tankard and paused as he noticed Lord Sheridan's line of sight.

"My lord, you seem quiet and in thought tonight. Does something trouble you about the garrison?"

"No, not at all, you are training them well. I am pleased with what I see," Lord Sheridan said as he spotted the soldier he was seeking. "Sir Kenneth, what is the name of the man sitting at the last table, on the right, third from this end?"

Sir Kenneth looked in the direction indicated by his lord. "That is Harlan. As you observed on the practice field, he is a merciless fighter, very driven, and aggressive. He keeps to himself, not many friends."

Lord Sheridan picked up his tankard again, sat back in his chair, and took a long drink of ale as a plan began to develop in his mind. He watched Harlan as he shoved others out of his way while reaching for a turkey drumstick from a trencher.

Harlan bit into the meat with such gusto that he ripped a large section of it from the bone and swallowed it whole like a beast devouring his prey. He picked up his empty tankard, banged it upon the table, and set it down as he took another bite from the drumstick.

A wary wench approached carrying a pitcher, picked up the mug, and began to fill it with ale. Harlan grabbed the wench around the waist, pulled her next to him, and pressed his nose into her shoulder drawing in her scent. The wench set his filled tankard on the table and tried to free herself. With the greasy turkey drumstick in hand, he pressed it to the back of her head and forced his mouth onto hers. She squirmed and pushed upon his shoulders hoping to escape. He kissed her savagely before setting her free. The wench reeled backward from his arms, put the back of her hand to her mouth, and wiped away his spit. A metallic taste filled her mouth as she looked at the back of her hand and confirmed it was red. He had bitten her lip to ensure he would receive what he wanted. Using her dirty overskirt, she pulled it up to her mouth and applied pressure to stop the bleeding as she continued onto the next empty tankard.

Harlan looked toward Lord Sheridan and sneered. *The fat bastard*, he thought, o*nly the luck of his birth allows him to sit in the prominent chair as the Lord of Thornwick. Like all men with power, he uses others for his own advancement and cares not for their misfortune. One day I shall be so lucky.*

Perfect, Lord Sheridan thought as he raised his tankard toward Harlan.

Harlan ignored his lord's silent salute and returned to satisfying his appetite.

As the meal came to a close, the empty trenchers were taken away by the wait staff. Tankards were gathered and taken to the kitchen for washing. Benches and tables were stacked neatly. The meal had come to an end, but Harlan continued to sit on his bench and eat.

Lord Sheridan held up his tankard. A nearby wench refilled his cup as he pointed to Harlan.

"Tell that man when he is finished eating, I would like to see him in my library." Lord Sheridan stood, and a servant pulled his chair out of his way.

"Yes, my lord." She picked up a half-eaten trencher from the High Table and headed in the direction of Harlan.

Lord Sheridan left the Great Hall carrying his filled tankard. Ale sloshed from his mug as he swayed from side to side through the hall and into his library. He sat down at his desk, opened an account book, and wondered how much he should pay Harlan for the task. An idea twisted within his mind as his attention was drawn to a knock upon the doorway. Harlan took an uninvited step into the library.

"Come in and close the door," Lord Sheridan said as he slammed the account book shut and waited for Harlan to shut the door.

"I am giving you a special assignment." Lord Sheridan looked up at the warrior's face and noted his enormous height. "You are to go to Wildenham and kill Lord Clayborn. In exchange for your service, you shall be knighted."

Harlan fought the urge to smile at the opportunity that was usually granted to a worthy knight. *The arrogant tub of lard wants me to do his dirty work*, he thought. *Well, it is going to cost him.*

"I would like my knighthood now." Harlan demanded even though he was confident he would complete the assignment unharmed. He folded his arms across his chest and lifted his chin in a silent challenge.

"Very well, kneel." Lord Sheridan rose from his desk, took his sword from its sheath, and stood before Harlan. He tapped him on each shoulder with the blade. "There. You are a knight. From now on, you will be known as Sir Harlan. Rise." Lord Sheridan returned his sword to its sheath.

"Once I kill Lord Clayborn, what of his daughter?" Sir Harlan had overheard conversations between the men who spoke of her acclaimed beauty and dreamed of such a woman to warm his bed at night.

"You may do whatever you wish with Lady Christine, but Wildenham is mine," Lord Sheridan said unsmilingly.

"You may have Wildenham, but I want Thornwick and I shall rule it with my new wife." Sir Harlan proclaimed.

Lord Sheridan was more than willing to give up his ramshackle residence.

"Agreed, leave tomorrow morning and report to me upon your return."

Sir Harlan's mouth turned up at the corners, displaying his broken, crooked teeth. When he returned, he would be bringing his new bride to their new home. *My, my, my, won't Sir Kenneth be surprised when he will receive his orders from me*, he thought as he nodded, turned, and left the library.

Quite confident his plan would come to fruition, Lord Sheridan tossed the contents of his tankard into the fire before setting it on a nearby table. He stumbled out of the library and a wicked grin grew upon his face. He was in the mood to celebrate with a female companion as he staggered up the staircase to the bedchambers. If he were lucky, perhaps he could find an unlocked door of a wench's chamber. At the end of the hall, he tripped up another staircase and into the servant's corridor where he tried each door until he heard one click open and entered.

Chapter 9

"I wish you would wait another week and give your body more time to heal." Rowena tried to convince Lord William as she looked at the morning sky and watched the threatening rain clouds that were gathering.

Adair pawed the ground eagerly while Lord William strapped his long dirk to the saddle, climbed atop his ebony war horse, and looked down into the apothecary's concerned eyes.

"Try not to worry. My arm is still a little tender, but the stitches are out, and I am growing stronger every day." He reassured.

Rowena knew he would be fine, but she also knew what awaited him within Wildenham's walls was a challenge that may change the course of his life. She had risen early to prepare a bottle of the tar water for his journey. Pride filled her heart as she looked at him sitting tall in his saddle and committed the mental picture to her memory. He was no longer the little boy she had found on the roadside beaten and bruised, who possessed a small sword with the Wildenham crest on its pommel. Having long outgrown the sword years ago, it remained hidden safely under her cot in the hut. Lord William now carried a crestless sword. He had commissioned a renowned sword maker to create a weapon to his specifications. It was perfectly balanced and forged from the finest steel. With the lethal sword strapped securely to his hip and Corvus on his shoulder, the ominous freelancer was an intimidating sight. He was dressed in black with a touch of gold thread embroidered on his tunic. Even though those he encountered may fear him, Rowena knew him for what he truly possessed, a kind and patient heart.

"Within Wildenham's walls is a spirit who is not at peace. Pour one drop on the floor of your chamber and tell the spirit to leave." She tied the pouch containing the bottle of tar water to the saddle next to another that contained bread and dried meat. "Godspeed." She hoped he would heed her warning as she took a step backward from Adair. She anticipated his reply, for his consciousness needed the security of knowing all would be well if he were killed.

"I will return in a week's time or send word if I am delayed. If I do not return, I can rest assured you are well cared for and all that is under the hearth is yours."

"You will live, nevertheless, fare thee well." Rowena turned toward the hut to conceal the look of concern upon her face. *Whether you return or not will be your choice*, she thought.

Lord William reined Adair and the three travelers made their way through the woods. The war horse paused at the edge of the road, unsure of which way to turn. Corvus turned his head and looked at his master quizzically. Lord William turned and looked in the direction of Wildenham. He took a deep breath and sighed before reining his horse toward the kingdom. He made a clicking noise with his mouth encouraging Adair into a trot. Lord William grew uneasy as he expanded the distance from his comfortable home to confront the unknown within the nightmarish kingdom of his childhood. He was determined his time away from Rowena would be brief. He would kill Lord Clayborn, adjure Wildenham to whoever was paying him for his service, and return to reside with the apothecary in the tiny hut nestled in the solitude of the woods.

After many hours of riding, he stopped by the roadside to let Adair rest and graze in the tall grass. He took bread and dried meat from the leather pouch, sat on the roadside, and handed Corvus a tidbit of bread. The raven gobbled the serving whole and looked to his master for more. Lord William broke off a chunk of bread, popped it into his mouth, and gave Corvus another piece as well. As he sat and ate, Lord William watched a peasant family pass by carrying a few piglets. Perhaps they were going to sell them at a market. He split the last piece of bread with Corvus, rose from the ground and led his horse to a nearby stream where the three drank their fill before continuing their journey.

It was difficult to determine the time of day as he looked to the threatening gray sky. He was thankful the rain had held off as he encouraged his horse into a gallop.

Cresting the top of a hill and the end of the day's journey, Lord William slowed Adair to a trot as majestic Wildenham came into view. His hands turned clammy. He grasped the reins tightly as a cold sweat broke out on his forehead. His stomach churned and grumbled reminding him that it was time for the evening meal.

The kingdom's drawbridge was down to allow his entry, but with night soon to fall upon the land, it would be pulled up and closed for its citizens' protection. Lord William encouraged Adair to quicken his pace.

As he approached Wildenham, it seemed smaller than he remembered. He noticed there were a few changes, but much remained the same. Lord Clayborn's colorful banners atop of the gatehouse flapped in the breeze.

He wondered if anyone in the garrison or Keep's staff would recognize him. His appearance had changed over the years, but in many ways he was the same. As he rode through the village, he noted the good condition of the buildings. The faces that peeked out from behind the doorways and through the windows of the huts were emotionless and curious.

He crossed the drawbridge and was stopped at the gatehouse by a guard who inspected Adair, Lord William, and Corvus sternly.

"Your name, sir."

"Sir William of Lincolnshire." Lord William lied convincingly, for he had learned long ago to keep his lordship title a secret and always state a false residence to reduce any suspicion of his profession.

The guard turned to a scribe who wrote down the information onto parchment. When the entry was complete, he turned back to Lord William.

"You may enter."

Lord William nodded his head in appreciation and urged Adair forward. He kept his horse at a slow pace as they went through the outer bailey. Goose bumps rose on his arms as the walls of Wildenham and its haunting memories enclosed around him. Many of the shops were still in operation. All seemed to be clean and well organized, which was an improvement from when he left. It appeared Lord Clayborn was competent in his duties as Lord of Wildenham.

A man flew through the air from a pub doorway startling Adair and causing him to sidestep and prance nervously. The drunk landed face down in a dark puddle sending mud splashing outward.

"Easy," Lord William said as he pulled the reins and patted Adair's neck.

"And don't bring your bloody arse over the threshold again unless you bring coins with you!" The bartender stood in the doorway slapping his hands together as if congratulating himself on a job well done.

Lord William reined his horse around the man who lifted his face from the mud.

"I can see why Rowena likes to limit my drink." He whispered to Corvus.

Making his way into the inner bailey, the Keep came into view. It was an impressive sight. The windows were aglow from evening fires and lit torches.

He reined Adair at the stable, lifted Corvus from his shoulder, and tossed him into the air.

The raven flapped his wings and flew away to hunt. His master would call when he was needed.

A stableboy came forward and took the horse's bridle. Lord

William dismounted, untied the dirk from his saddle, and strapped it to his belt.

"What's your name, lad?"

"Thomas, sir."

"Well, Thomas, cool him down, feed, and water him well." Lord William reached into his belt bag and flipped a coin toward the lad.

"Thank you, sir. I shall." The lad caught the coin and led Adair away.

Lord William entered the Keep. Merriment and laughter echoed from the Great Hall. He assumed the evening meal was in progress. He walked through the corridor and stood in the doorway of the large room. The long tables seated many people who shared trenchers that contained a variety of meats and roasted vegetables. He noted the tapestries on the walls had changed as he rotated his head to locate the High Table. At its center was Lord Clayborn sitting in his father's chair and to the left was a beautiful young lady, possibly the Lady of Wildenham. She seemed too young to be his wife, but one never knew. There were additional men and women who also sat at the High Table. He assumed the men were Lord Clayborn's knights and the women attended to the needs of their lady.

To show his respect, Lord William approached the High Table, knelt onto one knee, and requested an audience with the Lord of Wildenham. Lord Clayborn paused from eating and looked down at the stranger.

"We have a guest? How unusual. Rise, sir, and state your business." Lord Clayborn was intrigued, and those within the Great

Hall grew quiet and took note of the tall, dark stranger dressed in black.

"My lord, I am Sir William of Lincolnshire. May I request a few nights stay to rest myself and my horse from our weary travels?" Lord William kept his eyes on Lord Clayborn while his host made his assessment and rendered an answer to his request. He was tempted to glance at the beautiful woman, but restrained out of respect.

Lord Clayborn scrutinized his visitor, taking note of his clothing and build. He looked like a black demon with piercing hazel eyes and noted the sword at his side and long dirk.

Lady Christine glanced at the stranger before reaching for her tankard of spiced wine.

"Sir William of Lincolnshire, you may stay for as long as you wish. Please find a seat and join us for the evening meal. I will have Wilfred, my steward, show you to your chamber when you are ready to retire," Lord Clayborn said as he pointed toward the tables before him.

"Thank you, my lord." Lord William bowed in gratitude and turned to view the tables for an empty seat. A few men at the table to his left made room for the kingdom's guest. He accepted the seat humbly and thanked them for their kindness. A serving wench arrived at his side with a filled tankard of ale. Taking a drink, he allowed his eyes to look in the direction of the beautiful young lady at the High Table. She looked bored. Her eyes were downcast at the tabletop. As if she knew she was being watched, she glanced in his direction and looked away as if to dismiss him instantly. Lord William shifted his eyes to Lord Clayborn and found the lord's eyes upon him. To disguise the uncomfortable feeling of guilt that overcame him, Lord William raised his tankard in a silent toast to his host and his host returned his toast with a smiled. Perhaps Lord Clayborn was entertained by his interest in the lady. Lord William had to admit, she was breathtakingly beautiful.

As the evening continued, he sat quietly and ate while listening to the conversation of the men at his table. He observed the decoration that adorned the room and stared at a magnificent tapestry that hung on the wall across from him. Most tapestries told a story that usually entailed Greek mythology, but this story was unfamiliar to him. He admired the colors of the thread and silk in the detailed border. His eyes widened with surprise as he recognized his family crest at each corner of the tapestry.

The man sitting across from him turned to see what had intrigued the guest. Stripping a hunk of meat from the bone he was holding, he turned back to Lord William.

"It is beautiful, isn't it?"

Lord William looked from the tapestry to the man who had spoken. The man smiled as he continued to smack his lips while chewing a mouthful of food.

"Yes, quite," Lord William said in reply.

"A sad, sad story behind it though. Lord Bradford had it commissioned by a group of nuns at Saint Michael's Abbey in memory of his son."

"What happened to his son?" Lord William was curious to hear the man's version of the story.

The man, who was eager to share the story, hunched over the table toward Lord William and lowered his voice to a whisper.

"I was told that his son disappeared one night. Being his father's only heir, Lord Bradford had his men searching for the lad right up until the day he was killed by Lord Clayborn. Many believe the tapestry contains a hidden message. Strange occurrences within the Keep are said to be Lord Bradford's ghost haunting each room in search of his son."

The man straightened upright on the bench, grabbed his mug, and took a large swig of ale. He set the mug upon the table, nodded his head in satisfaction of his storytelling skills, and smiled. Lord William smiled in return, took another bite of meat, and turned his head to look at Lord Clayborn, his father's killer.

The Lord of Wildenham leaned close to the lady's ear and whispered. She looked toward the ceiling as he returned to sit upright in his chair. It was obvious she thought little of his comment.

Perhaps the young woman is his wife or at the very least betrothed to another, he thought as he broke off a chunk from a loaf of bread and put it in his belt bag for Corvus.

Once Lord William had finished a fruit tart and washed it down with ale, he was approached by Wilfred.

"Sir William, I am Wilfred, the steward." He introduced himself and displayed a slight bow.

The lines had deepened upon Wilfred's face. His hair had thinned and turned gray. His body seemed withered as he stood with rounded shoulders. The steward's disposition as a loyal, kind, and soft-spoken soul seemed unchanged, so it was no surprise that he had retained his position on Wildenham's staff.

"It is nice to meet you, Wilfred." Lord William stood up

from the bench and looked down at the steward. Wilfred took a step backward in order to look up at the guest's face.

"If you will please follow me, I will take you to your chamber."

Wilfred and Lord William left the Great Hall and climbed the staircase to the bedchambers above. Lord William made a mental note of his surroundings. He would need a rapid escape once he fulfilled his assignment. As they passed an open doorway, Lord William was certain the luxurious bedchamber had once belonged to his father and now belonged to Lord Clayborn. Taking an additional step, he ducked his head instinctively as if he had bumped into a heavy cobweb. He stopped walking abruptly, brushed the top of his head with his hand, and looked upward, but there was nothing there. A tickle from a silk ribbon or thread over his right forearm caused him to raise his tunic sleeve. He stared at his arm as the sensation continued, again there was nothing there.

Realizing Lord William had stopped, Wilfred halted and turned around.

"Sir, is something amiss?"

The feeling on his forearm had subsided. Lord William gave a quizzical look to the steward. Dare he explain what had just happened?

"I don't mean to insult your staff, but I thought I had walked into a cobweb."

Wilfred remained unshaken; for he knew the ghost of Wildenham was known to touch guests to make himself known, but thought it best to downplay the occurrence.

"I will ensure the staff cleans the hall upon daybreak. Shall we proceed?" Wilfred continued down the hallway. Lord William pulled his sleeve down, brushed the top of his head, and looked toward the ceiling once again. Out of the corner of his eye he saw someone standing in the doorway of the bedchamber. He turned his head toward the door and saw a shadow disappear behind the wall. He looked to see if Wilfred had witnessed the occurrence, but found the steward had continued down the hallway. Lord William glanced back to the doorway. The shadow had disappeared, so he quickened his steps to join the steward.

Lord William was certain the next bedchamber door they passed had once belonged to his mother. He surmised his mother's bedchamber now belonged to the lovely lady who sat at the High Table. Understanding Wilfred's role within the Keep, the steward would know the information that would satisfy his curiosity.

"Is Lord Clayborn married?" Lord William took a step closer to the steward.

"No, the Lady of Wildenham passed away several years ago."

"The young lady at the high table is?"

"His daughter, Lady Christine."

"Is she married?"

"No."

"Betrothed?"

"No." Wilfred had learned long ago to limit the amount of information he divulged. He stifled a laugh. The odds were against the young man in winning the heart of Lady Christine. After having her heart broken by a womanizing knight, the suitors who followed had tried and failed to gain her favor. One particularly frustrated suitor compared her to an untamable wild horse. Many within the kingdom thought the label fit her well and used it often.

They continued to walk through the candlelit corridor and ascended another staircase. Wilfred stopped at the first chamber's doorway.

"Here is your chamber. I took the liberty to have your leather bag of personal items brought in from your horse," he said as he opened the door. "I anticipated your need for embers and had them placed in your fireplace. Shall I add a log or two to ward off the chill of the night?"

"I can do so, thank you."

"Shall I light a taper for you?" Wilfred offered as he indicated the unlit candle on the mantel.

"Please." Lord William stepped aside and allowed the steward to do his job. He watched Wilfred select a rush from the floor, hold it to an ember until it set aflame, and light the taper.

"The garderobe is at the end of this corridor. I will have a tray of food brought to you in the morning," Wilfred said as he picked up the taper, walked across the small room, and set it on the nightstand next to the head of the bed.

Lord William selected two split logs and some kindling from a stack of wood next to the fireplace and placed them on the embers. The kindling smoked and crackled before bursting into flames. Fingers of the fire wrapped around the logs adding a golden light and warmth to the room.

"Thank you," Lord William said as he looked around the chamber. There was a small window to the right of the nightstand and a bench beneath it.

Wilfred made his way toward the door.

"Is there anything else you need before I leave you for the evening?" The steward paused in the doorway.

"That is all, Wilfred. Good night and thank you for your hospitality." Lord William took off his sword and strapped it to the bedpost next to where his head would lay.

"Good night, Sir William." Wilfred left the chamber and closed the door.

Lord William opened the window and whistled. He stepped away and unfastened his belt and dirk, took off his tunic, and laid them on the bench. He loosened the tie on his breeches as Corvus landed on the windowsill and looked into the room. Lord William rotated his left arm. It ached. He touched the scar to ensure the wound had remained closed. *Perhaps a few days in Wildenham will be necessary before I am able to kill Lord Clayborn and return*, he thought. He reached into his belt bag and took out the piece of bread.

"I saved you something from the evening meal," Lord William said as he tossed the tidbit onto the floor. Corvus hopped down from the windowsill, grabbed the bread with one of his clawed feet, and began to eat.

Lord William blew out the candle and slipped beneath the covers.

"Lady Christine, interesting." He whispered to himself and wondered what fate had in store for her once her father was dead. He closed his eyes as darkness crept into his mind and drifted off to sleep.

Chapter 10

Lord William cringed as he woke from his slumber. He ran his hand across his stomach and felt lines of raised skin. He rolled onto his left side and opened his eyes. The room was dark except for the amber glow peeking through the cracks on the ashen embers in the fireplace. He blinked his eyes several times and tried to focus on what appeared to be a shadowed figure hovering in the corner of his room.

Corvus slept perched on the headboard and awoke as Lord William whipped back the covers, sprang out of bed, and grabbed his sword from its sheath. He readied himself to encounter whoever had entered the chamber, but when he looked to the corner of his room, it was empty.

He lowered his sword and went to the door. It was bolted shut. He stepped to the fireplace, picked up a poker, and stirred the embers to set them aglow. He scrutinized his abdomen in the golden light and discovered several bloody scratches. He ran his hand over the welts and looked toward the bed. It was common for cots to contain fleas, bed bugs, or even lice, but they usually left markings different than what he had suffered. Whatever creature was in his bed, he was unwilling to endure any more of its abuse. He rolled his tunic into a pillow and lay down upon the bench. He would request a different cot from Wilfred in the morning.

*   *   *

Lord William rose at first light. He sat on the edge of the bench and tried to rub a kink out of the back of his neck. His body was stiff, and his arm ached as he rolled out his tunic and tried to straighten the wrinkles. Seeing his attempt was futile, he slipped it over his head and pulled it down. He lifted the covers on his bed and searched his pillow, but found it empty of pests. A knock at the door caused him to drop the blanket and look in its direction. Corvus hopped from the headboard of the bed and perched himself upon his master's shoulder.

Lord William opened the door and greeted the steward.

"Good morning, Wilfred."

Wilfred was startled to see the large black bird upon Lord William's shoulder. Knowing his place, he ignored the raven.

"Good morning, Sir William." Wilfred stepped aside to let a stout servant girl enter the chamber. She carried a tray of bread, cheese, and meat and a tankard of ale. She walked across the room, set the tray on the bench, and batted the lashes of her big brown eyes at Lord William.

"Thank you," he said as he selected some cheese from the tray. She smiled, curtsied, and left the room. Lord William popped the cheese into his mouth and reached for a small piece of bread.

"I hope you slept well," Wilfred said as he watched the raven.

"I was wakened during the night and acquired scratches upon my stomach. Pests, I presume. Would it be too much trouble to request another cot?"

"I will see to it at once." Wilfred assured even though he suspected the true cause of the injury to be something other than mere pests.

"Wilfred, would it be possible that I train with the garrison today?" Lord William raised his hand toward Corvus and handed the raven a bit of bread.

"I cannot answer that question. You will have to ask Lord Clayborn for permission." Wilfred stared as he watched the raven eat the piece of bread whole.

Jackson had followed the servant from the kitchen with his nose sniffing the aroma from the tray and entered the chamber. He rubbed his face on the edge of the door, walked across the room, and arched his back against the bedpost.

"And who is this?" Lord William noticed the black and white feline and sat down on the bench next to the tray. From his master's shoulder, Corvus watched the cat too. The raven tilted his head to the right and then to the left as if to get a good look at the feline with one eye at a time.

"That is Lady Christine's cat, Jackson. As you can see, he is overfed, and she spoils him rotten." Wilfred motioned his hand in the cat's direction.

"Jackson?"

"Yes. His father's name was Jack. Therefore, he is

Jack's son – Jackson." Wilfred nudged the cat with his foot toward the doorway.

"Wilfred, he can stay." Lord William squatted and held out a piece of meat toward the cat. Corvus watched the succulent tidbit as the cat waddled toward the offering. Jackson sniffed the meat, licked it twice, ate it greedily, and began to purr.

Wilfred sighed in disgust and shook his head slightly from side to side.

Once the meat disappeared into the feline's mouth, Corvus turned his head toward his master and pinched his ear with his beak. Lord William handed him a piece of meat as well.

"If there is nothing else, I must tend to other duties." Wilfred nodded his head in respect.

"Thank you, Wilfred." Lord William selected another piece of cheese from the tray, popped it into his mouth, and took a long swig of ale as he turned and looked out the window at the beautiful sunny day.

Jackson sat on the floor before him and tipped his head to the left as he watched Lord William's hand move from the tray to his mouth.

Corvus stared at the feline with contempt.

Lord William petted Jackson on the top of his head and gave him another bit of meat. He offered a small chunk of bread to the jealous raven. Corvus pecked it from his lord's hand and flew out the open window as his tolerance for the feline had reached its end.

Lord William finished his meal, strapped on his sword and dirk, and picked up Jackson before leaving his chamber and closing the door. He ruffled the top of the cat's head as he walked through the hallway. In appreciation of the attention, Jackson purred as he lowered his head, butted it against Lord William's chin, and snuggled against his chest. Lord William stopped before what he assumed to be Lady Christine's bedchamber. He knocked on the door.

"Enter."

Lord William looked down at Jackson for the feline's reaction to the sound of his mistress's voice. The feline seemed comfortably nestled within his arms with little interest in leaving. He was certain Lady Christine was alone in her bedchamber since one of her ladies had failed to answer the door. Out of respect for the lady's reputation, he knocked again.

He could hear stomping toward the portal before it was flung open.

"I said for you to enter." Lady Christine stood before him in her thinly woven chemise. Lord William kept his eyes upon her face as he watched her cheeks turn a rosy hue. Lady Christine crossed her arms over her chest to conceal the transparency of the undergarment.

"I believe he belongs to you." Lord William averted his eyes to Jackson and scratched him under his chin. Jackson lifted his chin, closed his eyes, and purred loudly. He held the chubby cat away from his body and waited for her to uncross her arms.

Lady Christine snatched Jackson from the stranger and cuddled him closely.

Lord William stared into her defiant brown eyes. *She has spirit*, he thought as a silent challenge of dominance between them seemed to linger.

The man's hazel eyes pierced her soul. They were almost evil and quite unsettling. Lady Christine lowered her nose to the top of Jackson's head. She ruffled his fur, but peeked through her lashes as her eyes were drawn back to the stranger who stood before her.

"Good day." Lord William nodded his head, turned, and continued through the hallway toward the staircase that led down to the Great Hall.

Lady Christine stepped into the hallway and watched the stranger leave. As a shiver went up her spine, she stroked Jackson under his chin to calm her uneasiness.

Lord William felt her eyes upon him as he turned right at the top of the staircase and stopped.

Fearing he would catch her staring, Lady Christine stepped quickly into her bedchamber.

When Lord William turned his head in her direction, he saw the fleeting billow of her undergarment and heard her bedchamber door shut. With a slight grin on his face, he descended the staircase and entered the Great Hall.

Lord Clayborn was entering the Great Hall at the opposite side of the room accompanied by two of his knights.

"Pardon me, Lord Clayborn," Lord William said as he approached.

"Ah, Sir William, I hope you slept well."

"Your accommodations are superb and much appreciated, thank you." Lord William complimented, but in truth, he preferred his sleep uninterrupted.

"May I introduce to you Sir Gunther and Sir Farrell, my trusted knights."

"It is a pleasure to meet you, Sir Gunther, Sir Farrell." Lord William shook each knight's hand in greeting before readdressing Lord Clayborn. "May I have permission to practice with your garrison today?"

"Yes, of course. My men will be pleased to have you on the field," he said as he looked to each of his knights.

"Sir William, practice is held throughout the day. You may join us on the field whenever you are ready." Sir Gunther welcomed and looked forward to the challenge of a new sparring partner.

"Thank you, Sir Gunther. If you will excuse me," Lord William said as he gave a slight nod of his head and left the Great Hall. He exited the Keep and went to the stable.

Thomas sat on a mound of straw, but jumped to his feet when he noticed the approaching guest.

"Good morning, Thomas."

"Good morning, sir."

"Would you be so kind as to saddle my horse?"

"Yes, sir," Thomas replied, as he scurried off to fetch Adair.

Lord William took note of the well kept stable and surrounding buildings while he waited patiently. He had to admit, Lord Clayborn kept Wildenham in fine condition.

Hearing the sound of hoofbeats behind him, Lord William turned around and found Adair standing before him with Thomas holding his bridle.

"That was rather quick, Thomas. Let me see how well you did." Lord William jested as he circled his horse pulling on the saddle strap and verifying that each buckle on the saddle and bridle was secure.

"Well done." He stated as he reached into his belt bag, took out a coin, and tossed it to the lad. Conal led a pony out of the stable as Thomas caught the coin and grinned from ear to ear. "Be sure to share the coin with the other stableboy as well."

"I will. Thank you, sir," Thomas said as he watched Lord William climb atop his great destrier and ride away.

Lord William urged Adair into a leisurely pace as he rode through the baileys. Many of the shops were as he remembered. The candle maker with his candles hanging in bunches from dowels. The broom maker had various styles of brooms and whisks hanging both inside and outside of his store. The blacksmith with its smoke billowing from the chimney as a constant clang-tap-tap-clang rhythm resonated from within. The tinsmith displaying boxes and pitchers, whose quality of work was well renowned. The kingdom's ale house with the alewives busy and brewing their finest for all to enjoy. The popular pub with its patrons inside enjoying a pint or two and the usual drunks sleeping outside in the street was hard to miss. He dismounted at the leather smith and purchased a decorative satchel for Rowena. He strapped it to Adair's saddle, took the reins in his hand, and began to walk with his horse following obediently. He passed many other shops and observed the interaction of its people before he climbed atop Adair and headed to the front gate. *Wildenham is self-sufficient, and many seem proud to call it their home*, he thought.

He rode over the drawbridge of the gatehouse, through the dusty streets of the village, and dodged young children while they played as their mothers went about their household duties. Lord William reined Adair before a small hut and stared at it intensely.

He thought he had spent time there as a child and a vague memory of its interior containing a table and few chairs formulated within his mind. Whenever he needed to escape the wrath of his father, he would go to this hut and play with his best friend, Harry. Together they would fish in the river that ran through Wildenham or play hide and seek in the fields of grass that grew as tall as their shoulders.

Adair had grown tired of standing. He jerked his nose forward, pulled on the reins, and brought his rider back to reality. Lord William urged his horse forward as he continued to tour the village. He noted a few of the huts were in need of repair. He rode past men who were tending to the crops in the fields. The weather had been kind, and the crops looked as if the harvest would be plentiful. Lord William made a clicking sound with his mouth and Adair broke into a trot. They made their way to the practice field while listening to the resonating echoes of wooden swords clashing in the distance. Lord William slowed Adair to a walk as he approached the archers and watched them draw their bows and let their arrows fly toward targets in the field. He observed mounted warriors ramming a quintain with their poleaxes and lances. Arriving at the area where men were practicing with swords, Lord William reined his large horse next to Conal's pony, dismounted, and was approached by Sir Gunther.

"It is good of you to join us," Sir Gunther said as he wiped his sweaty brow with his sleeve and looked up at Lord William.

"I am looking forward to it." Lord William took off his sword, dirk, and belt bag and tied them to his saddle. He opened his saddlebag and took out his leather arm bracers.

Conal stepped forward.

"May I assist you, sir?"

"Thank you." Lord William held out his arm and handed Conal the bracers. The stableboy took one bracer and wrapped it around Lord William's forearm. He laced it tightly, dressed the other arm, and stepped back.

"There you go, sir." The stableboy stated proudly.

Lord William inspected the bracers.

"Well done, thank you."

Lord William walked over to a stack of practice swords that lay within a low wooden bin upon the ground, selected one that looked sturdy, and tapped it on a wooden post to ensure the sword was solid. He turned to Sir Gunther and followed him to a vacant spot on the sparring field.

Both men took a guarded stance.

Lord William kept himself in check as he tried to determine the skill level of the knight he opposed. Sir Gunther was a good fighter, but easy to read. Lord William's left arm begin to ache, but he continued to spar. Out of the corner of his eye he spotted a pair of warriors dismounting from their horses. As the two walked past him, he caught a glimpse of long blonde hair and a towering soldier who followed closely behind.

"It is nice of you to join us, Sir William," Sir Farrell said as he passed.

The momentary distraction caused Lord William to lose his focus and gave Sir Gunther the opportunity to hit his tender arm.

"Augh!" he said under his breath as he grabbed his arm and spun away from Sir Gunther. He stepped back to get another look at the small knight who turned to face Sir Farrell and readied for an attack. Lord William's mouth dropped open as he recognized the small warrior. It was Lady Christine.

Sir Gunther came to his side.

"Sorry." He apologized as he followed his opponent's line of sight to Lady Christine.

"No need to apologize. It was my mistake," Lord William said as he rubbed his arm. "I am surprised to see her on the field practicing." He admitted to Sir Gunther.

"She practices often. Her father prefers she stay within the Keep, but as you can see, he has little control over what she does." The knight commented with a smirked.

The two men watched Lady Christine spar with Sir Farrell.

It was obvious to Lord William that the knight was keeping his strength in check. Lord William scrutinized Lady Christine's footwork and noted her mistakes and lack of balance. *It is unfortunate that Sir Farrell ignores the opportunity to improve her skills*, he thought.

Lady Christine stumbled suddenly and fell. Sir Farrell stopped sparing.

"Humh, she would be dead." Lord William commented aloud to Sir Gunther.

Lady Christine snapped her head toward Wildenham's guest as the comment reached her ears. She narrowed her eyes conveying her agitation.

"I don't believe I asked for your opinion, sir," she said as she picked herself up from the ground, walked to where he stood, and stared up into his eyes.

"You didn't and I wasn't speaking to you." Lord William stated without flinching. "You misstepped and it would have cost you your life. Normally, your opponent wouldn't stop fighting. They would go for the kill." His eyes bore into hers. He was confident his conclusion of the mock fight was correct.

Something in his hazel eyes unsettled her. Was it anger? Was it hate? Or perhaps it was a wickedness she saw as she studied the gold flecks amongst the greens and browns? Even though she hated to admit, she had landed on the ground, and it was embarrassing to do so. She preferred to correct the mistake.

"Perhaps my sparring partner has been lenient, for I see in your eyes that you would show no mercy. Demonstrate where I misstepped." Lady Christine ordered as she backed away and readied herself.

Lord William looked at her readied, small body and then to Sir Farrell, who nodded in encouragement for taking on his feisty lady. Looking back to Lady Christine, Lord William understood Sir Farrell's reason for checking his strength. Even with the practice sword he could kill her with one blow.

"On one condition." He stated as he stood before her with his practice sword lowered.

She lowered her practice sword with a look of defiance on her face. Usually her demands were met immediately and never negotiated, but she was willing to listen to what he had to say.

"Which is?"

"That we walk through this slowly. Over time, when you have practiced the movements that are new to you, and your muscles begin to retain the routine then we will increase the speed," he said as he wondered if he may be getting himself into a difficult situation. He was in Wildenham to kill her father, not to give fighting lessons to someone who would soon lose her home and be forced to live on the streets. He looked to the Keep and then to her and let out a sigh.

"I agree." She conceded and waited for instruction.

"Follow my movements." He raised his practice sword. She did the same. He lowered his sword and corrected her foot placement to improve her balance. He began with the simple movement she seemed to be having difficulty mastering. He stepped forward, aligning his feet and jabbing his sword.

"It's all a matter of timing." Lord William explained as he repeated the movement and she followed.

After several minutes, Lady Christine's arm began to tire. She became weary of the tedious repetition of the movement.

"Oh, this is ridiculous. Show me something I don't know." She ordered impatiently as she lowered her sword and stomped her foot on the ground.

Lord William stared at her intently and tried to retain his patience. He thought of going to the Keep, killing her father, and being on his way. Living on the streets would do her some good, but if that is where she was to reside in the future, it was imperative to improve her fighting skills for self-defense. He took a deep breath and let it out slowly.

"Do you want to learn or not?" He gritted his teeth to maintain his composure as his hazel eyes glared into her defiant orbs again.

She could see she had pushed him too far. After all, he was a guest.

"I do." She replied calmly as she reined in her frustration.

Sir Gunther leaned toward Sir Farrell and whispered.

"That may be the only time we ever hear her utter those words to any man."

Both men concealed the smiles on their faces as they watched the lesson continue.

"We will add other movements once you have perfected what we are doing now. Until that time, do what I say," Lord William said sternly.

She nodded her head in understanding and they began to move in unison once again.

Sir Farrell leaned toward Sir Gunther and said, "He handles her temperament quite well."

"I agree. He has a natural authority about him. It may come in handy should he ever fill the role as her husband and Lord of Wildenham," Sir Gunther said as he looked to Sir Farrell with a slight smirk.

"I doubt the thought has crossed his mind. He doesn't seem the type." Sir Farrell commented as he turned his attention back to the sparring pair.

"Well, we shall see," Sir Gunther said with a grin upon his face.

Lord William stopped several times and repositioned Lady Christine's arm boldly or redirected the placement of her foot for additional leverage while those around them watched. Several soldiers imitated their movements in an attempt to learn as well.

Arriving bareback on a pony, Thomas dismounted. He went to Sir Farrell and delivered a message. When Lord William paused to correct Lady Christine, Sir Farrell saw the opportunity to interrupt the practice session and relay the message.

"My Lady, your father requests your presence in the library."

Lady Christine sighed with vexation. She anticipated her father's trivial reason for interrupting her practice.

Lord William accepted a wooden ladle of cold water from Conal. He drank it dry, handed it back to the lad, and requested another. Conal dipped it quickly and held it up. Lord William accepted the ladle as he heard his name and turned in Lady Christine's direction.

"Sir William, my apologies, for my father demands a moment of my time."

Lord William finished the second ladle of cold water and handed the empty ladle back to Conal. His face was stern and unsmiling.

"Thank you for your tutelage. It has been most helpful," she said as she grew uncomfortable by his stare.

"The pleasure has been mine, my lady." He tipped his head with a slight nod.

She turned away, threw her sword onto the pile of practice swords, and climbed atop her horse. Sir Farrell followed her quickly.

Lord William watched as the two trotted their horses toward the Keep. A slap on his back caused him to turn his head toward Sir Gunther, who was standing next to him.

"Well done." Sir Gunther complimented as he gave Lord William's shoulder a good squeeze.

"What?" He was puzzled by the knight's comment.

"The way you handled her and earned her respect. I believe she may fancy you." Sir Gunther tilted his head in Lady Christine's direction and slapped him on the back again.

Lord William watched the long flowing blonde hair blow in the breeze and disappear over the hill. He doubted the knight's assumption of Lady Christine's feelings was correct.

"She must know how to defend herself," Lord William said. "Shall we continue?" He raised his practice sword. Sir Gunther complied.

Chapter 11

Lady Christine walked with commanding strides into her father's library while Sir Farrell stopped outside of the door and waited in the hallway. Her father was sitting at his desk surrounded by stacks of books and pile of folded missives.

"Father, what is the meaning of this summoning?"

Lord Clayborn looked up from a missive held within his hand.

"My darling daughter." Lord Clayborn began.

"Don't 'darling daughter' me. When you begin a conversation with those words, it usually means that you are up to no good." She insinuated and stood before him with her fists upon her hips as if scolding a child.

Lord Clayborn chuckled. She knew him too well. He looked down at the opened missives that lay upon his desk.

"We have received several offers for your hand in marriage," he said as he picked up the missives emphasizing the number.

She snatched them from his hand and plopped herself down in the chair across from his desk. She opened the first missive, read it quickly, and wrinkled her nose in disgust.

"Oh, you cannot be serious. I will not accept Lord Seward. I know he is wealthy, but his face looks like a fish and his breath is equally as smelly," she said as she threw the missive on the floor and opened the next from the pile within her lap.

"Lord Marshall? It is obvious his true interest is to increase his wealth, is it not? Last I heard, his kingdom was falling apart," she said as she tossed his offer onto the floor as well. She scanned through the rest of the missives.

"Lord Edwin, Sir Calvin, and Sir Philip." She read the signature at the bottom of each missive and tossed it onto the floor.

"Really Father, none are worthy." She stated emphatically and stood.

"My dearest, I am not getting any younger. You must find a husband, for my peace of mind, if for nothing else." He begged, trying to convey the urgency.

"I'm sorry Father, but don't you want me to be happy?" She lowered her chin and peeked at him through her long eyelashes.

"I do, but you may be unable to afford that luxury. If you are unwed when my time comes, you will lose Wildenham." He stated the reality of the situation and hoped she would see reason.

"I will choose someday, but not today and I am confident that your demise will be far into the future," she said as she leaned over the desk and kissed him on his cheek before turning and skipping toward the door.

"Christine," he said sternly.

Lady Christine stopped and turned to face her father.

"What, Father?"

"You are my legacy and I need you to carry on once I am gone. I want to ensure you will remain within Wildenham's walls, understand the workings of the kingdom, and know how to make decisions that are in the best interest of everyone. When do you plan to focus your attention on your future responsibilities?"

"Father, we have plenty of time for me to learn." She turned and left the library.

"I hope you are right," he said aloud to no one, as he looked at the missives scattered upon the floor and shook his head.

Having her practice session cut short, Lady Christine went directly to her bedchamber, bathed, and dressed in a cranberry red and gold gown. It was her favorite. Tiny pearls embellished the bodice. The skirt was full with many layers.

With nothing pressing on her lady's schedule, Gilda was granted the extra time to add special touches such as ribbon and pearls to her hair. Before leaving her bedchamber, Lady Christine took a book and went to the flower garden to enjoy the waning rays of the afternoon sun. She sat on a bench and opened her book. After her third attempt to read the same page, she closed the book and allowed her mind to reflect on her practice. She recalled his hand rotating her wrist and straightening her shoulders into the correct position. She was startled by his first touch, but understood the necessity and grew more comfortable as the practice progressed.

The bush to her right began to shake. She turned her head toward it and watched in wonder as Jackson pushed proudly through a hedge carrying a limp mouse in his mouth. He waddled to his mistress, dropped the mouse at her feet, laid down on the stone walkway, and began to roll about.

　　　　　　　　The Freelancer

Unable to resist the feline's charm, Lady Christine bent over, rubbed the cat's fat belly, and picked up the mouse by its tail.

"For me, why, thank you. Are you sure you don't want to eat this one?" Lady Christine stood.

Jackson stopped rolling, looked to her face and paused, then continued to roll. He twisted and turned along the stone until his fur became covered with loosened hair.

Lady Christine tossed the mouse into the nearby bush, bent down, and pulled her hand along the cat's body removing the loosened hair and letting it fly away into the air. She looked toward the darkening sky as her stomach grumbled indicating it may be time for the evening meal. She left the garden and went into the Keep with Jackson following. As she emerged from the hallway and into the Great Hall, many had gathered and were ready to be served. The aroma of roasted meats and vegetables filled the air. She took her usual place at the High Table. Her father sat to her left with Sir Gunther and Sir Farrell to his left. Enid and Gilda sat to her right. She watched as peasants brought in platters of food to their table and filled their glasses with spiced wine or ale. Those who sat on benches had their mugs filled with ale and were served trenchers piled high with food.

All waited for Lord Clayborn to begin his meal. He selected a goose breast, ate a large bite, and reached for his full tankard, but it flew off the table and crashed on the floor before he could grasp it.

"Darn ghost." He chuckled in an attempt to make the incident seem trivial. The flying mug unnerved those in attendance. They were a superstitious lot and found the legend of the former

Lord of Wildenham quite haunting. A serving wench came forward quickly with another tankard, filled it with ale, and handed it to Lord Clayborn. He took a large swig and set it upon the High Table. The meal had officially begun. Everyone selected their choice of meat and began to eat.

Lady Christine reached for a roasted turkey drumstick, but paused as she noticed Lord William's late arrival. *Apparently another black tunic*, she thought, eyeing the ebony tunic trimmed with silver thread and his sword and dirk at his side. As he walked past the High Table, he was followed by Jackson with the tip of his tail curled to the right and held high. Lord William sat at the same seat as he previous night and held out a mug for a wench to fill. He grabbed a turkey leg and was about to take a bite when Jackson hopped into his lap and sat. The cat sniffed in the direction of the meat and placed a paw upon the table indicating he was ready for his meal. She scowled as she watched Lord William break off a piece of meat from the turkey leg and set it upon the table before the feline. Unable to turn down the opportunity, Jackson ate the meat, licked his mouth, and looked toward the turkey leg for another piece.

Lord William bit into the turkey leg and took note of the various objects and tapestries displayed within the room. His eyes paused upon Lady Christine. She was staring at him. Was it anger he saw in her eyes? He picked up his mug of ale and hoisted it in a silent toast toward her before taking a large swig.

Lady Christine refused to return his compliment. She watched as Jackson's paw reached up toward the turkey leg. Lord William tore off another piece and set it upon the table for the cat to eat. How could Jackson favor this stranger over her? Her jaw began to ache as she clenched her teeth tighter. *Jackson is only taking advantage of a free meal,* she thought.

Lord William continued to peel off pieces of meat and feed the cat. He set aside a chunk of bread for Corvus. When Jackson was no longer hungry, he licked his paws and rubbed his face, curled into a ball upon Lord William's lap, and went to sleep. Lord William listened to his tablemates' stories and added to the conversation throughout the meal.

After having their appetites satisfied and listening to stories while drinking a pint or two, a large man dressed in green and black marched into the Great Hall. Conversations stopped as those within the room turned their heads toward the stranger who knelt onto one knee before the High Table, stood, and introduced himself.

"My lord, I am Lord Redmond of Langston. May I request a night's stay and a meal?"

Lord William watched the stranger intently. He knew the man was telling a falsehood because he had slain the man with the very same name and title nearly a month ago. He doubted there was a second Lord Redmond from the same kingdom.

"Ah, Langston, a lovely kingdom or so I have been told. Will you be staying only one night?" Lord Clayborn inquired.

"Yes, that is all I will need," the man said with a sneer.

Lord Clayborn was impressed with the size and stature of the visitor.

"My dear," he said to his daughter, "this is…"

Lady Christine rose quickly causing both knights at the table to rise respectfully.

"Good night, Father." She resented her father's weak attempt at matchmaking.

The guest was stunned by the lady's rudeness toward her father as he watched her leave the High Table and walk across the room. She was even more beautiful than the rumors stated. He liked her feistiness and anticipating her warming his bed very soon.

Lady Christine walked toward Lord William. Without a word, she took Jackson from his lap and left the Great Hall for her bedchamber.

Lord William ignored the removal of the cat as he stared at the kingdom's guest, who scrutinized its mistress.

"Yes, Lord Redmond, you may share a meal with us. When finished, Wilfred will show you to a chamber." Lord Clayborn stated as he picked up his tankard.

The guest turned his attention back to his host.

"Thank you for your kind hospitality," he said, nodding in appreciation. He turned toward the tables, chose a seat with his back facing Lord William, and began to eat.

Lord William glanced at the imposter from time to time while he continued to listen to the conversation at his table. He noted the stranger remained silent, ate quite quickly, and kept looking in the direction of the High Table. When the guest finished his meal, Wilfred appeared before the visitor and offered to escort him to a chamber. Lord William watched the two men as they passed by him and noticed Lord Clayborn staring at him. The Lord of Wildenham raised his tankard in a silent toast. Lord William grabbed his mug and returned the gesture. He surmised he had earned Lord Clayborn's trust, and it would allow him easy access when the time came to complete his task. He hoped to fulfill his assignment soon and return home.

Lord William sat and visited with the men at his table as he continued to drink and listen to their tales of women and woes. Having lived most of his life with Rowena, he was enjoying the company of the merry men and found conversing with them quite enjoyable.

Servants took away the trenchers and began stacking empty tables and benches. Taking a cue from the activity, Lord William excused himself, picked up the chunk of bread, and began to make his way to his chamber. He paused momentarily at Lord Clayborn's bedchamber door and looked toward his daughter's bedchamber. He wondered if she was sleeping. Jackson came down the hallway toward him with his tail raised high.

"Hello, Jackson. Come to visit me again?"

Lady Christine's door swung open.

"There you are, you chubby cat," she said as she stepped into the hallway, scooped up Jackson in her arms, and stood before Lord William. She was wearing a dainty white chemise trimmed in lace. Her long blonde hair hung down over her shoulders in luscious curls.

Lord William stopped and stood with his mouth agape. He had never witnessed such beauty as his eyes scanned her body from head to toe.

Lady Christine's skin seemed to crawl with goose bumps. Her stomach fluttered nervously as she realized his stare was one of desire or perhaps intoxication. Either reason being equally as dangerous.

"I see you have enjoyed the evening." She stated harshly as she cuddled Jackson close to her chest.

The sound of her voice brought his eyes back to her face. His cheeks turned to a pinkish hue realizing she had caught him gaping disrespectfully.

"Yes, um, it was nice. I am unaccustomed to spending time in the company of others." He sighed as he recovered his composure. "Well, good night, Lady Christine," he said as he walked away abruptly and went to his chamber.

She turned to watched him leave. When he was out of sight, she entered her bedchamber, shut the door, and bolted it securely.

Once in his room, Lord William shut the door and noted Wilfred had lit a fire in the fireplace. He took off his sword and dirk and hung it on the bedpost. Corvus, who had taken advantage of the open window and perched himself on the headboard, woke from his sleep, ruffled his feathers, and rotated to face his master.

Noticing his feathered friend was awake, Lord William inquired.

"Did you have a good day?"

Agitated that his sleep was being interrupted with such a trivial question, Corvus tilted his head pretending to listen. Lord William held the chunk of bread before the raven and then tossed it onto the floor. Corvus had found the dead carcass of a rabbit and had a feast of his own earlier in the evening. He ignored the meager morsel, closed his eyes, and returned to sleep.

Lord William sat on the bench, took off his boots and tunic, and looked out the open window at the glowing lights of the village in the distance. He had to admit he had enjoyed his day at Wildenham.

As he lay beneath the covers of his bed, he decided his stay in Wildenham should come to an end. He would kill Lord Clayborn at the close of the next day and ride through the night under the cover of darkness making his way back to the hut and Rowena.

Chapter 12

Lord William woke from his slumber as his bed began to shake and vibrate. He sat upright and looked to the foot of his bed. The bed stilled instantly. He looked around the room, but found no one in his chamber. *Am I dreaming?* He noticed Corvus had been disturbed from his perch as well, for he was awake and looked confused.

The raven stretched his wings and retracted them next to his body. The bed began to shake again. The hair on Lord William's right arm stood upright as if electrically charged. He darted out of bed and looked beneath it, but found nothing. The bed stopped shaking. He stood cautiously and looked around the chamber.

"It is time." A voice seemed to whisper close to Lord William's left ear.

He snapped his head toward the voice, but no one was there. Pulling his sword and dirk from the sheaths, he took a defensive stance dressed only in his breeches.

Two strong hands touched his back and pushed him forward toward the door. Lord William spun around and sliced his blade through the air at nothing.

*   *   *

Lady Christine opened her eyes lethargically. She watched the dancing shadows on her bedchamber wall cast by the dying flames of the fire. She tried to identify the noise that had awakened her. *Did someone knocking on my door*, she wondered but now only heard silence. She looked toward the window and surmised daylight was hours away. Rolling onto her side, she adjusted the blankets with the hope of returning to sleep, but thoughts began to run through her mind. Realizing sleep was futile; she threw back the covers in disgust, swung her feet to the floor, and stepped on something bumpy and fuzzy. Recoiling her feet, she crawled down to the foot of the bed, pushed Jackson aside, and climbed out the end.

Jackson, unhappy to have his sleep disturbed, took advantage of the vacated warm spot in the bed and curled himself into a ball close to her pillow.

She grabbed a rush from the floor and touched it to an orange ember in the fireplace. The dry rush lit instantly. Lady Christine cupped her hand to shield the flame as she lifted it upward to a taper on the mantel and lit it. Returning to her bed, she cast the candle's light upon the floor and discovered three dead mice all in a row. She wrinkled her nose and looked toward her feline friend.

"Thanks Jackson, but I really don't appreciate presents such as these."

Jackson raised his head, gave his mistress a disinterested stare, laid his head onto her pillow, and resumed his sleep.

Lady Christine picked each mouse up by the tail. The three dead mice dangled from her right hand as she crossed the room.

She set the taper upon the floor, opened the window, and threw the mice out into the darkness. As she closed the window, her stomach grumbled, conveying its emptiness. Picking up the taper, she patted Jackson on his head as she went to the door, unlatched it, and went into the hallway. She stood still for a moment with the taper held high and listened. Other than the light from her candle, the hallway was dark, and all was quiet. She headed toward the kitchen, but soon stumbled over something on the floor. The palms of her hands smacked the stone floor as she landed face down. The candle tumbled onto the floor and its flame went out. Alone in the darkness, she picked herself up and stood rubbing her hands to relieve the pain. Her chemise clung to the front of her body as if it was wet. She found it damp to the touch and pulled the garment away from her skin as she tried to return to her bedchamber, but her foot bumped into something on the floor. She squatted and reached toward the object. It was a body. She retracted her hands, stood, and reached for the wall to steady herself. The stone wall was cool to the touch, and she leaned on it for support to collect her thoughts. Shuffling her feet, she inched her way toward her bedchamber using the wall as a guide. She leaned against an unbolted door and stumbled into the chamber. Once she regained her balance, she realized she was in her father's bedchamber. The candles in the candelabra flickered and the fire burned brightly within the room. She turned to see her shadow cast upon someone lying in a puddle of blood upon the hallway floor.

"Father!" She screamed as she recognized the lifeless body. She stepped into the hallway, kneeled, and cupped his face within her hands. "Father! No!"

*   *   *

Lord William turned toward his chamber door. *Did someone scream?*

"Father!"

It was a woman, he ascertained.

He opened his chamber door and ran into the hallway. Chamber doors opened with curious faces peering at him as he passed and made his way toward the hysterical cries. When he reached the woman, he discovered Lady Christine kneeling over her father's lifeless body. Lord William avoided the blood on the floor as he knelt across from her and placed his head upon Lord Clayborn's chest. He listened, but only heard the silence of death.

Moving as quickly as his aged legs were able, Wilfred arrived carrying a lit taper. He observed Lady Christine, who knelt over her father weeping, then Lord Clayborn's face that stared upward, and finally to Lord William, who lifted his head from the body and sat upright.

"Is he dead?" The steward leaned over the body and watched to see if Lord Clayborn's chest rose and fell.

"Yes." Lord William lifted the left side of Lord Clayborn's nightshirt and discovered a fatal stab wound to his heart. He stood and entered Lord Clayborn's bedchamber with his sword readied. He looked around the room. Everything seemed tidy and in place. Returning to the hallway, he leaned toward Wilfred and said, "It may be a good idea to inform Sir Gunther and Sir Farrell of their lord's demise. The murderer may still be within Wildenham's walls."

"I agree." Wilfred turned and relayed the order to a curious serving wench. She scampered away.

"Oh God, Father no. Don't leave me alone." Lady Christine pleaded as she covered her face with her bloodied hands.

Lord William stood silently as he watched Lady Christine rock back and forth on her knees sobbing over her father's body. He had never witnessed the grief of those who were left behind after he had fulfilled an assignment. He had killed many over the years; too many to count. Had he caused such suffering in those who survived after their loved one was dead?

Lord William held both weapons in his left hand, knelt down next to Lady Christine, and placed his hand upon her back.

She looked in his direction briefly before reaching for her father's face and brushing his messed hair with her finger.

Lord William looked at the face of the Lord Clayborn whose eyes were open and seemed to be staring toward the heavens. He was a man who appeared to care deeply for his daughter, but what would become of the unwed Lady Christine? Lord William knew she must decide between three alternatives. First, once word of Lord Clayborn's death reached the baron, she may be forced to wed someone of the baron's choosing. Second, leave Wildenham and seek refuge with a relative. Third, live on the streets. The hair on the back of his neck seemed to rise as he sensed the curiosity of those who had gathered in the hallway.

"The ghost finally got him." A serving wench whispered to another.

Lord William glanced at Wilfred. The steward was staring at him. He looked in the direction of the bedchamber that no longer belonged to Lord Clayborn. As he stood and rotated in a circle, his eyes scanned the faces of the onlookers. Many stopped their whispered conversations and stared at his silent inquiry. They served a lord who was now dead. Some were crying and feared their uncertain future. Lord William looked down at the bloody floor and closed his eyes offering a silent prayer. He thought of Rowena, his life as a mercenary, and the justification to return to both.

Lady Christine's sobs broke his concentration. He opened his eyes to see her head upon her father's chest and her arms around his neck. Gilda stepped forward to comfort her lady, but Lord William held up his hand indicating for the woman to stop her advance. God help him for what he was about to do. He raised his head and looked toward the steward.

"Wilfred, could you retrieve my tunic and boots, please?"

"Yes, Sir William." Wilfred turned to get the items. The bystanders parted to allow the steward to pass.

Lord William knelt next to Lady Christine and leaned close to her ear.

"Lady Christine, you must listen to me." He whispered. She cried even louder.

"Christine, listen to me," he said firmly.

She sat up slowly and looked at him through two tear-streaked bloody handprints on her face.

"Do you wish to remain in Wildenham?"

She looked at him as if his question made no sense.

"Do you wish to remain in Wildenham?" He repeated.

"I have nowhere else to go, no family to take me in," she said as the steward returned.

"Here you are, sir. I also brought what was on your bedpost as well," Wilfred said as he juggled the tunic folded over his arm, the boots tucked under his arm, the leather sheaths in one hand, and the candlestick in the other.

"Thank you, would it be possible to have a few of the staff put Lord Clayborn's body in the cellar until it can be buried tomorrow morning and have the hallway cleaned even though the hour is very early?" Lord William took the boots from Wilfred and stepped into them. He put on his tunic, strapped the sheaths around his waist, and inserted his sword and dirk.

"I think that is a wise idea," Wilfred said in agreement.

"May I borrow your taper?"

"It is yours." Wilfred handed Lord William the lit candle.

"When you have finished directing the staff on cleaning the hallway, could you join us in the chapel?"

"I shall be there directly," Wilfred said before turning to a few of the servants and giving instructions.

"Lady Christine, come with me," Lord William said as he bent down and put his arm around her waist.

She gave her father's face one last caress before being pulled away. Once standing, her head seemed to spin and her knees became weak.

Sensing her distress, Lord William kept his arm around her waist as he held the taper high to light their way. They navigated the staircase and hallways and entered the chapel where the light of two red glass sconces upon the altar emphasized the place of reverence. Lord William guided Lady Christine to a bench and helped her sit.

"All will be well." He reassured as he looked around the chapel.

Her tears were uncontrollable. They cascaded down her cheeks as she looked about and realized where she was. *Lord William has escorted me here to pray for my father's soul,* she thought. *How kind.*

"Where is the priest?" Lord William inquired as he glanced around the room and then to her for an answer.

"Father Frederick's chamber is there," Lady Christine said as she pointed to the chamber door. She made the sign of the cross, clasped her hands together, and began to pray.

Lord William went to the side chamber and knocked on the door. He waited patiently and heard rustling within the chamber before the door opened.

"Father Frederick, I need you to perform a marriage ceremony," Lord William said.

"My son, now, at this hour?" Father Frederick was confused by the unusual request.

"Yes, it is imperative."

"I will be with you in a moment," he said and shut the door in Lord William's face.

Lord William turned away from the abrupt dismissal to rejoin Lady Christine, but paused as he thought he saw what appeared to be a shadowed figure standing in an unlit corner at the back of the room. *Perhaps someone followed us to the chapel,* he surmised.

Lord William ignored the assumed servant and sat quietly next to Lady Christine. He rested the lit taper upon his knee and turned his head slightly in her direction to see if she was still crying. He watched as a tear rolled down her cheek making a clean streak through the bloody handprint on her face. His eyes were drawn downward to her once white chemise now saturated with blood.

He bolted from his seat to stand before her and held the candle above them as his eyes searched for a tear in her garment.

"Are you hurt?"

She stopped her silent wish for her father's peace, unclasped her hands, and looked down at her chemise. Using her thumb and index finger of each hand, she pulled her chemise away from her body.

"No. It is Father's blood," she said as she released her gown and clasped her hands to continue praying.

He set the candle on the altar before returning to his seat. While they waited, he listened to Lady Christine's whispered prayers and became mesmerized by the dancing candlelight on the crucifix above the altar.

Father Frederick entered the room, but stopped suddenly when he noticed the condition of Lady Christine and her clothing. He looked to Lord William for an explanation.

Lord William stood and approached the clergyman.

"Father, Lord Clayborn has been murdered. It is my intention to marry Lady Christine." Lord William stated confidently.

"Wed? Me? I do not want to wed you." Lady Christine stood curling her hands into tight fists.

"Christine, your options are limited." Lord William explained calmly. "The baron will either choose a husband for you or Wildenham will be given to another to rule and you will be forced to leave. Is there another you prefer to marry?"

She stared at him as his words registered and recalled her father's warning to take a husband before he passed. Lady Christine scanned her memory of requests she had received, but her mind was fuzzy and blank. The only option that came to mind was Lord Sheridan, but she would rather live in the streets than be married to him.

"No." She replied meekly and lowered her head.

All turned in the direction of Wilfred as he walked into the chapel carrying another lit taper to light his way.

Anticipating his soon-to-be wife's needs, Lord William made another request of the steward.

"Wilfred, could you have a basin of hot water, soap, and linen taken to Lord Clayborn's bedchamber?"

"Certainly, my lord." Wilfred may have been a little premature with his respectful address of his soon-to-be lord, but getting in one's good graces never hurt. He nodded his head and left to instruct the servants.

"Do you accept this man as your husband, my child?" Father Frederick redirected Lady Christine to the task at hand.

Lady Christine looked at Lord William. After enduring the heartbreak and jilting of her last love, she wanted to marry someone she could trust, someone she loved. She knew nothing of this man who stood before her, but had no other choice than to marry him if she wanted to remain in Wildenham. She lowered her head and looked down at her bloody chemise as she clasped the garment and pulled it away from her body again. She had always imagined wearing the elegant ivory gown that had been made especially for her wedding day. It was stored with the utmost care in her bedchamber and would remain there with its beauty kept in secret and unused for its purpose.

"Yes." She replied meekly as she released her chemise and brushed the crinkled material straight. She lifted her chin, but kept her eyes cast to the floor as tears welled and rolled down her cheeks in earnest.

"Let us do what must be done." Lord William whispered into her ear as he took her elbow and guided her to the altar.

How I wish father were here, she thought refusing to look at her future husband as she took her place beside him and together they stood before Father Frederick.

Wilfred entered the chapel and joined Lord William at his side.

"Everything is being done as you have requested, my lord."

Lord William looked toward the steward.

"Thank you, Wilfred." He turned his attention back to Father Frederick and the matter at hand. "Father, shall we begin?" Lord William held his hand up with his palm down and looked to his bride. She looked at his outstretched hand, then to his unsmiling face, and placed her unsteady, bloody palm on the back of his hand.

Father Frederick picked up a leather bound bible from the altar. He turned toward the couple and began to recite the ceremony in Latin.

Wilfred stood next to the man who would soon become the new Lord of Wildenham and listened to Father Frederick's words resonate within the small chapel. Over the years, the steward had served several lords, but this lord and lady were young, very young. He questioned their ability to rule and wondered what changes lay in store for the kingdom.

When queued, Lady Christine and Lord William said, "I do."

Father Frederick finished the ceremony by giving the couple his blessing. He opened the registry book, dipped a quill in an inkwell, and dated the entry. The newlywed couple signed the registry making their marriage official.

"Thank you, Father," Lord William said as he shook his hand.

"You are most welcome, my lord." Father Frederick looked at Lady Christine with empathy and clasped her hand between both of his.

"My lady, we shall give your father a respectful burial as soon as you are ready in the morning."

"Thank you." She withdrew her hand and turned to leave the chapel. Wilfred stepped aside to let her pass.

Lady Christine's legs were shaky and almost numb, but she forced one foot in front of the other. She was tired and wished to bathe to remove the bloody filth from her body. As she walked down the aisle, her stomach grumbled reminding her of the reason she had left her bedchamber.

Lord William picked up the taper from the altar, turned to follow his wife, but paused before his steward.

"Thank you, Wilfred, for all you have done."

The steward nodded his head in acknowledgement.

"My lord, Sir Gunther indicates the Keep is secure and the guards are on alert."

"Very good, get some rest, for tomorrow may be a very long day."

Wilfred watched the new Lord and Lady of Wildenham exit the chapel. He bid Father Frederick farewell and retired to his bedchamber.

Lady Christine climbed the staircase and walked through the hallway toward her bedchamber. She stopped before her father's bedchamber. A servant had placed several candles on the floor and was doing her best in the dim light to remove the remnants of blood. Lord William stopped behind his wife and stood quietly. She was aware of his presence as a light emanated from behind her and looked over her left shoulder to verify that he was there. She stepped around the busy servant and entered her bedchamber that was lit only by the glowing embers of the fireplace.

Jackson raised his head from the pillow and watched her walk around the room.

I need to wash. She thought she had heard someone request hot water for her to wash, but noticed it was absent. To add to her confusion, she looked to the doorway where a shadowed figure stood. It was her husband.

"I believe Wilfred had a basin taken to your father's…," he said, then restated, "our bedchamber."

Lady Christine's eyes widened as she realized what he might demand from her on their wedding night. She was unprepared to satisfy his needs. Would he show compassion for her current emotional state? She stared at the darkened shadow, the stranger who was now her husband, and took a step backward as he walked into her bedchamber.

Lord William sensed her apprehension. He stopped and stood a few steps away from her.

"Shall we go to our bedchamber and see if the basin is there?" He suggested calmly and held out his hand for her to accept.

She looked at his hand and then to his face. His concern seemed genuine, but she was suspicious of his intention. She went to her bed, picked up Jackson, and ignored his hand as she walked past him into the hallway.

Lord William lowered his offered hand and let out a deep sigh. He was trying to be civil. He thought he was doing what was right, what needed to be done by taking her as his wife and ensuring she remain within Wildenham. He followed her into the hallway, but almost walked into the back of her.

With her pathway blocked by a servant who was still cleaning the floor, Lady Christine had stopped and stared down at the blood that remained on the floor.

Understanding her dilemma, Lord William set the taper upon the floor and scooped her and Jackson up into his arms. His wife let out a gasp of surprise as he stepped over the busy servant and into their bedchamber. He searched the room until he located the basin on the table. His eyes were drawn to her stomach as he heard it grumble.

Lord William lowered his wife to the floor and took a step backward. Both stood in silence, unsure what they should do next.

Thinking it would be best to give her a few moments of privacy to wash and change garments, Lord William headed toward the door.

"I'll just go to the kitchen and get us something to eat." He stated before exiting the room.

Lady Christine watched the door close as her husband left the bedchamber. She set Jackson on the floor and turned around to look at the steam rising from the basin on the table. Wilfred had kindly set out her scented soaps and a stack of linen wash cloths and towels as well. Or perhaps he instructed Enid or Gilda do the task. Slipping her chemise over her shoulders, she let it fall to the floor and stepped out of it as she went to the table. She dipped the linen cloth into the inviting water, wet it thoroughly, and wrung it out. She rubbed the wet cloth on the soap until it began to lather. She inhaled the fragrance of the calming lavender and began washing her chest and abdomen. When she rinsed the linen, the water turned red. She stared in horror.

"Oh, Father."

Her bottom lip trembled as she wrung out the cloth and examined her body wondering which part to wash next. Her father's blood seemed to have soaked into every pore of her body. It was nearly impossible to find a spot that was unsoiled. Her heart began to pound, her breathing quickened, and tears streamed down her cheeks as she began to wash as quickly as possible. Lady Christine tried to rid her body of the blood, but no matter how much she bathed, there was always more. She continued to rinse the cloth and wash herself, scrubbing harder and harder until her skin was as red as the blood.

Chapter 13

Once in the hallway, Lord William picked up the taper from the floor and made his way to the kitchen. He walked through the arched doorway holding the candle high and toured the room. It remained unchanged from years ago with its pots and pans stacked on shelves and tables in the center used to prepare the food. A young lad slept on a cot next to the kitchen fireplace. Lord William assumed the lad's responsibility was to keep the fire lit through the night. The embers were ashen and dying. Knowing the lad would have to wake soon to rekindle them, Lord William stirred them with a poker, selected a few logs from the pile on the floor, and placed them upon the rejuvenated embers. The boy mumbled something incoherent, but remained asleep.

Lord William chose a wooden plate from a shelf, entered the storage room, and set down his candle upon a stool. He selected an apple from a barrel, a cheese wedge, and a small loaf of bread. He lifted a linen cloth and discovered a tray of fruit tarts, selected one, and placed it upon the plate in case his wife preferred something sweet. He found a bottle of spiced red wine and tucked it under his arm. He picked up the lit taper and left the storage room. Setting the candlestick momentarily upon a table, he selected two wooden mugs and a small cast iron kettle from a shelf. He placed the mugs in the kettle before slipping its handle over his arm, retrieved his lit taper, and headed back to the bedchamber.

The hallway floor was clean and the servant had left. He tilted his head toward the bedchamber door and heard hysterical crying coming from the other side. He opened the door hesitantly and scanned the room until he found his wife. She stood with her back toward him and wore a towel tucked securely around her body. She was gasping for air, mumbling incoherently, and scrubbing as if trying to rid her body of a terrible disease. He closed the door with his foot and set the contents within his arms upon the bench before the fireplace. He stepped next to her, set the lit taper on the table, and looked at the bowl of bloody water.

"Christine, calm yourself." He unfolded each finger of her clenched hand and removed the wet linen, set it on the table, and guided her to the bench where he encouraged her to sit.

"His blood is everywhere," she said as she tried to catch her breath and wiped the tears from her cheeks with the backs of her hands.

"I know." He went to the table and picked up the basin, the wet linen, and a damp bar of soap. He returned and set the basin on the floor next to his wife. He dunked the cloth in the red water, squeezed out the excess, rubbed it on the soap, and lifted her chin with his free hand.

Too tired to resist his touch, she closed her eyes to avoid his inquisitive stare.

With tender care, he washed the bloody handprints from her tear-streaked face.

Lady Christine opened her eyes when her husband released her chin. She watched as he rinsed the cloth and ran it over her arms and legs to ensure they were clean. Her face flushed from his unfamiliar touch. She turned her head away from him to hide her embarrassment.

"Where is another chemise?" He set the wet cloth upon the end of the bench.

Lady Christine's breathing had slowed. Her tears had stopped.

"There is another in my room, in the chest at the foot of my bed." She averted her eyes to the floor.

He took the lit taper from the table before going to her bedchamber. He entered and paused inside the doorway. The furniture was the same. Memories of his beloved mother flashed in his mind; her beautiful face, warm smile, and loving embrace. He looked to the bed where he had laid next to her when she took her last breath and death opened the portal for her soul to enter the nonphysical world. He had thought of her so little over the years. Perhaps the hate he had for his father had consumed what love she had instilled within his heart. He wondered if she would be pleased with his decision to remain in Wildenham.

Pulling himself from his thoughts, he selected a chemise from the trunk and returned to their bedchamber. His wife was gazing into the fire as if in a daze. He set the candle upon the mantel and knelt before her.

"Christine, lift your arms." He waited patiently for her to comprehend his request.

She looked into his eyes, then to the chemise in his hands, and did as he asked while he guided her arms through the sleeves and slipped it over her head. He pulled the gown over her body and reached underneath to loosen the towel. It would fall off once she stood.

"Unsure of your preferences, I tried to select a variety of food." He stated as he picked up the wooden plate at the end of the bench and set it on her lap.

She nodded as she tried to smile, but tears began to roll down her face again. *He is being so kind*, she thought as she blinked her swollen eyes lethargically.

Lord William picked up her hand and put it on the edge of the plate to ensure it would remain upon her lap.

She grasped the edge, but her eyes returned to the flicker flames.

He poured the wine into the kettle and placed it on the hook over the fire to warm. Returning to the bench, he noticed she had yet to select an item from the plate.

Jackson walked toward the couple, rubbed against Lord William's leg, and sat before him. The fat feline tilted his head from one side to the other until Lord William reached over to the plate, broke off a piece of cheese, and tossed it to him. Jackson bent down and smelled it. He sat up and batted it a few times with his paw as if to play with it like a mouse. He looked to Lord William as if disappointed.

"That is the best I can offer you," Lord William said and patted the cat's head.

Jackson lowered his head, licked the cheese, and ate it.

Lord William heard his wife's stomach grumble again.

"I thought the tart looked rather good." He suggested to his wife.

She looked down at the tart.

"It does, but I'm not in the mood to eat at the moment."

"I'm sorry for the loss of your father." He was pleased to have her conversing.

"Thank you," she said as she wiped a tear from her cheek. "He was a good man."

"I'm sure he was."

"I can't understand why my tears keep coming like waves in the ocean. I believe myself to be fine and the next second sorrow fills my heart and my tears begin again." She wiped away another tear.

Unsure of what to say, he sat quietly and watched the fire. When steam began to rise from the kettle, Lord William took a mug from the bench and dipped it into the kettle to fill it. He wiped the outside of the cup with his tunic to remove the dripping wine. Lifting the plate from Lady Christine's lap and setting it on the bench, he placed the mug within her hands and wrapped her fingers around it to ensure she held it. He guided the mug upward to her mouth. She sipped the warm wine. When she lowered the mug to her lap, he took the second mug from the bench, turned, and dipped it into the kettle. He sat back down on the bench next to his wife and took a large swig. The warm red wine was spicy and soothing.

"This is very good wine." He commented with the hope of pulling her into another conversation. Lady Christine remained silent. She continued to sip her wine and stare into the fire until her mug was half empty. As the warmth spread throughout her body, she began to relax. Her eyelids grew heavy. She fought to keep them open.

Lord William watched his wife from the corner of his eye as he lifted his tankard and took another swig. Her mug was beginning to tip forward. Her head bobbed while she fought to stay awake. He set his mug upon the bench and reached for her tankard.

"Perhaps you should go to bed. I will be there soon." He took her mug before it spilled.

Lady Christine opened her eyes as the mug left her hands and watched as her husband set it on the bench and reach for her elbow.

The towel fell to the floor as he helped her stand and guided her to the bed. He pulled back the covers. She slipped between the soft linen sheets and lay upon her side facing him. She closed her eyes as he pulled the covers over her shoulder.

Lord William looked down at his wife and hoped he would never regret his decision. *Such a beauty*, he thought. He walked to the fireplace and refilled his mug. He sat on the bench and sipped the warm, spiced wine as he watched the mesmerizing flames in the fireplace. With his wife sleeping soundly, he welcomed the soothing effects of his drink and became lost in thought. It was the first time he had failed to fulfill an assignment. His ego was bruised, but since his identity as a mercenary remained unknown, his reputation would go unscathed. Who had requested his service and why did they want Lord Clayborn dead? Whoever it was, they knew where to find Rowena. Would they retaliate against her for his failure? He would send a messenger to warn her of the impending danger and offer a safe residence within Wildenham's walls.

He pondered the true identity of the imposter who claimed to be Lord Redmond of Langston. What was his reason for telling the falsehood? Was he another mercenary? Would he be found within Wildenham's walls at daylight? If he was Lord Clayborn's murderer, would he try to attack Lady Christine as well?

A noise from the bed pulled him from his thoughts. He looked in its direction and heard Lady Christine sobbing as she rolled over in her sleep. To lose her father and become a wife within an hour's time would be too much for any woman to handle. How was he going to explain to her that he was the one who should have killed her father? In order to keep their marriage civil, he saw little need to divulge his true reason for coming to Wildenham.

He took the last large gulp of wine from his mug and set it on the bench. He reached for the linen towel that lay on the floor, used it to insulate his hand as he removed the hot kettle from the fire, and placed it on the stone hearth. He blew out the taper and barred the door of the bedchamber. Lord William took off his sword belt and hung it on the bedpost next to where his head would rest. He removed his tunic, tossed it on the chest at the end of the bed, and slipped beneath the covers next to his wife. She lay on her left side facing him. He admired each feature on her face that was highlighted by the flickering firelight. *She is a beauty*, he thought again. He had to admit she was a feisty soul and he hoped they would grow accustomed to one another as husband and wife. He rolled away from her onto his left side and let his heavy eyelids close. The hair on his arms stood on end as if sensing something was wrong, very wrong. Cracking his eyes open, he scanned the room and tried to focus on a dark shadow next to the fireplace. He could roughly make out the outline of a person, yet see through it to the paneled wall behind. The shadow seemed to come forward toward him, but retreated quickly and disappeared into the paneled wall. Lord William closed his eyes and let sleep overtake his weary mind.

With matters settled for the night, Jackson hopped up onto the bed and curled into a ball between his lord and lady. He covered his eyes with his paw and began to purr as he drifted off to sleep.

Chapter 14

Lady Christine lay on her back. A nagging pressure bearing down upon her chest caused her to wake from her restless slumber. She opened her eyes a mere crack to see Jackson staring into her face with his paws curled underneath him. She closed her eyes hoping to return to sleep, but it was too late. Jackson saw her eyes move and knew she was awake. He tapped his paw gently upon her cheek and then rested it upon her chest. She ignored his prodding and kept her eyes shut. She knew the feline wanted her to get out of bed and open the bedchamber door so he could go to the kitchen and receive his morning meal from the cook.

Jackson's impatience grew. He touched his paw to her face again and flexed his claws conveying his urgency to eat. Four little pinpricks broke the skin of Lady Christine's cheek.

"Jackson, go away." She turned her head away from his paw and closed her eyes tightly from the bright rays of sunshine beaming through the window that announced the beginning of the day. She stretched and forced her swollen and crusted eyes to open. Wiping away the residue to help clear her vision, Lady

Christine blinked her eyes as the ceiling came into focus, and she realized she was in her father's bedchamber. She turned her head to her left and found the bed empty. Pushing Jackson off of her chest, she sat up quickly and the covers fell away from her chest. Her husband was sitting in a chair at the table, fully dressed, and he was staring at her.

"Good morning." Lord William greeted.

She grabbed the sheet and jerked it to her chest. Her eyes narrowed as she stared at him. She remained quiet as she searched her memory and recalled her father's death, her bloody chemise, and candlelight wedding in the chapel. Her eyes widened at the thought of what may have occurred, but her mind seemed void of the tiny detail. Had she truly become his wife?

A knock at the door interrupted her thought. She looked toward the noise.

"My lady, we hate to interrupt, but Father Frederick wishes to know if you are ready for your father's funeral?" Enid enquired through the door.

"I will be there shortly." She responded harshly as she looked back to her husband and then searched the room for something to cover herself. Her father's robe lay on the chest at the end of the bed. She got out of bed and crossed her arms over her chest. She eyed her husband cautiously as she reached for the robe, put it on, and tied the belt securely. A fragrance of musk and cedar permeated her nose. She held the sleeve to her nose, inhaled her father's fragrance, and settled her nerves for the moment.

Lord William rose from his chair, pulled out his dirk, and walked toward her.

As her husband approached, she stared at the weapon and backed away until she bumped into the wall by the head of the bed.

Lord William pulled back the covers on the bed and cut his left hand with his dirk.

"We don't want servants getting the wrong idea, now do we?" he said grinning.

Lady Christine sighed as she watched him squeeze his hand into a fist and drip blood onto the sheet. *So, I have yet to become his wife,* she thought as he painted a large red blotch. She looked to his face in disbelief.

"Did I overdo it? I don't want to seem as if I am bragging." Lord William jested and displayed a devilish grin.

"You should know better than I." She confessed her virginal status and emphasized the loss of his. She looked to the ceiling. *Men and their egos,* she thought.

There was another knock on the door.

"I'm coming!" She yelled as she walked past her husband to open the door. Lord William straightened the blankets. He walked to the table, selected an unused linen from the previous night, and wrapped a cloth around his left hand to stop the bleeding.

"Good morning, my lord and lady and congratulations. Wilfred told us the good news." Enid greeted with a smile on her face as she entered the bedchamber. She carried a tray piled with enough food for several people. Gilda followed with two mugs of ale in one hand and clean sheets for the bed in the other.

With the bedchamber door open, Jackson saw his opportunity to make his way to the kitchen, but stopped short as a whiff of the breakfast food caught his attention. He turned and followed Enid as she passed him and placed the food on the table.

Gilda set the drinks next to the food. She plopped the clean sheets upon the chest at the foot of the bed and helped Enid pull back the covers. Both women paused when they saw the blood-stained sheet. They looked at each other with skeptical eyes conveying their shock silently. Both women turned their heads and looked at Lord William.

He displayed a proud grin on his face and gave a slight nod of his head. The women looked away as they changed the sheets and made the bed neatly.

"My lord, my lady, is there anything else you need?" Gilda inquired as she gathered the dirty sheets into her arms.

Enid picked up the bowl of bloody water from the floor and turned with the intention of emptying it down the chute in the garderobe when she looked down and saw a spot of blood on the floor. She took a dirty linen that lay on the bench, dipped it in the bloody water, and began to clean the spot.

"Enid, what are you doing?" Lady Christine walked over to her lady in waiting and looked down.

"I'm cleaning the blood that is on the floor, my lady."

Lord William went to Enid's side and followed the trail of blood that led to the bedchamber door. He turned to his wife.

"Did your father make a habit of bolting his door while he slept?"

"Yes, always," Lady Christine said as she forced herself to look away from her father's blood. *What a daft question*, she thought and glared at her husband from the corner of her eye.

Lord William scanned the interior of the bedchamber. *The murderer must have been waiting in the room*, he reasoned as he looked toward the garderobe.

When Enid finished cleaning the trail of blood, she emptied the bowl down the garderobe chute and gathered the remaining dirty linen including the bloody chemise that lay upon the floor.

"My dear, could you please introduce your ladies," Lord William said as he looked to his wife indicating her lack of duty.

"I'm sorry, my lord. May I introduce Enid and Gilda," Lady Christine said sarcastically and a little embarrassed in having her shortcoming brought to light. The women curtsied as they each heard their name.

"It is nice to meet you both." He stated with a nod of greeting.

"Please lay out my blue and gold brocade and tell Father Frederick we will be ready for my father's service after we have eaten and dressed." Lady Christine turned toward the table where her husband now stood.

"Yes, my lady." Enid carried the bowl of dirty linen as she exited with Gilda following and closing the door behind them.

Lord William pulled out the chair for his wife to sit down.

Lady Christine looked to the chair and then to her husband. His unsmiling face was one of insistence. She walked over to the chair and sat as he pushed her toward the table. Lord William pulled out the chair across from his wife and sat. Their eyes met briefly before each took their choice of food from the tray at the same time.

They sat in silence as if an invisible wall was between them and ate. Lord William glanced in her direction often, but always found her face turned away from him as if in protest or disgust. Perhaps she was uneasy in his presence.

"Let me put your mind at ease." He began.

Lady Christine looked at her husband's face.

"I have never forced any woman into my bed. We shall only become husband and wife after I have won the affections of your heart."

His wife looked at him in disbelief and narrowed her eyes.

"Then you will be waiting a lifetime." She replied as she popped a piece of apple into her mouth. Lady Christine ate it as quickly as possible, took a sip of her ale, and pushed herself away from the table. "My lord, if you will excuse me. I need to ready myself." She stated meekly as she rose from her seat and her husband stood and replied.

"William."

"What?" She stood still with a puzzled look upon her face.

"When in the privacy of each other, I prefer you address me by my given name, William." He explained and waited for her reply.

Lady Christine had little care for what he preferred. Her priority was to bury her father. After which time, she intended to take her proper place and run her father's kingdom as she saw fit.

"William," she said tilting her head to the side with a sarcastic curtsy before exiting the bedchamber and shutting the door.

Staring at the closed portal, Lord William sat back down and took a long swig of ale. *She is going to be a handful,* he thought to himself. He felt something brush against his leg and looked down to see Jackson. Lord William attempted to pet the feline, but Jackson moved out of his reach and headed in the direction of the bedchamber door.

"All right," Lord William said as he pushed himself away from the table. "I am interested to see how you and Corvus will get along." He assumed the raven had spent the night roosting on the headboard of his previous chamber and was currently hunting for his breakfast. He opened the bedchamber door. Jackson scampered out of the room. *Now to dress.* He hoped to find something appropriate to wear for the funeral. What little clothing he had brought with him on the assignment would have to be transferred from his chamber to his new dwelling with his wife.

Chapter 15

She paused outside her bedchamber door as a wave of sorrow washed over her. She blinked her eyes as they filled with tears. Perhaps it was the combination of her father's death, being married to a stranger, and the responsibility of running Wildenham when she possessed little knowledge of how to do so. She took a deep breath, opened the door, and was greeted by the smiling faces of Enid and Gilda. They had laid out her blue and gold gown upon her bed and stood waiting for her arrival. Their devilish smiles and curious eyes indicated their need for the details of their mistress's wedding night.

Lady Christine leaned on the bedchamber door as she closed it behind her. At the sight of her ladies' smiles, she burst into tears.

Enid and Gilda's happiness faded and their faces became blank with concern.

"Oh, my lady." Gilda comforted as she came toward her distraught mistress, put her hand upon her lady's arm, and guided her to sit upon the chest at the end of the bed.

"It couldn't have been all that bad." Enid added as she imagined the thrill of intimacy of one's wedding night.

Gilda looked at Enid with a threatening glare and contorted her face indicating her comment was inappropriate.

Lady Christine covered her face with her hands. Her tears were uncontrollable, but what was more troubling was the unexplained reason for them. She had difficulty pinpointing their justification.

"There, there, my lady." Gilda consoled as she patted her lady's shoulder. "We will get through today as best we can." She patted the top of her mistress's head and pulled her hair away from her face. "Your father was a good man, and we shall miss him dearly, but it is nice, however, that we shall remain within Wildenham and that we have a new lord."

Lady Christine wiped her red and swollen eyes with the backs of her hands and then wiped her runny nose with the sleeve of her father's robe. She stood and let out a sigh. She tried to pull herself together, walked around to the side of the bed, and touched one of the sleeves of her gown.

"Father always liked this dress. I think it was his favorite." She stated, trying to distract her mind.

"Shall we get you dressed?" Gilda suggested as she began to loosen the belt on her lady's borrowed robe. The two women worked together to have Lady Christine looking her best. Pearls and ribbon embellished her beautiful golden hair. Unfortunately, nothing could camouflage her puffy eyes and rosy nose. Enid handed her mistress a handkerchief to carry in her hand before opening the bedchamber door.

Lord William waited in the hallway dressed in his usual black attire. He turned toward his wife as she emerged from her bedchamber.

Lady Christine averted her eyes away from her husband in an attempt to hide the fact that she had been crying.

Lord William went to her side.

"Is all well?"

Lady Christine kept her eyes downcast as she nodded her head in confirmation.

They walked side by side through the hallway with Enid and Gilda following, down the staircase, and into the Great Hall. They found Wilfred waiting for them at the bottom of the staircase.

"My lord and lady, I have had your horses readied. Father Frederick has gone ahead and awaits your arrival." Wilfred informed as he walked with them.

Lady Christine took a breath to reply, but her husband did so for her.

"Thank you, Wilfred. We appreciate all that you have done," Lord William said.

Lord William placed his hand on the small of his wife's back and guided her to the stable where the stableboys were holding the reins of their horses.

Lady Christine stopped short.

"I can't remember the last time I rode a horse wearing a dress." She whispered to no one in particular.

Lord William looked at her panicked face, to her horse, and then to her dress.

"Would you like some assistance getting on your horse or shall I call for a bucket for you to use as a step?"

She was a little girl the last time she used a bucket to mount her horse. In her present stature, it would be a little embarrassing to have to use one now.

"I don't want to use a bucket," she said too proud to ask for help.

Lord William bent down and cupped his hands together. She slipped her left foot into his hands. He lifted while she straightened her knee and threw her right leg over the horse. He slid her foot into the stirrup and then climbed atop Adair. The Lord and Lady of Wildenham walked their horses through the castle and headed toward the cemetery.

*   *   *

News of Lord Clayborn's death spread throughout the kingdom. His body had been readied and carried by wagon to the cemetery. Peasants, knights, and nobles had gathered around the grave. Father Frederick gave a respectful service and concluded with a fitting eulogy. With her husband by her side, Lady Christine accepted a bouquet of wild flowers from Enid and placed them upon her father's body. She stood numbly and watched as her loved one was placed into the grave. Peasant men shoveled dirt onto the body until it formed a mound. They outlined it with stones enclosing her father in a tomb of eternal sleep. As she turned toward her horse, a peasant man stepped forward and knelt down upon one knee.

"My lady, what is to become of Wildenham and its citizens?"

Lady Christine looked down at the man and up to those who stood behind him with inquisitive eyes.

"You and Wildenham will remain safe, for I married Lord William upon my father's death." She looked up to her husband who stood to her right. He nodded kindly to the crowd in acknowledgement. Many wished them well as the couple made their way to their horses. After assisting his wife upon her horse, Lord William climbed atop Adair and rode along side of his silent wife back to the Keep.

As they reined their horses before the stable, Lady Christine slid down from her horse and headed for the Keep, hoping to avoid any conversation.

Lord William's leg brushed his saddle bag as he dismounted. He heard a sloshing noise from within the satchel. He lifted the leather flap of the bag and discovered a corked bottle with a note tied around its neck. He had forgotten that Rowena had tied the item to his saddle when he departed. He pulled the bottle from the bag, untied the satchel he had purchased for Rowena, and hurried to join his wife as they made their way through the hallway and into the Great Hall.

"Excuse me." Lady Christine dismissed her husband for some needed solitude. She climbed the staircase and made her way to her bedchamber. Enid and Gilda walked past Lord William and ascended the staircase behind their grieving mistress.

Lord William sighed as he watched the women leave. He lifted the note on the bottle to examine it, but heard a noise to his right and looked to see Wilfred waiting for a moment of his time.

"Yes, Wilfred." He lowered the bottle as the steward approached.

"May I offer to give you a tour of the castle and its workings? It may help you to adjust to your new role as Lord of Wildenham."

"That won't be necessary. I know my way." Lord William declined. His mind was concerned with another matter.

Wilfred tried to conceal the puzzled expression upon his face.

"I do, however, need a messenger. Actually two. Please have them come to the library." Lord William glanced at the tapestry as he passed by it.

"Yes, my lord." Wilfred nodded his head in understanding.

"Also, I need to speak with Sir Farrell." Lord William added over his shoulder before entering the hallway.

"Yes, my lord," Wilfred said with a nod of understanding.

"Thank you." Lord William entered the library and closed the door. It was imperative he send the missives as soon as possible.

Chapter 16

Lady Christine hurried her steps, entered her bedchamber, and burst into tears.

"What am I to do now?" She sobbed trying to catch her breath as she placed the palm of her hand on her stomach and paced back and forth.

Enid and Gilda closed the bedchamber door and looked to one another. Neither was brave enough to offer their advice.

"All of those people depend on me. I have little knowledge of the operations of Wildenham. Oh, how I wish father were here." Lady Christine's breathing quickened and dizziness forced her to collapse onto the window seat.

"My lady, you will carry on," Enid said as she kept her distance from her distraught mistress.

"I'm sure whatever efforts you make to run the kingdom will please your father who watches you from above." Gilda tried to sound reassuring, but the distraught look on her lady's face led her to believe otherwise.

"Wonderful, so when I make a mistake or misstep, father

will be there to cringe or laugh." Lady Christine brushed the tears away from her cheeks.

"We trust you will do the right thing when the time comes. Perhaps for today, you may want to check with the cook and see if the evening meal is to your liking." Enid suggested once she was confident her mistress could control her temper. She crossed the room and smoothed Lady Christine's hair where it had messed and tangled.

"I could what?" Lady Christine tried to understand her new responsibility. "An evening meal? That is the least of my worries. Who is the stranger I have married? I know nothing of him." She looked to her ladies and wiped away another tear.

"He seems very nice and over time, it may turn out to be a good match. It could be worse. You could be married to Lord Sheridan," Gilda said as Enid gave her a look of disdain for the comment.

*   *   *

The room was as he remembered. His father's carved wooden desk and chair placed at the opposite side of the room. The chessboard set on the small table with two chairs against the wall. He looked to the large window behind the desk that allowed the daylight to brighten the room. He remembered the two candlesticks nearly as tall as himself that held a dozen candles each. The walls decorated with the same oil paintings as years ago. Two inviting plush chairs remained before the unlit fireplace with a small table between them. He looked down at the bottle in his hand and read the attached note aloud.

"Your father's spirit does not rest. Place one drop on the floor of each room and tell him to leave." He thought it silly and wondered how Rowena knew he might need such a concoction.

Closing the door, he walked to the desk, sat in the chair with the intention of sending two messages, and set the bottle and satchel upon the desktop. He opened a drawer and found a stack of parchment and a small rectangle box containing a quill and ink. The bottle of pine tar water fell over onto its side. He looked at the upturned bottle and thought it was strange that it should topple, but set the bottle upright before lifting the box from the drawer and setting it upon the desk. He selected two pieces of parchment and closed the drawer. He opened the inkwell and dipped the quill as he tried to organize his thoughts. He needed to inform the baron of the changes within Wildenham, but Lord William was finding it difficult to choose the proper words that jumbled within his mind. How would he explain Lord Clayborn's death, his marriage to Lady Christine, and his true identity as Lord Bradford's son, the rightful Lord of Wildenham?

Out of the corner of his eye, he saw the bottle slide sideways on the desk, or at least he thought he did. When he turned his head toward the bottle, it had moved a little, but now stood stationary. He turned back to the missive and composed each sentence in his mind before writing it upon the missive. When he finished, he folded the parchment, opened another drawer and looked for a seal and wax. Unsuccessful, he tried a second drawer and discovered a small brass box. He took it from the drawer, set it on top of the desk, and lifted the lid. Inside was the seal of Wildenham and a red wax candle. He picked it up and rotated it between his fingers as he wondered how many times his father had used it. Now the seal of Wildenham and responsibility of the kingdom rested upon his shoulders.

The hair on his arms stood on end. He had a feeling he was being watched. He looked to the right and saw a man with glowing white eyes. Lord William could see through the figure to the bookcase that was behind the apparition and noticed the man's legs disappeared just below his knees. He looked at the floating body and recognized the stern face. It was his father.

A knock at the door startled the spirit. It transformed into a black shadowed figure, traveled up to the corner of the room, and disappeared.

Did I just see what I thought I saw? Lord William asked himself and looked toward the closed door.

"Enter." He ordered.

The library door opened and two messengers came into the room.

"Could one of you light this taper?" Lord William gestured to the candle upon his desk.

One of the messengers nodded and left to retrieve hot embers.

Lord William addressed the second piece of parchment to Rowena. He informed her of his marriage to Lady Christine, but paused, searching for a justifiable explanation. It was difficult to pinpoint any particular reason, so he omitted his reasoning. Now that he must remain at Wildenham, he was concerned for Rowena's welfare and stated his desire for her to live within Wildenham's walls where he could oversee her safety and needs.

The messenger returned carrying a kettle with embers. He dumped them into the fireplace and lit a rush. He lit the taper, but the flame extinguished as if blown out by a puff of wind. The messenger looked to his lord and then to the other messenger before attempting to light the candle a second time. The taper's flame disappeared again.

"My lord, I am trying my best, but it doesn't seem to want to stay lit." The messenger was flustered and attempted to light the candle a third time.

Lord William held up his hand, halting the messenger and stood from his chair. He looked around the room before picking up the bottle from his desk, walked to the center of the room behind the men, and shook the bottle before he uncorked it.

"Whoever is devious enough to blow out the candle is no longer welcomed in my library. You will leave this room and never return." Lord William tipped the bottle and allowed a drop of the wretched liquid to plop onto the floor. He heard a groan. Both of the messengers heard it as well and looked to each other for reassurance. Lord William tapped the cork back into the top of the bottle and returned to his seat.

"Perhaps it shall stay lit now," he said as he nodded his head toward the taper and set the bottle on the desk.

The messenger touched the flame of the rush to the wick of the candle. All watched the lit taper as it remained aglow. Assured it would remain lit, the messenger tossed the rush into the fireplace.

"Thank you," Lord William said as he folded the missive for Rowena. He took the red candle and touched its wick to the taper's flame. He let the wax drip onto both folded missives to seal them shut, blew out the red candle, and pressed the seal of Wildenham into the warm wax puddles.

Lord William handed one of the missives to a messenger.

"Please deliver this to the baron." He instructed. The messenger nodded and left the room.

Lord William picked up the second missive and the satchel and explained the assignment.

"Along the road toward Bristolwood, within a thick forest, is a woman. She has long gray hair and goes by the name Rowena. She is a well-known apothecary. Ask those along the way. They can point you to her whereabouts." Lord William handed both items to the messenger.

"Yes, my lord." The messenger replied as he stood, daring to broach a request.

"Is there something else?" Lord William inquired.

"Once I have delivered your missive, may I stop and check in on my mother. As of late, she has been quite ill." The messenger requested humbly.

Lord William thought of his mother and empathized with the young man.

"Take a few days to visit. If you know what ails her, perhaps Rowena can prescribe something."

"Thank you, my lord." The messenger grinned and left the library.

Lord William returned the red candle and seal to the brass box, closed the lid, and set it back in the drawer.

"My lord," Sir Farrell said as he stood in the doorway of the library.

Lord William paused with his hand on the drawer handle as he looked toward the door.

"Sir Farrell, please come in."

The knight did as instructed and stood before his lord's desk.

"You asked to see me, my lord."

"Yes, I would appreciate you continue your duty to watch over and protect my wife when I am unable to be with her." Lord William stated as he closed the drawer.

"I will do my best."

"Thank you."

Sir Farrell looked down at the floor and back to his young lord's face. *He is young, at least two and ten years my younger.*

"Is there something that concerns you?" Lord William recognized the knight's hesitation to speak his mind.

"My lord, I commend you for taking Lady Christine's hand in marriage. Many are pleased to know she shall remain within Wildenham as her father would have wished." Sir Farrell replied, looking his lord directly in the eye to convey his sincerity. "May I ask if there is a reason to fear for Lady Christine's life?"

Lord William studied the knight's inquisitive and concerned stare. He knew very little of this man who stood before him, but felt it best to share his thoughts and earn his trust.

"I don't know. Is Lord Redmond within Wildenham's walls?"

"I will ask at the front gate."

"Thank you. Please return once you have the answer."

Sir Farrell nodded, turned toward the door, and left.

Lord William leaned back in his chair, let out a sigh, and

wondered what he needed to address next. He reached for a drawer, opened it, and discovered a leather-bound journal. Taking it from the drawer, he untied the thin leather strap and opened it. Lord Clayborn's name was written in script on page one.

"Well, let's see what kind of lord you really were." He whispered aloud as he turned the first page and began to read.

Chapter 17

The sun was past midday when Sir Harlan trotted his tired horse proudly toward Thornwick's stable. After riding through the night, he was tired and frustrated, but quite pleased with himself.

Lord Redmond, fancy that, I have always wanted to be a lord, he thought as he dismounted and threw the reins to the stableboy hitting the lad across the face. *If only Lady Christine's door had been unbolted,* he sneered as he entered Thornwick's Keep and walked toward the Great Hall. As he emerged into the room, two servant women carrying dirty linen passed by on their way to the laundry.

"Where is Lord Sheridan?" Sir Harlan demanded. The women stopped and looked at the dirty stone floor. One of the servants pointed to a chair before the fireplace at the other end of the Great Hall.

Sir Harlan walked briskly past them, stood before it, and refused to kneel.

"It's done." He announced, staring down in disgust at Lord Sheridan. "And I believe Thornwick now belongs to me." Receiving a silent response, he began to pace back and forth before the fireplace.

Lord Sheridan took a drink from his tankard and lowered it to his right knee.

"Thornwick will become yours once I have Wildenham." He announced as he watched Sir Harlan pace. "For a man who just succeeded in killing another, you seem quite vexed."

"Her bedchamber door was bolted." Sir Harlan hissed as he turned to pace in the opposite direction with his nostrils flaring and his fists tightening until his knuckles turned white.

Lord Sheridan chuckled and said, "I stand corrected. You are disappointed, not vexed."

Sir Harlan stopped his pacing and stood with his legs apart and his fists upon his hips. He displayed an ugly scowl upon his face in reply to the comment. He was tempted to take his sword and run him through.

"No matter, by week's end we shall pay a visit to Wildenham before word can reach the baron. I shall become the Lord of Wildenham, and you may have Lady Christine." Lord Sheridan stated with a hint of sarcasm. A chuckle escaped his lips as he found it difficult to contain his excitement.

"And rule Thornwick." Sir Harlan added adamantly.

"Yes, and rule Thornwick, as I shall rule Wildenham." Lord Sheridan took another swig from his tankard.

Sir Harlan began to smile.

*   *   *

Wilfred stepped into the library and waited patiently for Lord William to finish the page he was reading. As the Lord of Wildenham turned the page, he looked toward the steward.

"My lord, there are several peasants waiting in the Great Hall that wish to speak with you." Wilfred informed as he motioned toward the doorway.

"Thank you, Wilfred." Lord William closed the journal and returned it to the drawer. He rose from his chair, grabbed the bottle by its neck, and snuffed out the candle while Wilfred waited by the doorway for his lord to join him.

The two men left the library, walked through the hallway toward the Great Hall, and paused in its doorway, befuddled by what they saw. Lady Christine sat proudly in her husband's chair upon the raised platform used for the High Table. She was answering a question from a peasant man.

"I'm sorry, my lord, but I am accustomed to placing only one chair upon the dais. I did not know that Lady Christine would be joining you. For future reference, would you like both chairs placed on the High Table floor?" Wilfred realized his mistake.

"Yes, I think that would be wise." Lord William agreed. "Could you take this to my bedchamber?" He handed the bottle to Wilfred.

"I would be happy to do so, my lord." Wilfred left to carry out the task.

The small crowd quieted as Lord William took commanding strides into the Great Hall and walked behind his wife to retrieve her chair that sat next to the wall. He picked up the chair, walked to the front of the dais and faced his wife, placed it to the left of his chair, and looked to the empty seat suggesting his wife should move to her appropriate chair.

How dare he demand I move from my father's chair, Lady Christine thought. Feeling quite proud of the way she handled the menu for the evening meal, she was determined to take her rightful place in her father's chair and carry on where he left off. Lady Christine raised her chin in defiance and refused to move.

"Do you need some assistance?" Lord William lifted both of his hands toward her, offering to help.

"You wouldn't." She threatened and narrowed her eyes.

Lord William scooped her up into his arms, turned, and placed her into her seat with a plop. He nodded his head in satisfaction and brushed the palms of his hands together before turning toward the crowd.

"Thank you, my dear, for your assistance in answering the inquiries of these good people. I will try to be more punctual in the future." Lord William stated loudly as he nodded his head toward his wife and addressed those in attendance.

Many in the crowd snickered and smiled as their lord sat in his seat. Lady Christine's face turned red, but she smiled at her husband and the peasants as if the incident was nothing more than a jest. She rose to leave, but her husband put his hand upon her arm causing her to stop midway.

"My dear, I would appreciate your assistance and would like you to remain," he said with a commanding tone.

She looked down at his hand that grasped her left arm and then to his face. He stared into her eyes.

"Let's do this together, shall we?" He suggested in a whisper and removed his hand from her arm.

Her eyes shifted to the inquisitive stares of the peasants who stood waiting to voice their concerns. Her father understood each peasant's role and vital function in order for Wildenham to operate smoothly. She wished she would have paid more attention during her father's lectures. Those who stood before her now depended on what little she could remember. She wanted to continue her father's legacy and above all, make him proud. Unfortunately, she assumed her husband possessed even less knowledge of the kingdom's operations than she did. For now, she would appease him and resumed her seat to observe and assist her husband wherever possible. She stiffened her back and lifted her chin as the next concerned field worker stepped forward.

Sir Farrell walked through the hallway and into the Great Hall where he saw his lord and lady upon the raised platform.

Lord William waved the knight forward as he finished responding to the man's concerns.

Sir Farrell made his way around the crowd of peasants, stopped before his lord and lady, and knelt.

"What have you discovered?" Lord William indicated with his right hand that his knight should stand.

"Thomas said he was roused to ready a horse for the person of your inquiry who left Wildenham before sunrise, my lord." Sir Farrell reported as he stood.

"As I suspected, thank you."

Sir Farrell nodded and left the room.

"Who left Wildenham?" Lady Christine whispered while she continued to look toward the peasants.

Lord William leaned in her direction, for what he had to say was for her ears only.

"Our guest, Lord Redmond of Langston." He stared at the next peasant who stepped forward.

"That is not unusual. Many who request a night's stay will leave before sunrise."

"This man was not who he said he was."

"So he lied. Most men do when it suits their needs," she said sarcastically as she looked in his direction.

"Lord Redmond of Langston died not more than a month ago." Lord William explained as he turned his head to look at his wife.

"How do you know?"

"Because I killed him." Lord William stated as he looked her directly in the eye. "And I'm not lying."

Lady Christine studied the gold flecks in his hazel eyes and the sternness of his face that conveyed truth and determination.

"Whoever that man was, I promise you, I will discover his true identity." Lord William stated as he turned his head to face the peasant who knelt before them.

A howl echoed from the staircase. Everyone in the room looked in the direction of the noise. A shadow lingered in the upstairs hallway, floated to a wall, and disappeared. Murmurs spread through the small crowd.

Feeling the need to downplay the situation, Lord William kept his composure and waited until those within the room had grown quiet before nodding to the man to speak and address his issue.

Chapter 18

The sun dipped below the tops of the trees casting a shadow upon the road. The messenger looked to the sky and sighed. He had kept his horse at a wicked pace since leaving Wildenham and knew he was running out of time. It would be necessary to camp by the roadside for the night if he was unsuccessful in locating the apothecary. He had stopped several people along the way, but they were of little help. Many would point down the road to indicate he should continue on his current path. His eyes began to wander along the roadside for a suitable place to camp before darkness made his travel dangerous. His horse was tired and needed rest. He slowed it to a trot as they rounded a bend in the road and encountered a young lad who was walking lethargically and carrying a small leather pouch. He reined his horse next to the boy.

"Can you tell me where I may find a woman by the name of Rowena?"

The boy coughed while nodding his head, indicating he could be of assistance. He looked back down the road in which he had came and yelled.

"Rowena, wait, there is a man who wishes to see you!"

The lad turned back to the messenger and said, "She should be just over the hill by the side of the road. She has long gray hair and should be carrying the pheasant I just gave her in payment of this." He held up the pouch and coughed again. "If she is not there, then wait until morning and she will find you."

"Thank you," the messenger said as he kicked his heels into the sides of his horse, urging it into a trot.

Rowena remained hidden within the foliage of the woods as the stranger passed her and continued down the road.

Feeling as if he may have gone too far, the messenger pulled the reins to stop his horse. He looked at both sides of the road in search of the woman. He heard a rustling coming from behind him and turned his horse around. He looked to the left of the roadside to see an elderly woman with long gray hair emerge from the dense forest.

"You asked to see me." Rowena stated as she stood in the road with a dead pheasant dangling from her hand.

"Lord William requests that I give you this." The messenger informed her as he reined his horse next to Rowena. He pulled the sealed missive and satchel from his saddle bag, reached down from atop his horse, and held them before her.

"Lord William, you say?" She realized he had used a proper title.

"Yes, Lord William of Wildenham."

Rowena took the items from his hand. *So Lord William has accepted the responsibility that is rightfully his*, she thought. She was curious, however, for his reason in doing so. She looked to the darkening sky.

"Your name?"

"Henry."

"Well Henry, night will soon be upon us and I have a pot of stew and bread to eat for dinner. I would appreciate your company and am eager to learn of what has happened at Wildenham since Lord William arrived. You and your horse may sleep in the stable," she said as she turned around to lead him through the woods to the hut.

"Thank you, you are very kind." Henry dismounted from his horse, held the reins, and followed the apothecary as she stepped into the foliage and disappeared into the dark woods.

Rowena remained silent as she wove her way to her hut. When they reached the clearing, Rowena pointed in the direction of the humble stable.

"You may take your horse and bed it down in there. Join me inside when you have finished," she said as she continued to walk to the door of the hut while opening the missive.

Henry nodded and took his horse to the stable. It was a small structure, almost lean-to like, made of sticks with a moss roof. He pulled aside a long sapling of the tiny corral to allow himself and his horse inside. He discovered a bucket with water, some hay, and a wooden box with gnawed edges that contained a few oats within the shelter. He unsaddled his horse, set the saddle on a wooden barrel that stood in the corner, removed the horse's bridle, and tossed it across the saddle before leaving the stable. He closed the corral by lifting the sapling and putting it across the opening. Henry went to the hut and entered the opened door. As he looked around the room, goose bumps began to rise on his arms. The apothecary had hung the pheasant by its feet from a hook on the fireplace. There was a bed next to a stone wall. Shelves covered nearly every space on the remaining walls. The shelves held jars and crocks that contained various herbs and concoctions. A narrow ladder led upward to a loft.

Rowena set a bowl of stew on the table and noticed the messenger gaping at the contents of her home.

"Close the door and please be seated," she said as she took a second bowl, scooped a serving of stew with a large spoon, and filled the bowl. She placed the second bowl across from her guest. They both pulled out a chair and sat down at the table opposite one another.

"Thank you, this looks delicious." Henry stated politely.

"I am happy for the company." She watched him eat a spoonful of stew. She poured two mugs of water from the pitcher and placed one before him. He took a sip to cool the hot stew within his mouth.

"Very good stew." He complimented as he swallowed and ate another spoonful.

Rowena smiled and replied.

"Thank you."

With niceties out of the way, her curiosity was piqued, and she was unable to withhold her question any longer.

"The missive indicates Wildenham has a new lord and he is married to Lady Christine. Who is Lady Christine?"

"Lord Clayborn's daughter."

Rowena sat back in her chair and watched the messenger eat. She closed her eyes. The vision of a beautiful woman flashed within her mind. She opened her eyes.

"She is beautiful," she said aloud.

Henry paused in his eating and looked at the apothecary.

"Yes, very." He agreed.

"Why did Lord William marry her?" Rowena leaned forward and took a bite of her stew.

"Lord Clayborn was found dead on the floor outside of his bedchamber, murdered, they say. I believe Lord William married her so she could remain in Wildenham." Henry took another bite of stew.

Rowena was hesitant to ask her next question in fear of his reply, but her curiosity forced her to speak the words. She sat forward and scooped another spoonful of stew.

"Who killed Lord Clayborn?" She paused with a spoon midway to her mouth.

"They do not know."

Rowena ate her readied serving and pondered the presented facts, but her thoughts were interrupted by her guest.

"Lord William said I was to ask you for a remedy for my mother. She is ill, and I plan to visit her on my way back to Wildenham. I don't mean to impose, but it would ease my mind knowing I did something to help her." Henry conveyed as he paused eating.

"I will have something ready for you to take with you in the morning." Rowena had seen several with the same symptoms and assumed his mother may be suffering from the ailment.

"Thank you. I truly appreciate your effort." The messenger returned to eating his meal.

*   *   *

As servants cleared tables and snuffed out the dinner candles, darkness seemed to close in upon those who remained within the Great Hall of Wildenham.

Lord William watched the shadows of the candlelight dance upon a wall as a servant passed a tall candelabra. His wife had been quiet during the meal. He sensed she was angry. Having little knowledge of women and their complicated emotions, he had learned one important fact about their silence. It would only be a matter of time before she released her vexation upon him. He picked up his tankard and finished its contents. A serving wench rushed forward to refill his mug, but he waved her off indicating he had enough. He looked in the direction of his wife. She had finished eating.

"Shall we retire?"

His wife turned toward him with an expression of disgust upon her face. Lady Christine rose from her seat and stood. Her husband did the same.

Even though it was early in the evening, many assumed the newlyweds were eager to seclude themselves in their bedchamber as they watched their lord and lady ascend the staircase.

"You were quiet the entire meal," Lord William said as they stopped before their bedchamber and held the door open for his wife. "Are you well?"

"Perfectly well." She pushed her words past clenched teeth as she tried to rein in her temper until she crossed the threshold. Once in the bedchamber, she turned around to face him with her hands fisted and propped on each hip.

"I did not appreciate you humiliating me in front of the peasants as you did in the Great Hall earlier today. I was listening to their requests and concerns as my father would have done." She turned and plopped down upon the bench before the fire with her arms folded across her chest.

Lord William closed and bolted the bedchamber door. He sighed and looked at his wife who seemed to have had her feelings hurt and was pouting like a child. Unsure of what to say or do, his male instinct told him to tread lightly. He decided to keep his voice calm as he approached the bench, stepped over it, and sat down. He looked at the profile of her stern face and tried to find a reason that justified his actions.

"I appreciate your assistance today, but as Lord of Wildenham, it is my job to sit in the lord's chair and listen to the concerns of the people."

She snapped her head in his direction.

"It is my father's chair and the responsibility should be passed down to me." She stressed with a raised voice.

"It is my chair now and I hope to fulfill his duties successfully, with your guidance, of course." He replied kindly. "I apologize if I embarrassed you today, but I must display leadership to those who watch my every move. As the Lady of Wildenham, you are being watched with equal regard."

Lady Christine looked away from her husband and stared at the dancing flames in the fireplace. She knew he spoke the truth. At best, she could try to fulfill her father's wishes by advising her husband in his decisions.

Her silence led Lord William to believe he had made his point. He looked around the room and noticed the window was closed. Lord William rose, walked over to the window, opened it, and whistled. The raven may have fallen asleep while roosting in a tree, but would follow the sound of his master's call and arrive soon.

Ignoring her husband and the noise that he made, Lady Christine heard scratching at the bedchamber door and rose, crossed the room, and opened the door. Jackson waddled into the room. She closed the door, bolted it, and turned to see Corvus land on the windowsill.

"What is that raven doing there? Shoo it away." She ordered, wrinkling up her nose.

"I will do no such thing. This is Corvus, my pet."

"You have a pet raven?" She questioned as she looked down at her cat. "Jackson will not tolerate that bird and will most likely eat him by morning." She stated as Jackson caught sight of the raven and crouched down into his hunting stance as if he became suddenly invisible.

Corvus turned his head and looked at the cat with one eye as if sizing him up for a fight.

"I would hope Jackson is smart enough to know his place when encountering a raven," Lord William said with a smirk on his face.

"It's a bird. He kills them all of the time," she said as she crossed her arms over her chest confidently.

"Not this bird he won't," Lord William said as he chuckled and unbuckled his sword, walked around the bed, and hung it on the bedpost. He took off his tunic and shirt and tossed them onto a chair. Understanding Wilfred's efficiency, he assumed his clothing had been moved from his previous chamber and stored within the chest at the bottom of the bed. He would search for them in the morning.

Lady Christine stared in horror as the firelight reflected off his shiny scarred back.

"My God, were you tortured?" She realized how little she knew about her husband. Was he a criminal?

He turned to see her face. Was it one of disgust or fright?

"Yes, long ago." He replied and walked back to the bench and sat down.

"What did you do?" She was dumbfounded and remained standing, frozen in place.

He stared at her inquiring eyes and then to the floor. Dare he tell her? He looked to her face again and replied.

"I fell short of my father's expectations."

She had difficulty believing his reply and walked to the bench and sat.

"Your father?" she said in disbelief as she leaned forward to see her husband's face. "Your father did that to you?"

"Well, he ordered someone else to administer the punishment."

"No father should treat his son with such cruelty." Lady Christine found it difficult to fathom the pain he endured from the abuse. She looked away from her husband and watched the flames wrap around the logs in the fireplace.

Lord William glanced behind him to see Jackson creep across the floor and stop below the open window where Corvus was perched. The cat's jaw seemed to quiver as if he was talking to the bird. The raven looked down at the feline with intrigue. Lord William looked at the table and spotted the bottle of tar water. He thought to use its contents to insure their privacy.

"Is your father still alive?" She reflected on her own loss.

Lord William turned his head toward his wife. Her question seemed genuine.

"No," he said as he shook his head slightly and looked down at the floor. He wondered if she knew her father had killed his father to gain control of Wildenham. *The irony of it all*, he thought. Each of their fathers wished to pass the kingdom down to them. With the recent turn of events, both of their paternal guardians had received exactly what they wanted.

Lord William rose and picked up the bottle from the table. He went to the center of the room, shook the bottle, and uncorked it. Lady Christine watched her husband.

"What are you doing?"

"I have noticed a black shadow within the Keep and even within this room." He tilted the bottle in an attempt to estimate when a drop would fall.

"Yes, Lord Bradford's ghost. He is in my bedchamber as well." She commented as she watched her husband curiously.

"Well, I intend to rid him from this room." Lord William explained as a drop of the pungent tar water fell to the floor. "Be gone from this room and do not return, Lord Bradford!"

"Does that actually work?"

Lord William sealed the bottle and returned it to the table.

"We will find out," he said as he returned to his seat.

As husband and wife sat uncomfortably silent, time was

marked by the crackle of the burning logs. Lord William admired the detailed woodwork of the fireplace as he searched his mind for a topic to discuss.

"Father Frederick conducted a nice service in your father's memory," he said. It was the only topic that entered his mind from the day's events.

She nodded in agreement.

"I have asked Sir Farrell to continue to be your escort." He stated in an attempt to converse again.

"Is there reason to fear ... " She was cut off by the sudden sound of fluttering and wrestling.

They turned toward the noise to see Jackson leap upward toward Corvus. The raven jumped into the air, flapped his wings, landed on the back of the cat, and pecked Jackson's head. The cat hissed and rolled on the floor with the hope of getting the attacking bird off of his back.

To save the chubby feline, Lord William whistled and Corvus flew to his shoulder and landed. A few of the bird's feathers were askew. Jackson took the opportunity to scurry under the bed for safety.

"This is unacceptable. They will never adjust to one another. That bird must stay out of this room." Lady Christine insisted as she pointed to the raven.

"I think we should give it time. Corvus may lose a few feathers and Jackson endures a few pecks on the top of his head, but they may adjust to one another," he said as he reached up and petted the bird.

Lady Christine bolted to her feet.

"I disagree and I want that disgusting bird out of here when I return. It probably has lice." She stated before crossing the room and opening the bedchamber door.

"Where are you going?" Lord William watched his wife walk away.

"I am going to change my clothes." She stated harshly over her shoulder and left.

"She is trying my patience, Corvus." He looked toward the bed to see Jackson's little white nose peek out from beneath it.

Corvus turned his head as he noticed the cat. He decided the feline was a safe distance away and flew to the headboard of the bed to roost.

"The two of you are going to have to come to terms with one another, and the sooner, the better." Lord William scolded as he stood and faced them both. Corvus turned his back to his master and Jackson's nose disappeared under the bed.

"It seems as if everyone is turning their back on me tonight," he said aloud to himself.

Chapter 19

Rowena rose with the sunrise. She put bread and cheese in an oil cloth and tied it with a leather string. She sat at the table and reread Lord William's missive. *Such a kind lad,* she thought. Retrieving pen and ink from a shelf, she wrote her reply on the bottom of the parchment, folded, and tied a piece of twine around it. She traced her fingertips over the engraved leather of the satchel and appreciated his gift. She missed Lord William's company, but knew he was following the correct path for his life. It was for the best.

Knowing Lord William would want a few of his personal items; she lifted the stone of the hearth, opened a chest, and searched for the leather pouch. Unsuccessful in her search, she tried another chest and another before finding it. She opened the pouch, dumped the ring into the palm of her hand, and held it up to the light. The amethyst and diamonds sparkled. Rowena had little desire to possess such an object, but admired its beauty.

She returned the ring to the pouch and set it next to the other items on the table. Rowena went to her cot, lifted the bedroll, and retrieved Lord William's childhood sword. She wrapped the sword in oil cloth and tied it securely with a leather string to keep it out of sight from onlookers who possessed greedy hands.

She pulled jars from the shelves and mixed an herbal tea in a bowl for the messenger's mother. She lined a small tin box with oil cloth, dumped the bowl's contents into the container, and sealed it tightly.

Rowena gathered the items under her arm, left the hut, and went to the stable. Henry was returning from the stream with a flask filled with water.

"Good morning." Rowena greeted. "I hope you slept well."

"Good morning and yes, thank you. I did sleep well." Henry had his horse ready and tied the flask to the saddle.

"I have a few things that I need you to take to Lord William." Rowena handed the items to the messenger and he put each one into a saddle bag with the sword sticking through the opening at the top. He tied the flap securely to ensure all of the items would remain inside.

"This is for you to eat along the way." Rowena handed him the parcel of food. "And this is for your mother." She gave him the tin box.

"Thank you. You are too kind." Henry complimented and climbed atop his horse. "Thank you for your hospitality and fare thee well." Henry urged his horse forward with the hope of finding his way to the road.

"Fare thee well," Rowena said as she watched him disappear into the foliage.

*　　　*　　　*

After receiving permission to enter the castle, Lord Sheridan and Sir Harlan trotted their horses into the outer bailey of Wildenham.

"I have always admired this kingdom," Lord Sheridan said. He was in a grand mood as he inspected the facilities, shops, and livestock while picturing himself as the Lord of Wildenham.

Sir Harlan grunted in acknowledgement. He was more interested in getting his hands on Lady Christine, bedding her, and returning to Thornwick as its lord.

They continued their leisurely ride into the inner bailey and reined their horses before the stable.

Thomas came forward and took the reins of their horses. The smart lad recognized both men. Lord Sheridan had visited many times over the years. It had been nearly a week since the tall man had roused him very early one morning wanting to depart before daybreak. Thomas watched the men as they entered the Keep. A troubling uneasiness stirred within him causing goose bumps to pucker his skin. He led their horses to a stall, climbed atop his pony, and left the stable at a gallop to fetch Lord William at the practice field.

*　　　*　　　*

Wilfred was passing through the Great Hall when he noticed the two men. He stopped to observe Lord Sheridan parading around the perimeter of the room with his thumbs tucked into his belt. The lord had an approving smile upon his face as he pointed to a wall hanging and admired its beauty. The steward stared at the back of the other tall gentleman who appeared disinterested in Lord Sheridan's comments. *There is something familiar about him*, the steward thought.

When Lord Sheridan pointed to the tapestry that Lord Bradford had personally commissioned, it lifted on one edge and rippled strangely, causing both men to eye it suspiciously.

"Lord Sheridan, what brings you to Wildenham?"

Both men turned in the direction of Wilfred.

"We wish to express our condolences to Lady Christine for the loss of her father."

Wilfred's eyes shifted to the man who stood to the left of Lord Sheridan. He recognized the former guest of Wildenham.

"How nice to see you again, Lord Redmond," Wilfred said politely.

Sir Harlan nodded his head in acknowledgement, but remained silent.

"I believe Lady Christine is out of the Keep at the moment. Please be seated. I will send a servant with refreshments for you to enjoy while you wait for her to return." Wilfred motioned with an open palm toward two benches before the fireplace. He bowed slightly, watched them settle into their seats, and left the room. Rushing to the kitchen as fast as his elderly legs allowed, he shouted orders.

"Samuel, go and tell Thomas or Conal to fetch Lord William from the practice field."

Samuel's eyes widened at the request. His only responsibility was to keep the fire lit through the night. Noting the agitated state of the steward, he assumed the situation to be serious and scurried to the stable while Wilfred continued to bark orders.

"Ellie, put together two tankards of ale and fill a pitcher as well. We have two guests in the Great Hall. I want to ensure they remain pleasant. Daisy, fill a tray with bread and cheese. Hurry girls! We must not keep our guests waiting."

The women gathered the necessary items, straightened their dresses, and went to the Great Hall while Wilfred paced nervously. He knew Lady Christine was in her bedchamber reading. He hoped she remained there until her husband arrived.

*   *   *

Lord William sliced his practice sword through the air and struck Sir Gunther's wooden shield. Sir Gunther blocked and returned the attack.

Bouncing bareback upon his pony, Thomas reined it before them.

"Lord William! Lord William!"

Lord William stopped his sparring.

"What is it Thomas?"

Sir Gunther relaxed his stance, turned, and looked in the lad's direction as well. Sir Farrell, who was overseeing the practice of two soldiers, walked over to the two men to listen to the lad.

"Lord Sheridan and that man are here."

Lord William noted the panic in the lad's face.

"What man?"

"The man who woke me early to saddle his horse on the day Lord Clayborn was found dead. They are in the Keep!" Thomas turned his pony toward the Keep and kicked it into a gallop.

Sir Farrell ran to his horse.

Lord William's concern increased after witnessing the knight's panicked reaction to the news. He turned to Sir Gunther.

"Who is Lord Sheridan?"

"Lord Sheridan is the Lord of Thornwick and a suitor for Lady Christine's hand in marriage." Sir Gunther informed as both men threw their practice equipment onto the pile and jumped onto their horses.

The three men spurred their steeds into a gallop and passed Thomas. Thomas kicked his pony to encourage its short legs to move faster, but he was unable to keep pace.

Samuel's arms were wrapped around Conal's waist as they bounced atop their tiny pony toward the practice field. As Lord William and his knights came into view, Conal reined the pony to allow Samuel to convey Wilfred's message, but the men passed them by at a galloping pace. They turned their pony around and followed.

Corvus sat atop the stable watching some chickens feed below, but the thunderous sound of hoofbeats made him look in the direction of the noise. He saw his master enter the inner bailey. Dust billowed into the air as Lord William reined Adair to a sudden stop. The raven extended his wings and took flight.

The Lord of Wildenham and his knights dismounted.

"Leave the horses saddled!" Lord William yelled back to the stableboys who trotted their ponies into the inner bailey.

Corvus landed on Lord William's shoulder as his master paused to observe Thornwick's saddled horses in the stalls. He walked briskly and entered the Keep.

As Lord William passed through the hallway toward the Great Hall, he heard a man yelling, presumed it be Lord Sheridan, and Wilfred trying to handle the situation calmly. He stepped into the Great Hall followed by his two knights. Lord William stared at the back of a stoutly fellow who he presumed to be Lord Sheridan and noted a rather large knight who sat upon a bench with his legs crossed at his feet and his arms folded over his chest disrespectfully.

Wilfred looked toward the doorway, spotted his lord, and breathed a sigh of relief.

"My lord, this is Lord Sheridan. He has come to call on Lady Christine." Wilfred explained as he excused himself and exited the room in haste.

Lord Sheridan turned to face Lord William.

"Lord William?" Lord Sheridan emphasized the title sarcastically and widened his eyes in disbelief. The young man who stood before him seemed too young to hold such a title. "Wildenham has a new lord?"

"Yes," Lord William replied as Corvus stretched his wings, flapped them twice, and then tucked them into his body.

Sir Harlan stood from his bench, placed himself behind Lord Sheridan, and refolded his arms across his chest.

*   *   *

Sitting comfortably upon the window seat in her private bedchamber, Lady Christine took a sip from her tankard of wine and set it on a nearby table. The bright sunlight from the window made it her favorite spot for reading a book. She turned the page and continued to read, but an incessant squeaking made it impossible for her to concentrate.

Jackson had cornered a tiny mouse. It was challenging the feline. It squeaked and bounced up and down on its hind legs with its forelegs raised as if attempting to punch the cat in the nose. It had managed to get itself under Jackson's tummy and continued to jump. Jackson was trying his best to dodge the mouse so he could snatch it up and end its incessant squeaking.

"Oh, Jackson, that little mouse has such spirit and courage. We must let him live." Lady Christine placed the ribbon she used to mark her page into the book, closed it shut, and stood from the window seat. She set the book upon the table and picked up the tankard. It was half full. She scanned the room for a vessel to pour the wine in, but found nothing. She opened the window and looked below to see if anyone may be there. No one was in sight. She dumped the contents of her mug and closed the window.

With the help of Jackson, she was able to back the mouse into the corner by the bedchamber door. Lady Christine scooped the tiny rodent into the mug and pushed Jackson aside. She looked down into the tankard at the mouse. Its tiny black eyes stared back at her defiantly as it twitched its nose.

"Thank you for your help Jackson, but this little one deserves to live." She told her cat as she put her hand over the mug to cover the mouse and watched the feline continue to search the room for the rodent.

Lady Christine removed her hand from the top of the mug and lifted the latch on the door. As she pulled the door open, she could hear voices echoing from the Great Hall. She stepped into the hallway to release the mouse, but froze as she recognized Lord Sheridan's voice. Moments passed as she strained to listen to what was being said. Remembering the mouse, she looked into the mug, but it was empty. Her hair began to shift and pull as if something was crawling in it. She covered her mouth with her left hand in an attempt to stifle a scream as she tried to remain calm and set the mug upon the floor. Leaning her head to the side, she felt the mouse's paw touch her face. She shook her head with the hope of jarring the creature loose, but the clever mouse traveled onto her back. She stood up and turned in a circle as she continued to rustle her clothing. She saw the vermin scamper down the hallway and breathed a sigh of relief.

Knowing Lord Sheridan was below in the Great Hall, she flattened herself against the opposite wall and tiptoed close to the railing that overlooked the room. Lady Christine heard her husband's muffled voice. She listened to the echo of footsteps and strained to hear the exchange of words between the men.

Lord Sheridan stopped pacing and stared at the young lord.

"Well, you must have just acquired the title. When did you become the Lord of Wildenham?"

"On the night of Lord Clayborn's death." Lord William kept a watchful eye on the sword hand of the large knight, who uncrossed his arms and lowered them to his side. He noted the scar on the man's cheek and assumed he had acquired it during a battle. His greasy brown hair hung in strands around his face.

Lord William stared at the knight's ocean blue eyes that stared back at him.

Lord Sheridan recalled the night he was unable to sleep knowing Sir Harlan would return with the good news of the death of Lord Clayborn.

"Who appointed you as Lord of Wildenham?" Lord Sheridan questioned sarcastically.

"I did, when I took Lady Christine as my wife. I have also taken the liberty to notify the baron of the current events and changes within Wildenham." Lord William explained trying to anticipate Lord Sheridan's next question and noted the registration of shock upon the knight's face.

Lord Sheridan turned away from Lord William to obtain a moment to absorb the information. He curled his hands into fists and exhaled. He anticipated waltzing into Wildenham, taking over the lordship, giving Lady Christine to Sir Harlan, and living happily ever after as the kingdom's ruler. *So much for an easy takeover of Wildenham*, he thought. Lord Sheridan turned around to face Lord William. There was something haunting about the young lord all dressed in black, with long dark hair, piercing hazel eyes, and the raven upon his shoulder.

"Who are you?"

"I am Lord William of Wildenham," he said, stating the obvious as he crossed his arms across his chest in defiance.

Lord Sheridan continued to study the young man before him. His eyes darted back and forth between Lord William and the raven.

"Lord William you say?" Lord Sheridan tried to recall Lord

Bradford's lost son's name. *William? Is it just a coincidence? Or could it be that the prodigal son had returned from the dead*, he wondered.

Lord William remained silent.

Lord Sheridan tapped his right hand's fingertips on his lips as he began to pace back and forth in thought and glanced toward Lord William from time to time. He stopped suddenly, lowered his hand, and faced the young lord.

"You fit the description of the mercenary who lives in the woods with an apothecary. He is known to patrol the road between Wildenham and Bristolwood at night. Could you be the legendary mercenary, perhaps employed to murder Lord Clayborn?"

Sir Gunther and Sir Farrell exchanged inquisitive looks.

Lady Christine pressed her ear toward the Great Hall. She held her breath as she awaited her husband's response.

Sir Harlan pulled his hair away from his face to reveal the scar he received during the thwarted raid. If his memory was correct, he was attempting a robbery along the same road. He touched the scar on the side of his face and narrowed his eyes.

Lord William stared at Lord Sheridan. *How can he assume a mercenary had been hired to kill Lord Clayborn, unless he employed one*, he wondered.

"I did not murder Lord Clayborn," he replied avoiding the confirmation of his true occupation. He glared at Sir Harlan and was certain the imposter was the true murderer.

Lady Christine covered her mouth with her hand to stifle her labored breathing as she realized her husband gave an indirect answer. Questions invaded her mind. *Am I married to a mercenary? Is he telling a falsehood and murdered my father? Did he kill him to marry me and become the Lord of Wildenham? Will he kill me next?* Her heart was beating so loudly she was afraid it would be heard downstairs by the men. She tried to slow her breathing as she continued to listen.

"I do believe, Lord Sheridan, that you employed another to do the job." Lord William continued as he stared at Sir Harlan.

Sir Harlan lifted his chin in a silent challenge.

"If I did, well, at least he succeeded," Lord Sheridan said condescendingly.

Lord William lifted his chin in defiance. He missed the opportunity to kill Lord Clayborn, but chose the more daunting task as husband to his daughter and fulfilling the role as the new Lord of Wildenham.

"Now that you have seen for yourself that Wildenham is in good hands, perhaps you should leave." Lord William stated sternly.

Sir Gunther and Sir Farrell placed their hands on the hilts of their swords.

With the unfavorable odds of three men against himself and his knight, Lord Sheridan conceded.

"Until we meet again, and it will be soon." He sneered as he left the Great Hall with Sir Harlan following.

Lady Christine crept quietly back to her bedchamber, shut the door, and bolted it.

Lord William looked in the direction of the bedchamber as he heard the bolting of the door echo down into the Great Hall. He turned toward his knights.

"Perhaps we should ensure they find their way off Wildenham's land."

Lord William and his knights exited the Keep and watched Lord Sheridan and Sir Harlan climb atop of their horses before climbing atop their own readied mounts to follow the two men of Thornwick.

Lord Sheridan and Sir Harlan spurred their horses into a gallop with the hope of leaving the Lord of Wildenham and his knights far behind.

*   *   *

Lady Christine paced the floor. Wicked thoughts tormented her mind. *He admitted to killing Lord Redmond. What kind of a madman have I married? "Took me as his wife." He did not take me. I agreed to marry him!* She thought to escape, run away, but then again, Wildenham was her father's kingdom. *No, I will not leave*, she concluded. She decided to remain in the safety of her bedchamber until she resolved her predicament and planned to stay far away from her murdering husband for as long as she was able.

Chapter 20

As a curtain of darkness fell upon Wildenham, and the evening meal was ready to begin, Henry reined his tired horse at the stable just as Lord William and his knights returned.

"My lord, Rowena has sent a few things for you." Henry stated as he retrieved the items from the saddlebag.

Lord William and his knights dismounted. The Lord of Wildenham approached the messenger while his knights went to the Keep. Henry handed the apothecary's gifts to his lord.

"Thank you, Henry." Lord William could feel a ring through the leather of the small pouch and assumed it was his mother's ring. He put the pouch and missive in his belt bag. He assumed the wrapped object was his childhood sword. "How is your mother?"

"She is improving. I believe Rowena's potion did the trick." The messenger replied as he followed his lord into the Keep.

"I'm glad she is doing well."

"Me too. Thank you, my lord."

The Lord of Wildenham joined his knights at the High Table while servants carried out trenchers of food. Lord William laid the small sword across his lap, noticed the chair to his right was empty, and looked to his wife's ladies for an explanation.

"She will not come out of her bedchamber, my lord." Enid conveyed.

Lord William stopped Wilfred as he passed by the High Table.

"Wilfred, is something keeping my wife?"

"I am told she will not leave her bedchamber." He emphasized which bedchamber she occupied and looked toward Enid and Gilda.

"Is she unwell?"

"I do not know, my lord." Wilfred bowed and left to direct a servant, who carried a trencher, to a particular table.

Lord William looked up to the balcony as he noted Wilfred's reference. He clasped his childhood sword within his hand as he rose from his seat, ascended the staircase, and stepped into their bedchamber. Wilfred had yet to light the tapers. The flickering firelight in the fireplace was the only light in the room. His wife was absent. He took a moment to set the sword on the mantel and returned to the hallway. He went to her bedchamber door. It was closed. He stood for a moment and listened. All was quiet. Perhaps she was asleep. He knocked gently and held his ear close to the door, but heard only silence. He knocked again.

"Christine, are you well?"

"Go away." She sat upon the window seat staring down onto the garden.

"Are you coming down for dinner?"

She looked toward the bedchamber door and yelled.

"I said go away! Leave me in peace!"

Lord William stared at the door.

"Could you open the door? I want to see that you are well," he said calmly.

She stood, put her fists upon her hips, and yelled again.

"I do not want to see you! Go away!"

Is it anger or fear that I hear in her voice, he wondered. He remained calm.

"Christine, please open the door."

His listened, but heard nothing.

"Christine?"

When his inquisition was met with silence for the second time, he became concerned. Was she ill? Was she angry with him? Whatever the issue, he was determined to get to the bottom of it.

"I'm coming in."

"Oh, you can try, but I highly doubt you will succeed!" She crossed her arms across her chest, turned away from the door, and looked out the window.

With that much spunk, she cannot be ill, he thought. Lord William went to their bedchamber, shut the door, and stood before the panel to the left of the fireplace. He looked at the rosettes and hoped he remembered the sequence to open the portal. He pushed the series of rosettes, twisted the right center rose, but the portal remained closed. *Wrong one*, he thought. He tried another sequence and the portal opened with a click. When he pulled it fully open, he was met by a wall of cobwebs. He brushed them away with a sweep of his hand, stepped into the passage, and closed the door behind him. Enclosed in darkness, he reached his hands in front of him and walked forward the few steps until he touched the door that entered his wife's bedchamber. He felt for the handle, turned it to unlatch the door, and pushed it open cautiously. The room was illuminated by two tall candelabras framing the opening of the window seat. She was standing with her back toward him as she looked out the window. He entered the room and closed the door behind him.

Lady Christine heard the click of the portal and turned around to discover her husband in her bedchamber.

"My dearest wife, what upsets you so?"

She looked to the bolted bedchamber door.

"How did you get in here?" She unfolded her arms. They stiffened by her side as her hands balled into fists.

He ignored her question and approached her. She backed away until her heel hit the window seat.

"Are you well?" He took another step forward.

"I am." She replied and continued to retreat toward the night stand.

"What keeps you from the evening meal?"

Lady Christine felt her heel hit the nightstand. She reached behind her, opened a drawer, retrieved a dagger, and pointed it toward her husband.

"Stay back." She warned.

Lord William looked at the dagger and stopped his advance. He knew he could disarm her within the blink of an eye, but overpowering her would only make matters worse. He held up his hand, cautioning her to remain calm as he made his way to the window seat and sat down. He waited for her to settle her nerves and thought a distraction may be helpful.

"Shall I have Wilfred bring up a tray of food?"

"I'm not hungry," Lady Christine said sternly as she narrowed her eyes.

Lord William surmised her emotional state. *She is afraid, but for what reason?* He recalled the echo of a door being bolted after Lord Sheridan left the Great Hall. *Perhaps she overheard Lord Sheridan's accusations*, he thought. He sat and waited for her to find the courage to say what was on her mind.

Her husband made her nervous as he sat without speaking and kept glancing in her direction. She was afraid to ask if what she overheard was true or perhaps she was more afraid of the truth, but she hoped he would clear up the confusion within her mind as she found the gumption to ask.

"I was in the hallway today and I overheard your conversation with Lord Sheridan." She waved the dirk in small circles before her as she spoke. "Are you a mercenary?"

Ah, the moment of truth, he thought.

"I am."

Lady Christine looked away from her husband. *I have married a murderer.* She snapped her head in his direction as if to accuse.

"Did you kill my father?"

"No," he said as he looked directly into her eyes to convey his honest reply.

Her arm began to ache. She lowered the dirk, sat upon the bed, and allowed the weapon to rest on her lap.

"Who did?" She whispered and looked down at the floor in search of the answer.

"Indirectly, it was Lord Sheridan, or at least I believe it was."

Lady Christine peered at her husband in disbelief.

"Lord Sheridan?"

"The mysterious Lord Redmond was with him when he visited today."

"The imposter? So?"

"So, if you recall, he arrived at Wildenham the day after I had arrived. He is quite tall and wears black and green leather attire. He had asked your father for a night's stay. That very same night your father was murdered."

"I do not pay attention to those in attendance during the evening meal." She confided.

Lord William recalled the image of her sitting at the high table and ignoring those within the Great Hall.

"Perhaps I should explain my theory. I sustained an injury during my last assignment. It was necessary to give my body time to heal. During that time, I believe it was Lord Sheridan who requested my service. He may have become impatient and sent his knight to kill your father."

"How do you know he is one of Lord Sheridan's knights?"

"He appeared to be affiliated with Lord Sheridan. Usually, a mercenary prefers to remain anonymous and travels alone." Lord William explained.

"How do you know Lord Sheridan hired you to kill my father?"

"I do not know for certain, but I have a strong inclination that he did." He waited for his words to register within her mind. He combed his hand through his hair.

Lady Christine let out a small cry.

"You were going to kill my father! How do I know you will not kill me?"

Lord William had been forced to kill only one woman in order to conceal his identity and make his escape.

"I did not kill your father and I have no intention of ever harming you."

"How am I to believe you? How can I forgive you for what you intended to do?"

"Currently, you have no other choice but to trust my word. Forgiveness will, hopefully, come with time." He looked at the floor and waited for her response.

Lady Christine knew he was right. At best, she would have to watch her husband's every move and question his intentions.

"I have tried to piece the night's events together. I believe the murderer was waiting in your father's bedchamber, perhaps in the garderobe, when he made his attack. I am curious, however, as to why he would return to the scene of the murder."

Lord William glanced at his wife. She was staring at him.

"Do you enjoy killing people?" She inquired bluntly.

He was surprised by her question, but searched his mind for an answer before replying.

"No, but we can talk about that some other time." He tried to avoid the subject. Sensing her disproval of his lifestyle and dwelling on the topic was counterproductive to winning her trust.

Lord William looked around the room as silence stretched between them. He saw the small heart he had etched into the panel of the fireplace for his mother. He recalled her scolding and her promise to keep it a secret. The cherished memory brought a grin to his face.

Lady Christine found his silly smile insulting.

"What are you grinning about?"

"Do you see that heart carved into the panel of the fireplace?"

She looked in the direction he indicated.

"Yes, I have noticed it before."

"I remember the day I carved it as a gift for my mother. She promised to never tell my father."

She searched the profile of his face.

"You have visited Wildenham when you were young?

Lord William turned his head and looked at his wife. It was time he shared the truth.

"There is a lot that we do not know about each other and for now, I need you to trust me." He watched her carefully as he stood slowly. She tightened her grip on the dirk, raised it from her lap, and squirmed where she sat on the bed.

He looked at the weapon and let out a sigh. He walked away from her and unbolted the bedchamber door.

She was shocked when he turned his vulnerable back toward her and watched with intrigue as he took a rush from the floor, held it to the embers of the fire until it set aflame, and lit a taper that sat on the mantel.

He picked up the taper and looked in her direction.

"I want to show you something." He stood to the right of the fireplace before the wooden door made of fifteen framed small panels, three wide and five long, each decorated with a carved rosette in its center. As he did on the other side of the portal, he began to push a series of rosettes.

She rose from the bed and walked toward him cautiously. With her heart beating rapidly, she kept the dirk in front of her and pointed directly at her husband.

He twisted the left center rosette and the portal opened with a click. He turned to look at his wife.

She stared at the open portal and then to her husband.

"This is how you entered my bedchamber?"

He ignored her question and opened the door wide enough for them to enter. He led the way into the chamber and held out his hand to encourage her to follow. She refused his hand and stood where she was.

"Come, I want to show you where this leads." He reassured as he lowered his hand.

She took a few cautious steps and entered the small chamber apprehensively.

"Could you tuck the dirk into your bodice while we are in close quarters?" he said as he looked down at the top of her head.

She looked at the blade of the dirk. It was poking him in the stomach. She looked up into his eyes and did as he asked. She could retrieve the weapon easily if needed.

Once they were both inside, he reached behind her and closed the portal. With only candlelight to illuminate the tiny passage, Lord William turned and stood to one side as he reached for the other door.

"Can you see the latch?" he said as he held the taper over the object he indicated.

"Yes."

"You must turn the handle to release the lock." He demonstrated to clarify his meaning while she watched. When the portal opened, they walked into their bedchamber.

Lady Christine entered and turned to her husband as he emerged into the room.

"How did you know about this passage?"

"This used to be my father's bedchamber. Your bedchamber once belonged to my mother." He shut the door of the passage.

"Your father's bedchamber?"

"Yes, you see, my father was Lord Bradford. He was the Lord of Wildenham before your father."

She stared at her husband as she tried to recall the past.

"I remember living at a different castle and my father said he was traveling in search of a new home for us. When he returned, we packed our belongings, left our home, and came to Wildenham. I was seven years old." She looked at her husband for understanding. "If this was your home, where were you?"

"I had tired of the abuse from my father and left at age eleven. I lived in the woods with Rowena."

"Who?"

"An apothecary. She took me in and cared for me. In turn, I cared for her by gathering wood, catching our food, and eventually became a mercenary. A few years after I had left Wildenham, I received word that my father was dead and the kingdom overthrown."

Lady Christine looked at her husband as the direction of his implication became clear. Her eyes widened. Her face hardened defensively.

"Your father killed my father in order to obtain Wildenham." He stated bluntly.

"My father would never have done that!"

"Not even for his daughter?" He stated calmly.

She remained silent. She knew her father would have done anything for her, but would he have gone to such drastic measures? Was her husband telling a falsehood?

"I hold no grudges or hatred. There was little love lost between my father and me," he said with a grin to lessen the tension.

She had a feeling he spoke the truth.

"Now, you need to know how to open the portal," he said changing the subject.

They turned around to face the rosette door.

"The series is the same on both sides. First, push this one." Lord William pushed the rosette above the center right knob. "Second, push this one." He pushed the rosette below the knob. "And then the very center rosette on the door and turn the knob." He did so and rotated the rosette knob. The portal opened. He shut the door and it clicked.

"Now, you do it." He told his wife as he took his place behind her to observe.

She did so proficiently and turned for his approval once the portal popped open.

"As usual, you are a quick learner."

She rewarded him with a slight smile.

"But there is more I must show you." He pulled the door open and urged her forward. Holding the taper high, he closed the door. He moved the taper to the right to display another panel with rosettes.

"This was my father's private chamber and the door has a different sequence of rosettes that must be pushed to allow it to open." He took a cleansing breath. "Now if I can just remember."

He handed the taper to his wife and focused on the task at hand.

Lady Christine paid careful attention and tried to memorize the sequence of rosettes as her husband pushed the rosette above the knob, below, to the left of the previously pushed upper rosette, to the left of the lower pushed rosette and then to the left of the knob. He turned the rosette and heard a click. He allowed a grin of satisfaction to appear upon his face as he looked down to his wife, accepted the taper from her hand.

"I was eleven years old on the night I left Wildenham. I came to this room and stole coins from my father's chests that lie within this chamber." He pulled the door open and held the candle upward. They stared at the doorway that was blocked by a curtain of cobwebs.

"Goodness, how long has your father been dead?" She thought out loud as she shifted her vision to her husband and she tried to calculate how long she had lived at Wildenham.

He looked down at her and said, "By my calculations, ten years." He stood lost in thought.

His hesitation caused Lady Christine to grow impatient.

"Well, are we going in?" She had little desire to break the barrier of the cobweb wall and preferred he went first.

Chapter 21

"Apparently the last person to enter this chamber was my father," he said as he brushed away the cobwebs and allowed his wife to enter before him. He followed her into the chamber and closed the door until he heard it click.

"It's warm in here." She said as she stood in the small room.

He held the candle above her shoulder.

"It is warm because it is between the fireplaces of the adjoining bedchambers."

The room dripped with cobwebs and dust covered its contents. The cot was to their right and his father's desk to their left. Lord William went to the end of the cot and tossed open the lid on one of the chests. It was full to the top with a variety of coins. He kicked several others that sat upon the floor. The thud that echoed from each indicated they were full as well.

Lady Christine examined a portrait of a family displayed on the wall above the desk. The woman was beautiful and had an amethyst and diamond ring on her left hand. She looked to the child's face.

"Is this you?"

He looked in her direction and noticed she was staring at an oil painting. He went and stood behind her, held the candle up to the painting, and examined it. He was young, perhaps four years old, and remembered posing for the painting shortly before his mother's passing. He smiled as he gazed at his mother with her beauty captured for eternity. She looked happy. He remembered her wearing the lovely gown and noticed she wore the ring that he now possessed.

"Yes, that is me."

"Your mother was beautiful."

He shifted his eyes to his father and his mouth went from an admiring smile to a frown.

Lady Christine looked down at the top of the desk and saw a missive and sword. She picked up the letter and blew away the dust.

"I believe someone knew you would be here," she said as she held the missive for him to see. He looked down at what she held in her hand and recognized his name in his father's script. He took the missive, sat upon the cot, and placed the candle upon the floor. He broke the wax seal and began to read.

William, my son and heir,

The watchmen have informed me of your departure, and it grieves me so that you have gone. Perhaps I was too hard on you, but I was trying to groom you to take my place. I sincerely hope you are able to forgive my harshness. Wildenham and its people are a great responsibility. If it is within my

power, my fondest wish is to help you arise to your rightful
place as Lord of Wildenham. Until the time when I breathe
my last breath, I will continue to search for you and hope
you will return to claim what is rightfully yours – Wildenham.

> *Your father,*
> *Lord Bradford*
> *Lord of Wildenham*

He lowered the missive and looked toward his wife, who had picked up the Sword of Wildenham, blown off the dust, and presented it to him. He gave her the missive as he took his father's sword from her and examined its hilt embellished with jewels and a lion made from black onyx. He withdrew it from its scabbard to feel its weight. It was a good sword that had been passed down for generations. Now, it belonged to him. He returned it to its scabbard, stood, and set it back on the desk as his wife placed the missive next to the sword.

Lord William looked around the small room.

"I remember using the back passage the night I ran away." He picked up the candle, walked to the opposite end of the room, and pushed aside the curtain of the only tiny window in the room. There was a half moon in the night sky.

"Follow me." He turned to his left, paused to verify his wife was following, and descended the stairway. Downward they went until they came to a door and Lord William unlatched it. They entered the back of a closet.

"This was my bedchamber when I was a child."

There were shelves on one wall with cooking utensils, crocks, and cast iron pots. He made his way to the exterior door that led into the kitchen.

"You are jesting," she said in disbelief.

"Unfortunately, I'm not. My pallet was placed under the shelves." He turned and pointed to the floor beneath the shelves before pressing his ear to the door and listening to the activity on the other side of the portal. The kitchen staff was busy with the evening meal. If they exited the closet, it would raise the curiosity of the servants and expose the secret.

"We will have to return," he said as he turned around. She did the same.

Both husband and wife retraced their route toward the small chamber. As they passed through the tiny, secret room, Lady Christine paused as she looked at the family portrait again. Lord William stood behind her and looked in the direction of her line of vision.

"What intrigues you?"

"Nothing. Everything. I'm just trying to understand."

He reached past her for the latch and lifted it to open the portal. They left the tiny chamber and went toward their bedchamber. Lord William closed the doors to both chambers, set the candle on the table, and watched his wife as she looked around the room trying to absorb the information he had revealed. Unanswered questions clustered within her mind. She turned to look at the only person who could answer them.

"My father killed your father, didn't he?" There was an ache in her stomach as she realized her husband had spoken the truth.

"So I have been told. I'm sure Wilfred could shed some light on the matter if you are in need of additional information or verification."

"Wilfred was a servant for your father?"

"No, he was the steward and a good one I might add." His stomach growled. "Shall we have our evening meal, together, here in the bedchamber? I can ask Wilfred to have a tray readied?" He suggested.

A quiet meal would be nice, she thought.

"Yes." She took the dirk from her bodice and set it on the table.

Lord William opened the bedchamber door and saw a servant girl passing in the hallway. He instructed her to bring their evening meal to their bedchamber, closed the door, and turned to see his wife sitting on the far end of the bench before the fireplace. He stoked the fire and added another log before sitting on the opposite end of the bench. He looked at his poised wife. *Such a spirited beauty*, he thought.

"I would like to hear the whole story, from the beginning." She turned her knees in his direction.

He nodded in affirmation as his wife tried to recall what she was able to comprehend.

"Let me understand. Your father, Lord Bradford, was the Lord of Wildenham."

"Yes."

"Your mother died when you were young, and you are their only child."

"Yes."

"And you left on your own accord at age eleven?"

"Yes."

"Why? You were so young."

"I could no longer endure the abuse."

Lady Christine looked to the fire as she recalled the scars on her husband's back.

"So, the scars on your back……" She looked at him again and paused to allow him to finish her thought.

"Are a permanent reminder of when I fell short of my father's expectations. I was usually shackled to the wall in the dungeon and whipped."

The picture painted within Lady Christine's mind caused her to cringe.

"I would have left too." She admitted. "Where did you go?"

"I left just as daylight turned to dusk. A cook told me to stay off the road at night and to camp in the woods, but I wanted to get as far away from Wildenham as I could. I had become sleepy, but knew Adair would continue without my direction. I was attacked, robbed, and left for dead. Rowena found me. I accepted her offer to live with her. She cared for me as I did for her."

"You stayed with her all of those years?"

"I had nowhere else to go. I didn't want to come back here," he said as he looked around the bedchamber and motioned with his hand toward the walls.

There was a knock at the door.

"Enter." Lord William ordered.

The bedchamber door opened. Wilfred and a servant girl

entered with Jackson following. The steward and servant each carried a tray that contained a full course meal and tankards of spiced wine.

"Here on the bench will be fine." Lord William instructed as he motioned with his hand to indicate each tray's placement between him and his wife. "And could you open the window, please?"

With his appetite satisfied by his evening meal from the cook, Jackson hopped up on the bed, curled into a ball, and went to sleep.

"Will that be all, my lord?" Wilfred opened the window. The servant girl exited the bedchamber.

"Yes, thank you, Wilfred," Lord William said as he noted his wife was looking at the steward as if for the first time.

"Have a pleasant evening, my lord, my lady," the steward said as he left the bedchamber and closed the door behind him.

Lady Christine drank from the tankard, lowered it, and gazed at her husband curiously.

"When did you become a mercenary?" She was finding it difficult to believe she was married to a murderer. He had treated her with nothing but kindness and respect since their lives had been thrown together.

"I believe it was before I turned one score of age. Looking back, some would say I was an angry child. I hated my father for what he did to me. I hated the men who attacked me on the road. I hated everyone. I vented that hatred through practicing my training. Eventually, I began to patrol the road at night so that others would not suffer the same fate I endured the evening I left Wildenham. Word spread of my vigilance and the road became safe to travel after dark. Before long, I was sought out and employed to kill others."

"How many have you killed?" She dared to ask.

Lord William took a deep, cleansing breath and searched his mind. *How many have I killed*, he wondered. He assumed the number to be great.

"Too many to recall." He replied.

"Did you enjoy killing them?" Perhaps she was pushing him a little too far, but she needed to understand the man who was now her husband.

"There was little emotion involved. They were nothing more than a job I was hired to do." He confessed as he picked up a tankard and took a swig. It was a relief to share the secrets of his life with her. It was as if a burden was being lifted from his shoulders.

"And you were going to kill my father because it was 'a job' and nothing more?" Her question came across as an accusation. *How could one take a life so easily*, she wondered.

"I had reservations about returning to Wildenham. In truth, I did not want to come. As a child, I vowed to never return, but once I arrived, it was fascinating to see the kingdom again. Not all of my memories are bad. It was unfortunate, however, that I made the mistake of staying longer than expected."

"A mistake?"

"I normally stay only long enough to fulfill the assignment, a day at most."

"My father is still dead, whether it was by your hand, or another."

"It was not by my hand." He defended.

She reflected on his words as they ate their meal in silence. Lord William waited for his wife's next question. It calmed him to be in her presence, or perhaps it was the wine as he picked up his mug and took another swig.

"So, you believe you were hired by Lord Sheridan to kill my father." She stated the fact instead of posing a question before she shoved a piece of meat into her mouth.

"The missive was sent anonymously. They seldom say who is requesting my service. After seeing Lord Redmond, or whatever his name is, with Lord Sheridan today, I believe so." Lord William nodded positively to the statement.

"And you think this other man killed my father?"

"Correct," he said as he ate a chunk of bread and took a sip from his mug to wash it down.

"If you dislike Wildenham and its horrid memories from your past, why did you stay and marry me?"

Lord William reflected, trying to find a specific reason.

"As I watched you cry and grieve over your father, I wondered how many women I may have forced into the streets, as a result of killing their husbands or fathers. I did what needed to be done, sealed my fate as Lord of Wildenham, and married you so you could remain in Wildenham."

"So you did this unwillingly?" Lady Christine met her husband's intense stare. Their eyes locked as if his response should remain in the confidence of each other.

"No, it was my choice."

"But in truth, all of this, all of Wildenham belongs to

you," she said as she motioned with her hands pointing toward the room's contents.

"No, it belongs to us. Our fathers wanted each of us to inherit Wildenham. We have, and we shall rule it together."

Lady Christine took a sip from her mug and watched the flickering flames in the fireplace.

"I'm sorry." Lady Christine whispered as she turned her face to look at her husband.

"For what?"

"I am sorry for the loss of your father."

"In truth, I was pleased to hear of his demise. Christine, you do not need to apologize for your father's actions. After all, he did it out of love for you." Lord William justified as he wondered if he was doing the same.

She noted his use of her Christian name.

"I shared the secret passage and chamber with you for a specific reason. Using the words my mother once spoke to me, please heed my advice. There may come a time when you must act cowardly to save your life in order to live another day. If that time should arise when your life is in danger, promise me that you will seek the shelter of the secret chamber."

She stared at him quizzically. She was confident she could defend herself if the need should arise, but appeased his concern and agreed.

"I promise and I shall keep the secret of the chamber and passage."

He nodded his head and sighed in relief. Something had changed between them. His wife seemed compliant, a little more at ease, and they were conversing civilly.

Corvus flew into the room and perched on the headboard and cawed. Lord William tossed a chunk of bread onto the floor. The raven fluttered to the floor and began to eat.

Lord William looked to the door and made a mental note to bolt it before retiring when he saw the chessboard and table with two chairs had been brought from the library to their bed chamber. The last time he had played the game he had resided within Wildenham. He turned back to his wife.

"Are you up for a game of chess?" He assumed she was a competent player. "It has been many years since I have played."

His wife looked to the chessboard and then to her husband.

"All right," she said and moved her tray of food to the floor.

Lord William set his tray on the floor. He crossed the room, placed his half-filled tankard upon the table, and closed the window before retrieving the chessboard and setting it upon the bench. He sat and examined its pieces.

"Perhaps we should review how each piece moves." He suggested, looking to her for guidance.

"Very well. The Queens go on the square of their same color and White Queen moves first. I mean, the person with the White Queen moves first to begin the game." She explained as she pointed to the pieces.

Once Lord William possessed a better understanding of the game, he did his best to make it a competitive match as they played well into the night.

Chapter 22

Lord Sheridan and Sir Harlan traveled through the moonlit night. They were confident they had left Lord William and his knights far behind and allowed their tired horses to walk at a gentle pace as they continued toward Thornwick.

"Well, isn't that a turn of events. The young Lord William, son of Lord Bradford, has returned and claimed his throne." Lord Sheridan revealed.

"I thought you implied he was a mercenary?" Sir Harlan was growing weary of Lord Sheridan's chattering, but wanted to clear the confusion within his mind.

"He is a mercenary. He is the very same one I hired to kill Lord Clayborn."

"I thought I was to kill Lord Clayborn."

"Yes, yes you were and did. But I had employed the legendary mercenary to kill him before I asked you."

"Then why did you ask me to do it?" Sir Harlan was tired of being used.

"He was taking too long to get the job done."

"Is he the very same person who also patrols the roads at night?" Sir Harlan wanted to see if Lord William was one and the same person.

"So I have been told."

"And now he is the Lord of Wildenham, how ironic," Sir Harlan said with a snicker.

"This is entirely your fault!" Lord Sheridan accused.

"How is it my fault?" Sir Harlan tried to remain calm. After listening to his annoying companion's unrelenting ravings of anger and disappointment from the moment they had left Wildenham, his disposition began to boil with anger. He was growing weary of Lord Sheridan's accusations and disgusted from watching spittle fly from his mouth whenever he enunciated a word.

"If you would have gotten to Lady Christine and taken her away from Wildenham, then Lord William wouldn't have married her and I could have claimed the kingdom for myself!"

"I told you, the door was bolted. There was nothing I could do!" Sir Harlan hollered with all of his might. He reined his horse to a stop. "Are you daft? How many times do I have to tell you? I am tired of listening to your incessant whining," he said through clenched teeth as he put his hand on the hilt of his sword.

"I expected you to do one simple thing, one simple thing, and you didn't do it properly."

"I killed Lord Clayborn. I did your dirty work for you. That is what you asked me to do!"

"But you left the door open for someone else to waltz into Wildenham and take it all away from me!"

"It was never yours." Sir Harlan withdrew his sword, swiped it through the air, and severed Lord Sheridan's head from his body.

He watched the detached cranium bounce onto the ground. The decapitated body fell from the saddle. Lord Sheridan's startled horse trotted a few strides before stopping.

"Perhaps I can finally enjoy a quiet and peaceful ride home." Sir Harlan sneered as he sheathed his sword. He urged his horse forward, grabbed the reins of Lord Sheridan's horse, and proceeded down the road. Reining his horse suddenly, he realized his return to Thornwick would be pointless. Its lord was dead and even though he was now the Lord of Thornwick, his agreement with Lord Sheridan was made in confidence. *Sir Kenneth will take charge and the garrison will follow his lead. Those within Thornwick's walls will never accept me has their lord*, he thought. *Until the baron is notified and a new lord appointed, the kingdom may fall into disorder and chaos.* Realizing he would never hold the title of the Lord of Thornwick, Sir Harlan turned his horse around, stared down the road, and a wicked smile grew upon his face. He kicked his heels into the sides of his horse, stared down at the lifeless body on the road as he passed it, and headed toward Wildenham with Lord Sheridan's horse following. *It is time to get even with the Lord of Wildenham and take his wife, kingdom, everything*, he thought.

His horse took a few quick strides before returning to its slower pace, but Sir Harlan was too preoccupied to notice. He replayed the events of the past few days in his mind and wondered what he could have done differently to have made the mission a success. He imagined the reaction of those within Thornwick when Lord Sheridan failed to return. In truth, he cared little of their plight. He thought back to the night when his attempted robbery was thwarted by a stranger with a bird.

The return trip seemed long. Sir Harlan's head began to bob as his eyelids grew heavy. He had ridden most of the night and assumed he was close to Wildenham's land. He could smell smoke from fires within the village and directed his horse off the road with Lord Sheridan's horse following. He went deep into the woods. When he found a suitable spot, he tethered the horses and took the saddle and blanket from Lord Sheridan's horse. He used the saddle as a pillow and covered himself with the saddle blanket as he lay upon the ground to sleep. He would begin to plan his revenge on Lord William and his lovely wife at the break of dawn.

*   *   *

Jackson jumped off of the bed, stretched, and sharpened his claws on the leg of the table. It was time for his morning meal, but the bedchamber door was closed making it impossible for him to go to the kitchen. He hopped onto the small table, sat, and looked at his lord and lady who were still asleep.

Corvus tilted his head and watched the cat curiously. The raven noticed the window was closed, his stomach was empty, and he was eager to stretch his wings.

Jackson looked at the mug on the table and dipped his head inside to smell its contents. The wine was of little interest to him. He withdrew his head and pushed the tankard with his paw. It made a scratching noise as it inched across the table. The mischievous feline looked toward the sleeping couple. Lord William rolled onto his side. Lady Christine continued to sleep. Jackson looked back to the mug and pushed it several times moving it closer and closer to the edge of the table.

"Jackson, knock it off," Lady Christine said as she awoke from her slumber.

Lord William rolled back onto his back and lifted his head to see the feline sitting on the table. He dropped his head back onto his pillow and closed his eyes.

Jackson looked toward his mistress. She remained in bed. He pushed the mug the last few inches sending the mug and its contents crashing to the floor.

Lady Christine sat up quickly and threw her pillow in Jackson's direction. Jackson jumped to the floor long before the pillow reached him.

"Well, he did as you asked," Lord William said as he threw back the covers.

"He just wants his morning meal." She replied as she closed her eyes.

"I'll let him out." Lord William swung his feet to the floor and stood.

Jackson ran to the door, sat, and looked toward his lord. He meowed as Lord William approached, curled up one paw, and flexed his claws.

"I'm coming, your highness." Lord William mocked as the chubby feline stood on all fours and rubbed against his lord's leg.

"There you go," he said as he opened the bedchamber door. Jackson scurried out. Corvus saw his opportunity, took to flight, and exited the chamber as well. The raven assumed the cat was going to get his morning meal and hoped he would receive the same as he followed Jackson to the kitchen.

Lord William closed and bolted the door and thought of returning to bed, but his wife had taken his pillow and returned to sleep. He looked out the window at the morning sky. With a deep sigh, he ran his hand through his hair and headed to the garderobe. A list of items that needed his attention accumulated within his mind. During his tour through the village, he had spotted needed repairs to a few of the huts. He would oversee the repairs and ensure they were done properly before winter arrived.

As he emerged from the garderobe, he saw the sword he had left on the mantel and remembered the other items in his belt bag. With the bedchamber door bolted, he retrieved his mother's ring and missive, opened the letter, and sat on the bench. Rowena had declined his offer and indicated the items she had sent. He stood and tossed the missive onto the ashen embers. He picked up the sword, took off the protective cloth, and examined the hilt. It was identical to his father's sword, only smaller.

Lord William pushed the rosettes on both doors and entered his father's tiny chamber. He set the sword on the top of the desk next to his father's sword. He pulled the right drawer open, lifted the false bottom, and took out a small wooden box. He opened the box to reveal the black velvet lining. He opened the leather pouch and dumped his mother's ring into the palm of his hand. He held the dainty ring between his thumb and forefinger as he admired the gems. He sighed as he glanced up at his mother's face in the portrait, placed the ring in the box, and returned it to the hiding place.

As he closed the portals and dressed, he planned to eat whatever he could find in the kitchen for a quick breakfast before making his way to the village.

*   *   *

A midday gentle breeze filtered the sunlight through the trees causing Sir Harlan to squeeze his eyes tightly. He rose and pulled some jerky and stale bread from a pouch on his saddle. He made his way to the edge of the woods, sat hidden within the foliage, and watched the activity of Wildenham's village. He stared at the Keep as he chewed his morning meal and wondered if Lady Christine had risen. As he observed the activity of the kingdom, he contemplated how to get inside its walls.

Sir Harlan stopped in mid-chew as a man dressed in black riding an ebony destrier reined his horse to look at a hut on the edge of the village. A crow flew in circles over the man's head and landed upon his shoulder.

"The Lord of Wildenham, what brings you outside of the Keep? I would have thought your new bride would have you still in bed," Sir Harlan said aloud to himself as he bit into the jerky, ripped off another bite, and chewed.

He watched the residents of the hut emerge and greet their lord. They conversed while pointing to specific spots on the walls and toward the roof. Lord William dismounted and inspected the areas the peasants had indicated. He nodded in understanding, climbed atop his horse, and rode toward the Keep.

Sir Harlan finished the last of his jerky and bread and remained in his place of hiding while he continued to observe. Within a few moments, Lord William returned with a wagon that carried supplies and a few peasant men. The Lord of Wildenham and the men began working together to repair the hut.

Sir Harlan snickered to himself. *My, my, my, Lord William, the way you work alongside these people, one would believe you actually care about their welfare*, he thought as an evil smile appeared slowly on his face. *It is such a pity. If all goes my way, you won't be their lord for much longer.*

Chapter 23

Lady Christine woke to an empty bedchamber. She flipped the covers to her husband's side of the bed, stepped onto the floor, and stretched with her arms over her head. She had slept peacefully and hummed to herself while she used the garderobe. She thought of passing through the portal to her bedchamber, but knew Enid and Gilda would see her emerge. She remembered her promise to keep the passage a secret, exited the room, and entered her former bedchamber to find her ladies ready to dress her for the day.

"Good morning." Lady Christine greeted as she continued to hum.

"Good morning." Enid and Gilda returned the greeting simultaneously and looked toward each other questioning the noticeable change in the disposition of their mistress.

"Do you know where Lord William is on this fine morning?" Lady Christine smiled.

Enid looked toward Gilda and then back to her mistress.

"Morning? My lady, it is midday. I overheard him tell Wilfred that he was heading to the village."

"Really? Well, then, let's get me dressed." Lady Christine was too impatient to wait for her ladies. She began to take off her chemise. "Gilda, please tell Wilfred to have my horse readied and Sir Farrell that I wish to practice my sword skills."

"Yes, my lady." Gilda left the chamber to find Wilfred.

Enid grabbed a dress and undergarments from the wardrobe.

Lady Christine looked at the dress Enid held before her.

"No, I want my practice attire."

"But, my lady, do you not think you should dress the part of the Lady of Wildenham?" Enid encouraged her mistress to dress appropriately for her title.

"Enid, I am the Lady of Wildenham and I shall dress as I please."

Enid lowered the dress and exhaled as she complied with her lady's wishes. She returned the garment to the wardrobe and selected a practice outfit. She helped her mistress dress as quickly as possible and pinned her hair neatly out of her face.

At almost a run, Lady Christine exited her bedchamber and hurried through the Keep. She found Thomas holding the reins of her readied horse and Sir Farrell sitting atop his destrier when she arrived at the stable. The stableboy assumed his lady would be wearing a dress and had placed a set of small steps before the side of her horse.

"My lady, you wish to practice today?" Sir Farrell questioned to verify her request, for he had hoped to avoid his temperamental mistress and focus on the men's fighting skills.

The Lady of Wildenham looked at the steps and then to the stableboy's kind face. She used the steps unnecessarily and climbed atop her mare. Thomas handed her the reins, picked up the steps, and returned them to the stable.

"Yes, I need you to show me a few maneuvers that will impress my husband." She explained to her knight as she reined her horse, trotted it through both baileys, and over the drawbridge. She turned her head toward the sound of someone shouting at the edge of the village.

"I can do as you ask, but who are you trying to impress?" Sir Farrell was curious.

She reined her horse to a stop as she heard a man's stern voice coming from the village. Was that her husband shouting orders? She turned her horse, directed it between the huts, and through the street of the village. As she rode with Sir Farrell following, many of the residents curtsied and greeted their mistress. When she nodded in acknowledgement, they were pleasantly surprised.

She heard her husband call out to someone again and directed her horse toward his voice. *What can he possibly be doing,* she wondered. As she came around the corner of a hut on the outskirt of the village, she saw her husband at the top of a ladder. She reined her horse and watched from a distance as he accepted thatching from a peasant and handed it to another who laid it on top of the roof of the hut. He was working side by side with the village men. Some worked to reinforce a wall while others ensured the door could swing and shut properly.

Lord William turned to see his wife and Sir Farrell watching him from atop their horses. Assuming an issue needed his attention, he descended from the ladder and waved for his wife to come to him.

She encouraged her horse forward at a leisurely pace and reined it before her husband.

"Is there something amiss?" He glanced from his wife to Sir Farrell, who kept his horse at a distance. The knight shrugged his shoulders as if puzzled by his lady's behavior.

"No." She replied as she looked away from her husband's inquiring face to the hut.

"Did you come to gloat over your win last night?" He raised his eyebrows teasingly. The corners of his mouth turned upward in reference to their chess match.

She returned her gaze back to his face and watched him walk to the side of her horse. His grin turned into a look of concern or was it apprehension?

"No," she said with a slight smile upon her face. "You will improve as you become reacquainted with the game."

He agreed with her assumption, but still searched for the justification for her visit.

"Did you need something in particular?" He inquired.

"No, I was only curious as to why you were shouting." She had to admit he had a handsome face. She was especially attracted to the gold flecks in his hazel eyes that sparkled in the sunlight.

"The structure appeared weak. I wanted to ensure it was ready for the coming winter," he said as he turned toward the hut to admire the work that was nearly complete.

She was impressed to see him take an interest in the welfare of the people as she scanned the repairs to the building.

"For the sake of those inside, I am glad you spotted the needed improvements."

Unaccustomed to receiving compliments, he paused before he turned toward her and puffed up his chest with pride.

She returned her gaze to her husband and let out a sigh as the silence stagnated between them.

"I was just heading to the practice field with Sir Farrell." She commented as the topic of conversation entered her mind.

"Good. After I help finish with the repairs, would you mind if I joined you?" He ventured the suggestion as a bright light flashed from the woods. He looked for a possible source, but only saw bushes and trees. He turned his attention back to his wife for her answer.

"How much longer will you be?" She inquired.

"We are nearly finished with this hut, but there are others. I can direct the needed repairs on the next building and then join you after I have my midday meal."

She looked to the sky. The sun was past midday. She had slept longer than she thought.

"Could you have a meal packed for two and bring it to the practice field? I have yet to eat."

Lord William nodded his head to indicate he would do so.

"Good, I will meet you there." Lady Christine reined her horse and departed.

Sir Farrell nodded his head toward Lord William, turned his horse, and followed Lady Christine to the practice field.

Lord William stared at the woods one last time before returning to the task at hand.

*　　*　　*

Sir Harlan remained motionless. Only his eyes rotated as he watched Lady Christine and the knight ride away. When he looked back to Lord William, he discovered the man dressed in black staring directly at him. *Does he know I am here*, he wondered. He looked back to Lady Christine. Her horse went over a hill and disappeared from his sight as if sinking into the ground. His desire for Lady Christine increased with each passing day. He smiled to himself. He would wait an eternity if the result had her warming his bed. Eventually, the opportune moment would present itself. He would take full advantage of it when it did. He observed the workers and their lord continue with their repairs as an idea materialized in his head. *Yes, she will be mine and so will Wildenham*, he thought before going back to his camp deep within the woods.

Chapter 24

Lord William crossed his arms over his chest and nodded his head approvingly at the repairs to the small hut. He inspected the next residence with the men who eagerly pointed to each needed repair. He listened to their concerns and selected two men to supervise, climbed atop Adair, and headed for the stable.

Thomas came forward and greeted his lord as he took Adair's reins.

"Good day, my lord." Thomas patted Adair's nose.

"Good day, Thomas. Please give him water and keep him ready. I will be leaving again shortly." Lord William dismounted and headed toward the Keep.

"Yes, my lord." Thomas led the destrier to a trough of water.

Wilfred greeted Lord William in the Great Hall.

"My lord, I have set out your midday meal in your library."

"Wilfred, I appreciate your foresight, but could you have it packed and add enough food for two so that Lady Christine and I may eat on the practice field?"

"Certainly, my lord."

"Thank you, Wilfred."

As Wilfred made his way to the kitchen to instruct a servant of their lord's request, Lord William went to his bedchamber, washed his hands and face, and changed into a clean black tunic. Exiting the bedchamber and making his way to the Great Hall, he met Wilfred at the bottom of the staircase. The steward handed Lord William a leather pouch filled with his lord and lady's meal.

"Thank you, Wilfred." Lord William accepted the pouch from the steward, exited the Keep, and found Thomas waiting with Adair.

"Thank you, Thomas." Lord William tied the pouch to the saddle, took the reins from the stableboy, and climbed atop his horse.

"My pleasure, my lord." Thomas watched his lord depart.

Lord William nodded to those who greeted him along the way. He was adjusting to his new role as the Lord of Wildenham. He made a mental list of items he noticed that would need repairs as he rode through the outer bailey. Once over the drawbridge, he breathed a sigh of relief as he escaped from the watchful eyes of those within the castle's walls. He tried to recall the items on his list to etch them within his memory as he headed toward the practice field. He surmised most of the items could be handled with common sense, except one. His beautiful wife was an emotional puzzle that he was putting together cautiously. Their previous night had been quite pleasant. That is, once matters between them were settled. He hoped to continue to build upon what little trust he may have instilled within her and allow their relationship to deepen and grow.

He reined Adair at the top of a hill, turned him around to face the kingdom, and admired the castle and village. He had to admit that Wildenham was a quite lovely. Any lord would be proud to rule and oversee it. He redirected Adair and continued on his way to the practice field. He singled out his wife and observed her sparring as he reined his horse to a stop. He cringed as she became off balance, sliced her sword through the air, and stumbled sideways, falling to the ground. Sir Farrell extended his hand to help her rise.

Lady Christine realized her husband was watching. Out of pride, she ignored her knight's offer and rose from the ground unaided.

Lord William could see the vexation and humiliation on his wife's face. *So much for civility*, he thought.

She grew uncomfortable and self-conscious. She assumed her husband was finding fault in every movement she made.

"Enough," she said as the pressure from his scrutinizing became too great. Both lady and knight lowered their wooden practice swords.

She turned to face her husband and met his eyes defiantly. Frustrated with the new moves Sir Farrell had taught, her heart seemed to sink into her stomach as her disappointment with her inability to master and perform them perfectly became apparent. She hoped to display her new skill to her husband, but now she would be subjected to his ridicule.

"Must you always wear black?" She snapped, misdirecting her anger toward her husband.

Lord William looked at his tunic and breeches. He liked the color. It worked well when he patrolled the roads at night.

"What's wrong with black?" He responded innocently.

She ignored his question.

"And the repairs?" She slapped her sword against her leg.

Lord William dismounted and untied the pouch from the saddle. *Perhaps appeasing her curiosity would improve her mood,* he thought. *It can't make it any worse.*

"They are progressing." He walked toward the bench, sat down, and motioned for her to join him. She crossed her arms over her chest.

Sir Farrell appeared behind Lady Christine.

"Sir Farrell, will you be joining us?" Lord William addressed the knight.

"No thank you, my lord, but if you don't mind, I would like to return to the Keep." He preferred to eat his midday meal in solitude and away from his ornery lady's company.

"You may go, Sir Farrell." Lady Christine ordered as she dismissed the knight and continued to stare at her husband.

Sir Farrell ignored his lady's order and looked to his lord for his approval. Lord William gave a slight nod of his head indicating the knight may take his leave.

Lady Christine noticed the exchange between the two men. She narrowed her eyes as she looked from her husband to the knight.

Sir Farrell turned to leave and cringed inside as he caught sight of the disapproving look upon Lady Christine's face.

Lady Christine glared at her husband who was busy unlacing the pouch. *How dare he usurp my orders,* she thought.

"Am I not your equal?" She questioned. "Why is he to wait for your approval before leaving?"

Lord William looked at his vexed wife.

"Christine, I was only replying to his inquiry," he said calmly, hoping to defuse the situation.

"Don't 'Christine' me! He is my knight!" She stopped her foot to emphasize her point.

"He is our knight, no longer just yours, and he was following my orders." Lord William corrected his wife, knowing she was unaware of his private instructions for the knight to continue his duties as Lady Christine's guardian.

Needing a distraction and a moment to calm himself, Lord William retrieved two corked bottles of ale, bread, meats, cheese, and sweet cakes from the pouch and set them on the bench next to where he sat. He uncorked his bottle, took a long swig, broke off a chunk of cheese, and popped it into his mouth. He turned away from his wife's condescending stare and focused his attention on the practicing men.

She knew he was ignoring her. *Well, two can play at this game,* she thought. She threw her sword onto the ground, sat at the opposite end of the bench, grabbed a bottle, uncorked it, and took a drink.

The Lord and Lady of Wildenham ate their meal without conversation or acknowledgement of each other's existence.

Lord William tipped his bottle and drained the last drop of ale. He wished he had a second bottle to drink as he rose from the bench, unbuckled his sword from his belt, and took his dirk from its sheath. He laid them on the bench, went to the pile of practice swords, and selected replacements. He tucked the practice dirk into his belt, knowing he needed to rein in his temper before practicing with his wife. He looked to Sir Gunther and nodded.

Sir Gunther nodded in affirmation and readied his practice sword. He knew his lord was a good fighter and anticipated a difficult sparring session, but Lord William's pursed lips and narrowed eyes conveyed anger that would pulverize him into submission.

At the sound of nearby clashing swords, Lady Christine turned, nearly choked on a piece of dry bread she was eating, and watched in awe at her husband's swiftness and agility. His moves were beautifully choreographed and fluid. Sir Gunther's counters with his practice sword were merely a reflex to each of Lord William's swift attacks. She gasped inadvertently when her husband moved so quickly that Sir Gunther soon found himself on the ground with a dirk held against his throat.

"Well done, my lord." Sir Gunther complimented as he relaxed upon the ground and tried to catch his breath.

Lord William nodded, returned the dirk to his belt, and held out his hand to help his sparring partner rise from the ground. Once both men were standing, they slapped each other on the shoulder. Lord William looked in his wife's direction to see if she had finished eating. She was staring at him with her mouth agape.

"Are you ready to practice?" His question came across like a curt order.

Lady Christine closed her mouth and remained silent as thoughts of confusion flooded her mind. *He is a killing machine, so finely tuned, precise, accurate, and deadly. He transformed from the kind man of last night into a beast before my eyes. He can kill with one slice of his sword. No emotion, a merciless stranger who can murder without feeling.* Her heartbeat quickened as she shook her head from side to side. She remained seated.

His chest heaved up and down as he walked toward her.

She wanted to flee, but pride kept her frozen to the bench as she looked up at her husband who towered above her. She noted the beads of sweat upon his brow, his hazel eyes that seemed to bore into her soul, and his unsmiling mouth.

"You have finished eating. I don't understand your hesitation." He bent down and picked up her practice sword from the ground and handed it to her hilt first.

She looked to the sword and shifted her eyes to Sir Gunther, who was watching intently. The knight nodded his head in encouragement.

"I hesitate because you scare me. You're a monster," she said as she grabbed the sword from his hand, stood, and walked past him to the vacant spot on the field.

Lord William's breath expelled from his lungs as if he were hit in the stomach. He remembered the last time he was called such a name. *A monster*, he thought as her words struck a nerve, a very sensitive nerve left scarred by his father. He bowed his head and looked down at the ground.

Lady Christine turned to face her husband and stared at his back.

"Well?" she said sarcastically.

Upon recognizing the flippant tone in her voice, Lord William lifted his chin, turned to face her, and threw his practice sword onto the pile with the others.

"Sir Gunther, you can train her. I have better things to do." He turned his back on his wife as he picked up his sword and dirk from the bench, made his way to Adair, and climbed atop his destrier. He gave his wife a look of disdain before pressing his heels into the side of his horse and leaving abruptly at a galloping pace.

Sir Gunther came to his lady's side.

"What's that all about?" She interpreted her husband's behavior as rude.

"Pride, my lady. You hurt his pride."

"How did I do that?" She turned to her knight seeking an explanation.

"Shall I speak freely, my lady?"

"Please do."

"I believe your words have wounded him. He is a man of honor, not a monster as you have so publicly labeled him."

Lady Christine became aware of the men close enough to have overheard her accusation.

Sir Gunther continued.

"Is he truly a mercenary as suggested by Lord Sheridan?"

"He has claimed to be so." She confirmed, but chose to hide the detail of her husband's plan to murder her father.

"Lord William could have left after your father's death and allowed Lord Sheridan or any other lord or knight to wed you and claim Wildenham as his own. One must ask oneself, would Lord William rather live his life as a mercenary than as the lord of this kingdom? He has made a great sacrifice, did what was right, and he did it for you. I, for one, respect him, as should you." Sir Gunther sighed as he and his lady watched Lord William disappear over the hill.

"I want to return to the Keep," Lady Christine said as her heart seemed to fall within her chest. She handed her practice sword to her knight without looking in his direction.

"Very well, my lady." Sir Gunther knew his words rang true. Without Sir Farrell to guard her, he tossed both swords onto the pile and followed to ensure her safety. They climbed atop their horses and rode toward the castle. As they crested the hill, Sir Gunther saw Lord William vanish behind one of the village huts. He turned his head to see if his lady noted the same. With her head lowered, she appeared to be wiping a tear from her cheek. The knight looked away and remained silent.

They made their way through the baileys and reined their horses at the stable. Lady Christine dismounted as Conal grabbed her mare's bridle quickly. The Lady of Wildenham kept her head lowered and went directly to her private bedchamber where her ladies and a bath were waiting.

She sat numbly upon the bed with her back to Enid and Gilda.

"A rough day, my lady?" Enid sensed her mistress's distress.

Lady Christine flopped backward upon the bed and stared up at the beamed ceiling. The tears that had pooled in her eyes slid to the corners, rolled onto the side of her face, and disappeared into her hairline.

"It was not my choice to marry, but yet I am a stranger's wife." Lady Christine began.

Hearing the sorrow within her lady's voice, Enid felt the need to comment positively.

"My lady, he is a fine husband who made a decision, a sacrifice that changed his life as well and he did it for you."

"I know, Sir Gunther has lectured me on the topic. Unfortunately, I fear I have turned him against me." She wiped the tears from her eyes, rolled over onto her side, and looked at her ladies.

Gilda was confused.

"Sir Gunther?"

"No, my husband." Lady Christine stated as she rolled back onto the bed and placed her right forearm over her eyes. "I just need time to think."

Chapter 25

With the wall fully repaired, the second residence was fit for the coming winter. Lord William stood shoulder to shoulder with the men as they admired their accomplishment.

"Well done, everyone." He complimented, giving them a sense of pride in their work. "We shall continue with repairs tomorrow."

Lord William slapped a few of the men's shoulders before climbing atop Adair and heading back to the Keep for the evening meal.

After dismounting and leaving his horse with Thomas, Lord William entered the Great Hall and found it crowded with people. Nearly every seat was taken except for those at the High Table. It remained empty. Feeling the need for solitude, he signaled to Wilfred for a moment of his time. The steward answered a servant's question before going to his lord's side.

"My lord?"

"Could you have my meal brought to the library?"

"Certainly, my lord." Wilfred went to the kitchen to have a tray readied.

Lord William entered the library and closed the door behind him. He stirred the embers, placed a log upon them, and sat in the chair before the fire. He let out a deep sigh as he watched the flames wrap around the wood.

Perhaps it was a mistake to come here, he thought as he longed for the peaceful, simpler life he had with Rowena. *A monster?* Her cutting words echoed in his mind. *Maybe I am unfit to be a husband, or the Lord of Wildenham.* He thought he had chosen the best option for his wife and everyone in Wildenham. *Dare I entertain the thought of leaving Wildenham in the hands of my wife and returning to Rowena?*

*   *   *

Lady Christine's hands were damp. Her heart thumped rapidly while she dressed in a beautiful burgundy gown trimmed in gold for the evening meal.

"You look lovely, my lady," Enid said and Gilda nodded her head in agreement.

Lady Christine took a deep breath, left her bedchamber, and descended the staircase. She noted her husband's seat was empty as she took her place at the High Table along with the knights and her ladies. The meal commenced even though her husband's chair remained empty. Her fear in confronting her husband had caused her to lose her appetite. She picked up her tankard and drank the warm, spiced wine to calm her nerves before forcing herself to take a bit of meat from her plate and place it into her mouth.

Wilfred passed the High Table with a serving wench carrying a tray of food.

"Wilfred, what keeps my husband?"

The steward stopped, as did the servant, and hesitated to answer her inquiry.

"He is, my lady, in his library and has requested his evening meal be served to him there."

Lady Christine's mouth fell open. She looked in the direction of the library and rose from her chair. Sir Farrell and Sir Gunther rose out of respect while Enid and Gilda questioned their lady's intention.

"Never mind, Wilfred. I will take the tray to him. Please send another tray for me as well." Lady Christine instructed as she came around to the other side of the table and accepted the tray from the servant.

"Very well, my lady. Your tray will be there shortly." Wilfred and the servant headed toward the kitchen.

Lady Christine's legs weakened. Her heart raced as she made her way slowly to the library. She tried to swallow, but her mouth was dry as she knocked softly upon the door with her foot.

"Come in," Lord William said.

Lady Christine let out a sigh to ease her nerves as she managed the tray in one hand and opened the door with the other. She entered the room and closed the door behind her. It took her eyes a few moments to adjust to the dark room. The only light came from the amber glow of the fireplace. Its flames reflected off of her husband's face as he slouched in a chair staring into the fire. She noted the furniture remained unchanged since her last visit to the room.

"Just set it on my desk, Wilfred," he said without looking in the direction of the door.

"I met…." Lady Christine started to say, but her voice

cracked. She cleared her throat and tried again. "I met Wilfred in the hall and offered to bring your dinner."

Lord William looked toward his wife, straightened a little taller in his chair, and returned his blank gaze to the fire. He had pondered his situation and came to a decision. He was determined to return to his solitary life and profession and preferred to enjoy his last meal within Wildenham alone.

Lady Christine crossed the room, set the tray on the small table next to her husband, and sat on the edge of the adjacent chair.

He picked up the tankard of wine and took a long swig, hoping to dull the sting of her earlier insult. He lowered the mug to rest upon his thigh, continued to stare into the fire, and wished she would leave the room.

She looked in her husband's direction, but he ignored her.

"It has been pointed out to me, actually by several people, that I overstepped my bounds today. I am sorry if I offended you on the practice field."

Lord William remained silent and nodded his head once in acknowledgement of her apology. A rap sounded on the door.

"Come in," Lord William said.

Wilfred and a servant carrying a tray of food entered.

"Where would you like your tray, my lady?"

Lady Christine pushed her husband's tray aside to make room on the table.

"You may set it here," she said as she tapped the space next to her husband's tray.

The servant walked to the table, placed the tray down, curtsied, and left. Wilfred paused before the door.

"My lord, lady, is there anything else that you need?"

"No, thank you, Wilfred, that will be all," Lord William replied with a voice that seemed to lack emotion.

The steward noted the tension between the couple as he looked from one to the other. He nodded his head, exited the library, and closed the door.

The Lord of Wildenham took another swig from his mug and watched his wife take a bit of cheese from her tray.

The resonating crackles from the fire were the only sounds within the room as husband and wife remained silent.

Why does he not speak, she wondered as she looked around the room and recalled the last time she was in it was when her father encouraged her to choose a spouse. She looked at her husband who continued to stare into the fire. *His silence is unbearable. Perhaps he is so angry that he does not trust himself to speak in fear of what he may say.* Her eyes began to well and try as she might, the tears were unstoppable. *I vow to never call him a hurtful name again.* She turned her face away from her husband as she brushed her hand across her cheek, wiping away a tear.

He was drawn by her sudden movement and watched her brush away what was perhaps a tear. *Does she cry?* He listened intently and watched her continue to wipe away tears. *Why must women always cry,* he thought. He set his tankard down upon the tray, reached for her upper right arm, and clasped it gently.

"Rise and come here." He encouraged her arm upward and she complied.

Lady Christine's vision was blurred by her tears. She soon found herself sitting erect upon her husband's lap and her body stiffened with apprehension.

"Why do you cry?" He put his left arm across her lap and cradled her backside with his right. She kept her eyes downcast and fidgeted with her hands.

"I don't know. Perhaps I am just overwhelmed by the sudden changes in my life." She tried to pinpoint the reason for her tears, but had difficulty in doing so. *My father's death? My marriage to a man I don't know? Running Wildenham when I have little knowledge in doing so? Discovering my husband is a mercenary?*

Lord William could only imagine her thoughts and ascertain the words he could speak that may give her comfort.

"I was going to leave Wildenham tonight." He confessed.

Lady Christine snapped her head with a look of panic on her face as she stared into her husband's eyes.

"You're going to leave?" Her voice was one of innocence. "Forever?" Her mouth pouted. She fought to keep her emotions in control while wiping away tears that were flowing faster. "No, please don't leave me."

He watched a tear roll down her cheek. Her request seemed genuine and sincere. He was quite certain his wife was incapable of overseeing the kingdom alone. Lord William sighed as he resigned himself to his responsibility.

"For whatever reason, fate has thrown us together." He conceded.

She wiped away the tear from her cheek as she looked down to her lap and fidgeted with her fingers as Lord William continued.

"The responsibility of the kingdom and its people is now mine, ours."

"So you will stay?" She persisted.

"I will not turn my back on Wildenham, or you."

Lady Christine turned her tear-streaked face toward her husband. She glanced at his chin before looking cautiously into his hazel eyes that reflected the dancing firelight. Another tear escaped the corner of her eye.

Lord William lifted his hand from her lap and brushed a tear away with his thumb.

"I'm not a monster, but I believe if we are to make our union work, we must begin with the basics of a relationship."

Lady Christine searched her mind. *Is he implying a physical relationship? Love? How can I love someone I do not know?*

He watched her eyes widen as she glanced away in thought.

"What I propose is nothing drastic or abrupt. It is something we cannot give to each other. It must be earned." He looked into her eyes as they returned to his.

"Love?" She inquired.

"There are many marriages that do not involve love." He stated.

"Honesty?" She guessed.

"I would agree that it is necessary for a good marriage, but it is not earned. Honesty is promised."

"I do not know." She confessed.

"Perhaps you will discover it in time." He reached for his wife's tankard and handed it to her.

Lady Christine accepted the mug, drank, and rested it within her lap.

"Why is it that you know the answer to this mysterious question and I do not?"

"Perhaps it is because I am the one who posed the question," he said as he reached for a hunk of meat, popped it into his mouth, and chewed with a slight grin on his face.

Lady Christine reached for a chunk of bread, brought it to her mouth, and began to nibble. Her tears had dried. Calmness settled within her heart.

"You are a good fighter." She hoped to change the topic of conversation, but was a little shocked that the compliment had escaped her thoughts.

"Thank you, but in my line of work, one must kill or be killed." He admitted.

"I can only imagine."

"How was your practice with Sir Gunther?"

"We did not practice." She confessed. "He pointed out my rudeness and we returned to the Keep."

After a few moments of eating their meal in silence, Lord William spoke.

"My father used to call me a monster."

Lady Christine looked into her husband's eyes and saw his pain.

"Oh, I am so sorry. I did not know." She sighed. "My lips will never utter that word again. I promise."

They had finished eating their meal. Lady Christine remained on her husband's lap and gazed into the fire. Perhaps it was the wine, but she had relaxed and was somewhat comforted by her husband's proximity.

Sensing her tranquil state and aware of his drowsiness, Lord William encouraged his wife to lie upon his chest. She complied. They stared into the flames until they fell asleep.

*   *   *

Sir Harlan put another log on the campfire. The evening was cool. He pulled the horse blanket over his shoulders as he huddled closer to the warmth of the flames. He had killed a rabbit for his evening meal, skewered, and rotated it over the fire. He stared at the flickering flames while he waited for his meal to cook and smiled as he imagined his plan coming to fruition.

"Soon, very soon," he said aloud to himself.

Chapter 26

Lord William's neck ached. He tried to shift his weight to a more comfortable position, but something pressed down upon his body. He remembered he was holding his wife. He listened to her rhythmic breathing as she lay on his chest with her face nestled against his neck. He opened his eyes and discovered the fire burning brightly in the fireplace and a blanket covering them both. He looked to the daylight emanating from the window and noticed the table had been cleared of their trays. Lord William assumed Wilfred and a servant must have paid a visit to the library. He laid his head back on the chair, closed his eyes, and tried to ignore his need to use a garderobe.

Moments later when his wife stirred, he opened his eyes and raised his head again.

Lady Christine took a deep breath and her nose filled with a musky aroma. She opened her eyes and stared into her husband's neck. Realizing the ease in which she laid atop of him, she put her left hand on his lower stomach, sat up in a panic, and pushed herself off of his lap allowing the blanket to fall to the floor. Her face turned a pinkish hue.

Lord William grunted and clenched his teeth.

"Have a care." He pleaded as the pressure upon his bladder made it feel as if it would burst.

Realizing what she had done, Lady Christine's face reddened deeper.

"Sorry." She stated with a cringe.

"No need to apologize," he said as he stood. "Shall we head to our bedchamber? Your ladies will be waiting. Wilfred will have our breakfast ready as well."

She nodded, turned in the direction of the door, took a few steps, and stopped suddenly. Lord William bumped into her backside. She turned to face him.

"I can't go out there," she said in a whispered panic.

"Why ever not?"

"I have spent the night in the library. My dress and hair is a disheveled mess. They are going to assume, well, you know." Lady Christine blushed.

"They already assume it." Lord William informed.

Lady Christine's mouth fell open.

"We are husband and wife. This is our kingdom. I believe we are capable of doing as we wish with our private lives."

"But going out there will make it all the more public."

"Then they will see a happy couple." He assured.

"But it is so embarrassing." Her face conveyed a shameful humiliation.

"It is life and many are not ignorant of it."

"But we didn't do anything and their assumption is false and still very embarrassing." Lady Christine brushed her dress with her hands in an attempt to straighten the wrinkles.

"Besides, since Wilfred and most likely a servant visited earlier, I'm sure the entire staff is aware that we slept in here last night. Hold still," he said as he tried to secure a wayward curl of her blonde hair with its loosened pin. "There." He announced upon his success of the delicate task.

Lady Christine touched her hair to ensure it was pinned in place correctly and adjusted her dress while Lord William opened the library door.

She looked to her husband for reassurance. He nodded his head in approval and smiled confidently. Lady Christine stepped into the hall. Lord William followed closing the door of the library behind them.

The couple made their way into the Great Hall where a few servant women were cleaning. Lady Christine looked toward the women who displayed insinuating smiles as they curtsied, returned to their work, and giggled.

"Ignore them." Her husband whispered into her ear as he placed his hand on the small of her back. "They secretly wish they were you."

Lady Christine glanced at her husband's face. He was looking down at her with raised eyebrows and a mischievous smirk. Although his jest brought a grin to her face, she sighed in disgust and ascended the staircase.

They made their way to their bedchamber. When Lord William opened the door to let his wife enter, they discovered Wilfred had indeed left their breakfast on the table and opened the window. Corvus was absent from the room, but Jackson laid in the sunshine that shown through the window and napped contently upon the floor. Lord William shut the door behind them.

"If you will excuse me for a moment," he said as he paid a much needed visit to the garderobe. Upon exiting, Lord William saw a basin, a pitcher of water, and a stack of linen upon the bench before the fire. Thankful for Wilfred's foresight, he sat on the bench, washed his hands and face, and dried them with the linen while his wife used the garderobe. He moistened another cloth for his wife.

Lady Christine emerged and accepted the linen from her husband. She washed her face and dabbed it dry with another fresh linen from the neatly folded stack. When she looked toward her husband, he was presenting a chair for her to sit at the table. She glanced up to his face as she sat in the chair. He pushed it closer to the table before sitting across from her. A knock sounded at the door. They looked to one another before turning their heads simultaneously toward the bedchamber door.

"Enter," Lord William said.

When the door opened, Enid and Gilda entered, and Corvus flew through the open window, circled the room, and caused the women to duck with fright. The raven landed on the floor next to Jackson. The dozing feline opened his eyes a mere crack, looked up at the bird, and closed his lids shut.

Lord William tossed a chunk of meat to his pet.

Jackson smelled the aroma of the nearby meal, opened his eyes, and watched the raven. Corvus used his beak to break the meat into two pieces and let them fall to the floor. Jackson reached his paw toward the nearest bit of meat, pulled it toward himself, and ate it while the raven consumed the other half.

"My lady, where have you been?" Gilda inquired boldly with a concerned look upon her face.

Enid elbowed her partner in the ribs.

"What Gilda meant was, we called on you earlier and found the bedchamber empty. We were concerned." Enid clarified as she looked from her lady to her lord.

"Thank you for your concern, but I fear I consumed too much wine on an empty stomach and fell asleep in the library." Lady Christine assured as she looked to her husband for assistance in confirming her story.

Lord William selected a chunk of bread and topped it with a bit of meat and cheese. He took a healthy bite as the toe of his wife's slipper touched his shin. He looked into her widened eyes and then to Enid and Gilda and nodded, confirming his wife's statement.

"Very well, my lady, my lord, enjoy your breakfast. We will be waiting in your bedchamber when you are ready to dress." Enid and Gilda curtsied, left the room, and closed the door.

"Perhaps next time you could sound a bit more convincing." Lady Christine scolded as she began to eat her breakfast.

"My mouth was full. I did not want to appear rude." Lord William grinned as he picked up a tankard and took a swig.

Lady Christine gave him a suspicious glare before making her inquiry.

"Do you have any plans for today?"

"There is always something that requires my attention, but my priority is to oversee the continuation of the village repairs." He explained.

Her face had become sullen before she looked down at her meal.

His wife's disappointment was obvious.

"Perhaps I can join you later after delegating the responsibility. What do you have in mind?" He broached the subject.

She looked up from her plate with a twinkle in her eye.

"If you don't mind, I would like to resume my sword practice with you," she said almost shyly.

He sat back in his chair and ate a chunk of cheese.

"For you, I believe I can clear my schedule for the day." He displayed a smile and watched a smile appear upon her face before she bowed her head toward her plate and ate a slice of apple.

Upon finishing their meal, Lady Christine joined Enid and Gilda in her bedchamber to dress for practice while Lord William changed once again into black attire. Jackson continued to sleep. Corvus, in his usual place for roosting, ruffled his feathers and looked down at the lazy cat.

Once dressed, Lord William gave the feline a few quick pats causing Jackson to stretch, fan out his toes, and awaken from his nap. He lifted his head and watched Lord William leave the bedchamber. The Lord of Wildenham left the door ajar to allow the chubby cat to make his way to the kitchen for a snack. Bored by the feline's lack of enthusiasm, Corvus flew out the window to join his master.

Lord William waited for his wife in the hallway. Moments later she emerged from her bedchamber. The couple made their way to the stable where they asked for their horses to be readied. Corvus swooped down from the sky and landed on his master's shoulder. Lady Christine looked toward the raven.

"How long have you had Corvus?"

Lord William inclined his head toward the bird.

"He had fallen out of his nest as a hatchling. I took him under my wing, so to speak, and he has been with me for close to seven years now."

"Here you go, my lord, my lady." Thomas proudly announced as he led the horses from the stable. He held the reins as Lord William presented his clasped hands before his wife and offered his assistance. She looked into his eyes to see if his offer was genuine. Finding her confirmation, she inserted her left foot into her husband's hands. He boosted upward and she sat upon the saddle. Lord William took the mare's reins from the stableboy.

"Thank you, Thomas." He nodded and gave the reins to his wife.

"My pleasure, my lord." The stableboy stepped away from the horses.

Lord William climbed atop Adair. The couple reined their horses and rode to the village. With plenty of supplies still in the wagon, the Lord of Wildenham dismounted and reviewed the repairs for the day with his supervisors. Confident that the hut would be reconstructed to the stated specifications, the Lord and Lady of Wildenham rode to the practice field.

The men on the field stopped their practice and watched as their lord and lady approached.

"Another lesson?" Sir Farrell posed the question to Sir Gunther.

"She never quite made it through the last one." Sir Gunther commented.

The Lord and Lady of Wildenham dismounted. Corvus flew to a nearby tree. Lady Christine walked toward the pile of practice swords while her husband removed his sword and dirk.

"This ought to be interesting." Sir Farrell stepped closer for a better view with Sir Gunther following.

Lady Christine chose a sword, put the point to the ground, and stepped on the blade to ensure its strength. She turned to select a practice spot on the field.

"Wait," Lord William said as he selected two smaller swords to simulate dirks. He tucked one into his belt on his right side and handed the other to her, handle first.

"Put this in your belt on your right side." He instructed as he selected a practice sword for himself.

She took the dirk and secured it through her belt. Lady Christine looked to her husband. He nodded approvingly. *What crazed mercenary technique is he going to teach me now*, she wondered.

They selected a spot on the practice field. Lady Christine looked at the men who had gathered around them and prayed she would appear anything but foolish during her lesson. She glanced at her husband. His back was toward her. She looked to Sir Farrell, who stared at her intently.

Lord William turned his head to look at his wife. She had her guard down.

"ARRRRGGGGG!" He yelled as he ran toward her with his sword swinging from his side, upward, and down upon her.

Lady Christine's head snapped in her husband's direction. Her eyes widened with fear. It was all she could do to counter the attack. She knelt onto one knee, grabbed the tip of the blade with her free hand, and held her sword above her head. She squeezed her eyes shut as she felt the impact of her husband's sword. Lady Christine remained frozen and waited for a second attack, but another hit never followed. She opened her eyes and stared up into her husband's hazel orbs. He stared down at her with his sword still touching hers. Lord William retracted his sword and took a step backward. She put her sword down and stood.

"What was that?" She spat the words.

Lord William stood with his legs apart and set the tip of his sword on the ground between his legs.

"The element of surprise. Expect the unexpected." Lord William watched her eyes resume their normal size as she looked toward the men who surrounded them, nodding their heads in agreement.

She swallowed her pride and returned her gaze toward her husband. He took a step forward.

"You chose a good defensive move for the circumstance. However, could you grab the blade of a real sword and survive the attack without injury?" His voice was calm as he watched his wife analyze her move.

Lady Christine reflected on her husband's words as she analyzed her counter move and glanced at her wooden blade. She thought of an answer, looked to her husband, and replied.

"Unless I wore a mailed glove, part of my hand would have been severed. Even wearing the glove, it may have been broken." She admitted and watched her husband's head nod in approval of her answer. "But what else could I have done?"

He was pleased she was willing to learn and accept his

advice. He moved closer to her and repeated his foolish attack in slow motion.

"As you see my sword swinging around toward you, block it with your sword over your head and grab your dirk with your other hand."

She looked down toward her dirk to grab it.

"Look at me. Always keep your focus on the one who is attacking." He instructed.

She looked toward her husband who had frozen his position.

"Reach for your dirk blindly." He instructed. "You can feel where it is on your body. Keep your eyes on me."

She looked into his hazel eyes and fumbled for her dirk. Finding the handle, she clasped the dirk and pulled it from her belt.

"Good. Now as I bring my sword down upon you, counter it with your sword and thrust the dirk toward my heart," he said.

He continued the motion of his sword and touched it to her practice sword as he felt her push the dirk into his right hip. He grabbed her hand that held the dirk and redirected it to his heart.

"Your attack was not fatal. You must aim for the heart. Look for the bottom center of the rib, angle the blade, and push upward into the heart."

She nodded her head in understanding.

"The swiftness of your move may be the difference between life and death. It is all a matter of timing. Return your dirk to your belt and let's practice this maneuver until it is proficient."

Lady Christine shoved the dirk into her belt and readied herself. *It's all a matter of timing*, she repeated to herself. Her husband's next attack was slow and allowed her enough time to find the dirk. As husband and wife continued to practice, Lord William increased the speed of his attack as his wife's skill improved.

"By God, I think he has done it," Sir Farrell said as he turned away to watch the men practice.

Sir Gunther turned away as well and looked to his fellow knight for understanding.

"Done what?"

"He has tamed the wild horse." Sir Farrell smirked.

"That he has." Sir Gunther nodded and grinned in agreement. "Thankfully for us all."

*   *   *

Rowena stirred a pot of stew over the fireplace. The hair on her arms began to stand on end as goose bumps formed on her skin. Something was wrong or would soon be. She closed her eyes. A picture of Lord William appeared within her mind. She opened her eyes. Rowena grabbed bottles of herbs from a shelf and headed outside to a caldron that dangled from its tripod. She looked in the direction of Wildenham before setting the items in her arms upon the ground. There was danger on the way. She returned to the hut and took the pitcher of water from the table. She shoveled hot embers into a small kettle and placed a few logs in her arm. She returned to the tripod and kicked leaves under the vessel. She dumped the hot embers onto the leaves and threw the kettle onto the ground. The apothecary poured the water in the hanging caldron and set the pitcher on the ground. She found and placed sticks onto the fire that lit quickly. She took the two logs from the crook of her arm and set them on the fire. Carefully measuring, she began to add herbs and other items to the caldron. Rowena picked up a stick from the ground and stirred the contents as she mumbled an incantation. She closed her eyes and raised both arms toward the sky as she asked for strength and protection for Lord William.

An owl landed on a tree branch and watched the apothecary. As the contents of the pot began to boil and steam rose into the air, the owl flew through the steam and headed in the direction of Wildenham.

Rowena opened her eyes as she heard the flapping of the owl's wings and watched the bird depart. She had done all that she could to help Lord William during the challenge he would soon face. Lowering her arms, she watched the medicinal steam follow the flight path of the bird. The apothecary knew she would receive little rest until the fateful event came to a close. She returned to the boiling pot and breathed in its fragrance, for she would need its herbal strength in the coming days.

Chapter 27

After a vigorous and successful day of practicing, the Lord and Lady of Wildenham were tired and dirty.

"Well done." Lord William complimented as he tossed his practice equipment onto the pile. Corvus flew down from a nearby tree and landed on his master's shoulder.

"Thank you." Lady Christine discarded her wooden sword and dirk.

They climbed atop their horses, made a point to stop by the repairs of the village, and were pleased with the progress. Too hungry to take the time to dress appropriately for the evening meal, they entered the Great Hall and sat directly at the High Table. Corvus hopped from his lord's shoulder to the back of his chair. Jackson's nose lifted in the air as he entered the room, sat patiently on the floor next Lord William, and waited for a few scraps to fall his way.

Lord William picked up his mug, drank the contents, and set it back upon the table.

Ah, I was thirsty, he said to himself. A servant came forward and refilled his glass with ale.

Lady Christine looked toward her husband and watched him pull a piece of meat from a bone and place it into his mouth.

"Thank you for practicing with me. I believe I have learned some useful skills today." She turned her attention to a chunk of cooked fowl, put it in her mouth, and returned her gaze to her husband.

Lord William's hazel eyes sparkled with pride. He grinned.

"I take that as a compliment, but in truth, you are an excellent student and very quick at learning the skill." He picked up his tankard and took a swig.

She thought of their day together and the patience her husband possessed. He was stern, but kind in his own way and he was strong, very strong. She picked up her tankard and drank its contents before she spoke.

"The village is progressing nicely. Are all of the repairs finished?" She inquired.

"I suspect there are more, but I will need to inspect the other buildings tomorrow." He explained and appreciated her thoughtful inquiry.

The change in the Lord and Lady of Wildenham's behavior toward one another seemed to have a relaxing effect on those within the Great Hall. The conversation of those in attendance was a mere whisper. They glanced frequently at the couple in an attempt to read their lips or overhear what was being said. Seldom had Lady Christine ever smiled, but on this night her smile never ceased.

As the pleasant meal came to a close, Wilfred approached the High Table.

"My lady, I have taken the liberty to draw a hot bath for you. It is waiting in your former bedchamber and so are your ladies."

Lady Christine turned to the vacated seats on her right. She had failed to notice when Enid and Gilda had left the table.

"My lady, is there anything special you would like prepared for your meal in celebration of your eighteenth birthday? It is only a few days from today." The steward inquired.

"No thank you, Wilfred. After all, it won't be much of a celebration without father there."

Wilfred nodded and looked to Lord William.

"Shall I have a bath drawn for you as well, my lord?"

"No need, Wilfred. I will use my wife's bath." He looked to his wife. Her head snapped in his direction. Her eyes enlarged with fear of his intention. "That is, once she has finished." He clarified as he looked back to Wilfred.

Wilfred nodded his head and left.

Lord William returned his gaze to his wife, who let out a nervous sigh and seemed to relax.

They finished their sweet cakes in silence. Lady Christine's muscles ached and were stiff. She yawned and looked to the staircase.

Her husband noted her weariness.

"Perhaps you should take your bath before you fall asleep." He suggested as he rose from his chair. "I shall be along in a few minutes." He pulled her chair out from the table as she stood.

She agreed with a nod of her head and ascended the staircase. When she opened her bedchamber door, Enid and Gilda rose from their seats.

"My lady, you have had a busy day," Enid said as she began to help undress her mistress.

"I must admit, I am quite tired." Lady Christine submitted to her ladies tugging and pulling her garment until she was naked and lowered herself into the hot water. She sighed with relief as her aching muscles relaxed in the lavender scented hot water. She leaned her head back on the edge of the tub and closed her eyes. Each of her ladies dipped a cloth into the bath water, lathered it with lavender soap, and washed an arm and leg while Lady Christine closed her eyes. She was on the edge of falling asleep.

The bedchamber door opened silently. Enid and Gilda looked toward the portal and watched as Lord William stepped into the room with his finger held perpendicular to his lips signaling they were to remain silent.

A golden glow emanated from the candelabras. The fire had been stoked to warm the bedchamber. He saw his wife's long blonde tresses dangling from the tub. He imagined running his fingers through the silky strands and twisting each curl around his finger. No longer able to resist the temptation, he signaled for the women to leave. As they placed their cloths on the edge of the tub and exited the room, he closed the door, and picked up an empty bucket and placed it on the floor beneath his wife's head. He took a mug from a basket that also contained various soaps and linens. He knelt on the floor, reached over his wife, dipped the mug into the clouded water, and poured it over her hair. She sighed. He wet her hair thoroughly and selected a rose scented soap from the basket. He lathered his hands and placed them within her hair. Her tresses were silky, just as he imagined. He massaged her scalp and lathered her hair until it was thick with bubbles. He rinsed, toweled, and combed it gently until all of the tangles were removed.

"Enid, you have magic fingers," she said.

"So I have been told." Lord William admitted with a grin on his face.

Lady Christine's eyes popped open. She sat up in the tub and turned around to find her husband staring at her. She looked down to her exposed breasts and crossed her arms over her chest.

"Your face is dirty." He observed as he picked up a wet cloth. "Close your eyes."

She stared at him untrustingly.

"I don't want to get soap in them." He explained. She stared at him intently before complying with his request.

Lord William washed each feature of her face as gently as possible and draped the cloth over the side of the tub when he finished. He wished to tuck his knuckled index finger under her chin and lift her lips to his, but knew he would probably offend her if he followed through with his thought.

"There." He rose, grabbed a large linen from the stool and held it open before her. "Out with you, for I am eager to rid my body of this filth." He ordered as he held the cloth with both hands so he could wrap it around her naked body.

Her mouth flew open.

Understanding her virginal uneasiness, he turned his head to the side as if to look out the window.

"Close your eyes," she said.

He sighed and did as she requested.

She crouched behind the cloth he held before her, reached

her hand upward, and waved it in front of his face to see if he was peeking. He remained still. Assuming his eyes were closed, she took the opportunity to grab the linen from his hands and wrap it around her body. She tucked the edge to keep it secure and stepped out of the tub. When she looked at her husband, he was stripping off his clothes.

"What are you doing?" She inquired.

He paused with his shirt in his hand.

"I'm taking a bath." He replied.

"Not with me in here, you're not." She turned to leave the chamber, but he reached for her hand to halt her progress.

"I would appreciate a good scrubbing on my back." He stated.

She looked at him in shock.

"Please." He released her hand.

She let out a sigh.

Interpreting her sigh as a positive response, Lord William turned, threw his shirt upon the window seat, and began to undo the laces of his breeches.

Realizing his intention, Lady Christine turned around quickly and tried to locate her chemise. She discovered it upon the bed and slipped it over her head before loosening the linen and letting it fall to the ground. She turned around too soon and saw her husband's backside as he stepped into the tub and lowered himself into the water.

Oh my, she thought at the sight of his muscular physique. Her cheeks became hot. She was certain they were also red, quite red. She sighed and accepted the debt of returning her husband's favor.

Lord William sighed with relief as the warm water surrounded his body. He sat forward in the tub and waited.

Lady Christine selected a pleasant smelling soap that seemed more masculine in fragrance, picked up the wet linen from the side of the tub, dunked the cloth into the water behind her husband, being careful to avoid his backside, and lathered the cloth. She knelt down on the floor, looked at the scars upon his back that appeared shiny in the flickering firelight, and applied the cloth to his skin. She moved the cloth in slow circles working her way down her husband's back. When she finished, she set the soapy cloth on his shoulder. He picked it up and began to wash his arms, chest, and face while she took the mug from the floor, dipped it into the water, and poured it over his back to rinse away the soap.

"There," she said.

"Thank you." He replied over his shoulder and continued to wash.

"You are welcome." Lady Christine rose from the floor and headed for the bedchamber door. She paused as her hand touched the latch and looked back at her husband. He had finished washing, rinsing, and leaned back in the tub to soak. She let out another sigh, and returned to the tub.

She picked up the mug, leaned over his chest, and dunked the tankard to fill it. She was thankful the water was cloudy. She had to admit she was curious to see if his front side was as equally as impressive as his back side.

Lord William lay still as he watched the filled mug pass over him. He closed his eyes and exhaled as the warm water cascaded onto his head.

Lady Christine refilled the tankard and poured the water as close to his face as possible without getting it into his eyes. Once his hair was thoroughly wet, she selected the same bar of soap and rubbed it on both of her hands until there was a generous lather. She laced her fingers in the hair and tried to imitate the same massage she had received from him. She stilled her hands and went up onto her knees in order to look at his face to see if he was sleeping.

He opened his eyes and looked into her brown eyes. Their color reminded him of chestnuts.

"Are you finished?" He inquired.

She shook her head shyly to indicate she was not done.

"I thought you may be sleeping." She explained.

"I nearly am." He admitted.

She sat back down and finished washing his long ebony hair. She dipped the mug several times in order to rinse it, toweled it dry, and combed it straight.

"I am done." She announced as she rose and turned to leave the bedchamber.

"Thank you." He sat up and turned his head toward her retreating figure.

"You are welcome." She replied.

He heard the bedchamber door close behind him. Lord William soaked in the tub until he feared falling asleep where he lay. He stood, selected a clean linen, and dried himself. He wrapped it around his waist, grabbed his belt and weapons, and left his soiled clothes to be taken to the laundry. He picked up the taper on the mantel, lit it from a candle on a candelabra before extinguishing the remaining candles in the room. He stood before the passage, pushed the series of rosettes, and entered. He closed the portal until he heard a click and began pushing the rosettes on the door to the tiny chamber. When it clicked open, he entered. He sighed as he looked down at the swords and letter on the desk. He opened the top right drawer and retrieved his mother's ring and sat on the cot. He slipped it on the top joint of his index finger and looked up to his mother's portrait. *I think you would approve of her Mother*, he thought as an idea formed within his mind. *So, your birthday is soon, my dear. Perhaps we shall make it a special celebration.* Lord William made a mental note to have Wilfred schedule a tailor.

The hair on his arms stood on end. He turned his head to the right and stood cautiously as he saw his father materialize. Lord William took a step backward in an attempt to distance himself from the apparition. His father's body was floating in midair. The spirit's haunting eyes stared at him as if searching for an answer.

"What do you want of me, Father? Against my better judgment, I have sealed my fate and fulfilled your wishes." Lord William stated in a hushed tone.

His father nodded his head up and down slowly as if in agreement and then vanished into the wall of his wife's bedchamber.

Lord William glanced around the chamber. He was alone. He returned his mother's ring to its hiding place, exited the room, and closed the door.

He opened the portal into the bedchamber, entered, and closed it quietly. He discovered his wife in bed with her back toward him and assumed she was asleep. He searched through a stack of clean clothing and dressed for bed.

Jackson lay curled at his mistress's feet, but Corvus was absent. Noticing the window was shut, Lord William opened it before going to his side of the bed.

As he pulled back the covers, he heard the fluttering of wings and assumed it was Corvus. Lord William looked to the window, but saw an owl on the sill. A medicinal aroma filled the room. *Rowena*, he thought. *I believe an owl is a good sign, or perhaps she has sent it as a warning.* Whatever reason, he would advise his knights to be on their guard and watch for suspicious happenings. He got into bed, tucked his right forearm under his head, and listened to his wife's rhythmic breathing before closing his eyes and falling asleep.

Chapter 28

The next few days their daily routine was much the same. Repairs continued on the village. The Lord and Lady of Wildenham spent part of each day on the practice field. Lady Christine was growing accustomed to her husband's company. She strived to meet Lord William's expectations during practice and was pleased when she achieved a skill well enough to bring a proud smile to his face. Lord William's skill on the chessboard improved. He managed to win a game or two. Sir Farrell and Sir Gunther remained vigilant and assigned guards at the gatehouse. Without any guidance or preference from Lady Christine, Wilfred was doing his best to oversee the planning of her birthday celebration. As another day came to a close, those within the kingdom of Wildenham were happy, except Sir Harlan.

Sir Harlan paced like a caged animal on the edge of the woods. He watched the kingdom until all grew quiet. It was well into the night. With the villagers asleep, the time had come. His plan was simple. He would draw Lord William away from his wife and kill him. If need be, he would use Lady Christine as leverage against all who opposed him, then assume the role as Lord of Wildenham.

Sir Harlan walked the horses out of the woods and tied them to the branch of a fallen tree on the roadside just outside the village. He grinned as he grabbed a dried branch from the ground and crept toward the glowing light in the village square. All was quiet except for the snoring that came from within a few of the huts.

Sir Harlan moved silently between the buildings until he stood before the warming fire that burned within a circle of stones. He looked in all directions for any watchful eyes, but saw none. He placed the branch in the fire and waited for it to catch.

*   *   *

Lord William opened his eyes. The shadowed ceiling came into view as he lay on his back and wondered what had awakened him. He listened to the dying embers crackle and pop in the fireplace. He tilted his head toward the pressure upon his chest and saw the top of his wife's head and her right arm lying across his body. *She may have gotten chilled and snuggled me for warmth.* He liked her soft body next to his as he removed his right arm from behind his head and reached for a lock of Lady Christine's blonde hair. The tress felt as soft as a rose petal as he rubbed it between his index finger and thumb. He looked toward the window. It was still dark. Lord William placed his arm upon his wife's back. She snuggled closer to him. He peeked over her head and spotted Jackson sleeping between his legs. He looked up to the headboard to see Corvus roosting. All was as it should be as he closed his eyes with the hope of returning to sleep.

"Lord William!" Thomas yelled as he ran into the Great Hall. He was unsure of the direction of his lord's bedchamber, so he called as loudly as he could. "Lord William!"

Lord William opened his eyes. Corvus awoke from his slumber and looked in the toward the bedchamber door. Jackson stretched his body from his head all the way down to his little toes before stretching out lengthwise and continuing his sleep.

Lord William tried to untangle himself from his wife and hoped she would remain asleep. As he sat on the edge of the bed and ran his hand through his hair, he heard Thomas call again.

"Lord William!"

"What is Thomas yelling about?" Lady Christine opened her eyes and looked at her husband's back.

Lord William smelled smoke in the air. Corvus flapped his wings and flew out the window.

"I will go and find out. Stay in the bedchamber," he said to his wife. He tightened the lace on his breeches as he left the room and went into the hallway. He walked to the top of the staircase and spotted Thomas at the bottom with a terrified look upon his face.

"What is it?"

"My lord, the village is on fire. Come quickly!"

"Stay there, Thomas. I will be just a moment." Lord William ran back to the bedchamber and donned a black tunic and shoved his feet into his boots.

"What is it?" Lady Christine sat up and watched her husband dress franticly. She sniffed the smoke filled air.

"The village is on fire."

Lady Christine gasped, threw back the covers, and got out of bed. She put on her father's robe.

"Christine, have Enid and Gilda ready for those who have injuries. Once you have done so, return to our bedchamber until I send word." He looked at her for confirmation.

She nodded her head, indicating she understood.

He strapped on his belt, sword, and dirk and hurried out of the room. He quickened his steps down the hallway and staircase and joined the stableboy. Both lord and lad ran out of the Keep toward the stable.

Conal had Adair readied and held the reins tightly as the destrier pranced nervously. Thomas hitched up a horse to a wagon while Lord William loaded buckets, shovels, and pole hooks into the back. The Lord of Wildenham climbed atop Adair. The stableboys jumped into the front seat of the wagon. As they went through the baileys, they could see the fire reflected in the night sky. They watched glowing sparks fly upward as they came to a halt and waited momentarily for the portcullis to rise.

Lord William reined Adair a short distance from the burning buildings. Conal jumped down from the wagon to take the war horse's reins. Women and children cried as they stood in the village square and watched their husbands and fathers use pitchforks and buckets filled with water from the well to fight the blaze. The air was thick with smoke. It was difficult to breathe. As another hut caught fire, men shouted toward each other to be heard over the popping and snapping of the flames.

Lord William approached the huddled women and children and cupped his hands around his mouth to project it over the noisy chaos.

"Has everyone gotten out?"

"Yes, but several are injured!" A woman shouted as she came forward to her lord. She pointed toward a group of people who sat upon benches or laid on the ground while others hovered over them. Many had soot upon their faces and clothing.

"Help them to the Keep. My wife will see to their needs." Lord William ordered as he turned to see several men trying to pull down a roof in an attempt to contain the fire.

"Thomas, stay in the wagon and hand out buckets and tools as needed."

"Yes, my lord," he said as he climbed into the back of the wagon and picked up a bucket.

Lord William climbed into the back of the wagon to get the men's attention.

"Come get a bucket to fill from the well or a shovel to throw dirt onto the fire. The pole hooks are longer than your pitchforks and can be used to pull down the burning roofs." Lord William looked at the blaze and wondered how the fire could have spread so quickly. It was a windless night. However, it had been many days since the last rain and the dry conditions may contribute to the consumption of the flames.

He climbed down from the wagon, grabbed a pole hook, and hurried toward a hut to help the men pull the burning roof down to the ground before the fire spread any further.

A man screamed as his sleeve caught fire while another man snatched a shawl from a woman's shoulders and used it to snuff out the flames.

Men formed an assembly line and passed buckets of water

with the last man in line throwing its contents onto the fire and running the empty bucket back to the well for refilling.

"My lord!" Thomas yelled as he spotted a man dressed in green and black in the distance standing with his arms crossed over his chest and a smile upon his face.

Sir Harlan was pleased. His plan was working perfectly. He turned toward the Keep and walked away.

Thomas got down from the wagon. He dodged those who worked to extinguish the fire as he searched for his lord. He saw Lord William pulling down a roof and ran toward him. The heat from the blaze forced him to raise his hands to shield his face and keep his distance.

"My lord!"

Lord William turned to see the lad too close to the fire and feared for his safety.

"Thomas, I told you to stay in the wagon." Lord William scolded as he stepped away from the burning hut to join the stableboy.

"But that man is here, the man who was with Lord Sheridan."

"Where? Point him out to me."

"He was there." Thomas pointed to the vacant spot. "He turned and walked toward the gatehouse."

"Take this and get back to the wagon," Lord William said as he handed the pole hook to the stableboy. He ran to Adair, jumped on his back, and kicked his horse into a gallop.

Chapter 29

Lady Christine instructed Enid and Gilda to see to the injured and returned to her bedchamber. She paced the floor as she listened to the echoes of chaos from the village, smelled the smoke in the air, and saw the reflection of the flames in the night sky. Her father's village was burning. She was obligated as the Lady of Wildenham to help in any way she could. Against her husband's request, she opened the bedchamber door and went into the hallway. Stopping at the top of the staircase, she peered down into the Great Hall and saw several injured peasants entering. Wilfred directed them toward the fireplace and helped them sit or lay down for treatment for their injuries. Enid carried a basket containing bandages and salve followed by Gilda, who carried a basin and pitcher of hot water. Lady Christine began to descend the staircase, but stopped suddenly as her eyes were drawn to a large man dressed in green and black who emerged from the hall. He looked in her direction. A wicked smile spread across his face.

"There you are, you little trollop!" Sir Harlan began to push the injured out of his way as he came toward the staircase.

Wilfred stepped in front of the man, but Sir Harlan shoved him to the ground. The steward's head hit the stone floor with a sickening thump.

Lady Christine's eyes widened. Her heart began to race as her husband's description registered within her mind. She turned and ran back to their bedchamber. She shut the door, but in her panic she failed to bolt it. She clapped her hands rapidly and yelled.

"Jackson, hide!"

The startled feline stood quickly on all fours and looked at her with wild eyes as if she were crazy.

Lady Christine began pushing the rosettes upon the portal frantically and tried to turn the knob. The portal remained closed when she pulled.

"Damn it!"

"Where are you!" Sir Harlan yelled as he got to the top of the staircase.

She turned her head in the direction of the door and then back to the portal. She pushed the sequence of rosettes again and pulled the knob. It refused to open.

"Come on, open." She began to whimper as frustration and fear pushed her close to tears. She heard heavy footsteps coming down the hallway. She took a deep breath and tried again. This time she heard the portal click, opened the door, went into the passage, and clicked it shut as she heard her bedchamber door open with a loud bang.

Jackson jumped to the floor, ran under the bed, and hid in the farthest corner away from the doorway.

Lady Christine stood quietly in the dark, pressed her ear to the door, and listened to the footsteps within the bedchamber.

"Come on out, my lady. I have been waiting for this for a long time." Sir Harlan coaxed as he walked to the garderobe, searched, and found it empty. "The last time I was in this room, I had a nice chat with your father."

Lady Christine bit her lip and put her hand over her mouth. *I dare not make a sound*, she thought as she suppressed her anger, or was it fear. Her husband was correct. This man killed her father.

"It didn't last very long." Sir Harlan looked under the bed, but found only a scared cat. He was certain she went in the room, but perhaps he had the wrong bedchamber. He left to search another room, but when he stepped into the hallway saw Lord William standing at the top of the stairway with his sword drawn.

"Well, well, well. Lord William, I was just looking for your wife." Sir Harlan turned toward the Lord of Wildenham, touched the scar on the side of his face, and pulled his sword from its sheath.

Lord William looked toward the bedchamber and back to Sir Harlan. He was relieved his wife was absent from their quarters, but wondered where she may be.

"I doubt my wife would have much to do with the man who killed her father."

Sir Harlan snorted with a proud grin.

"I believe once I kill you, she won't have much choice." Sir Harlan charged forward and whipped his sword toward Lord William, who easily countered the attack.

Many in the Great Hall were distracted by the noise from above and looked up to the hallway at the battling warriors.

＊　　＊　　＊

Lady Christine thought she had heard her husband. It was difficult to understand what was being said, but the sound of clashing metal was easy to recognize and caused her to panic. *Is William fighting that madman?*

"Dear Lord, protect my husband." She prayed as she turned toward the portal of the secret chamber and felt in the dark for the opening. She searched for each rosette and pressed them in secession, turned the knob, and heard the door click open. She opened the door, entered, and closed it behind her. The room was pitch-black. She reached her hands out in front of her and walked cautiously until she touched the opposite wall. Lady Christine turned to the left and held onto the wall with her right hand while feeling with her left foot to find the stairway. She inched her way forward until her toes dipped downward at the edge of the step. Descending the stairway with caution, she reached the bottom and located the latch on the doorway. She lifted the latch and entered the closet. When she opened the closet door, she entered the kitchen. A few of the sleepy-eyed staff turned to look at her. She closed the door and went to the Great Hall. Everyone in the room was looking at the balcony. She turned her head toward the sound of clashing swords. Her father's robe fell open revealing her dainty chemise as she ascended the staircase and stepped into the hallway to witness her husband counter another slash of his opponent's sword. Both men looked tired and were breathing heavily.

Lord William charged Sir Harlan and their blades momentarily locked. The men used what little energy remained in their bodies as they resisted and pushed. Lord William's knees buckled, giving Sir Harlan the advantage.

Lady Christine's heart seemed to pause with fear, making everything move in slow motion.

"William!" She took a step toward her husband.

Hearing his wife's voice behind him, Lord William found the needed strength to push Sir Harlan backward until his opponent lost his balance and stumbled. Assured Sir Harlan would tumble to the floor, Lord William turned toward his wife to verify she was a great enough distance from the fight, but she came toward him.

"Get back!" He warned as he held out his unarmed left hand to push her away.

Sir Harlan had regained his balance and remained standing. His chest rose and fell rapidly. An evil grin grew on his face as the back of his opponent came into his line of sight. Sir Harlan's eyes narrowed. Determined to get what he wanted, he stood up straight and started toward Lord William with his sword swinging around from behind him in a large circle. He intended to strike his opponent at the base of his neck on his sword side and cut deeply.

Lady Christine looked past her husband toward the man in black and green and watched in horror.

His wife's widening eyes foretold of Sir Harlan's attack. For the second time in his life, Lord William knew he had made a deadly mistake, one that may cost him his life. He raised his sword over his right shoulder in an attempt to block the deadly strike.

Anticipating Sir Harlan's next move, Lady Christine ran, closing the distance between herself and her husband. She withdrew his dirk with her right hand, wrapped her left arm around his waist, and blindly thrust the weapon behind him toward Sir Harlan.

The dirk was jerked out of her hand as she felt her husband's arm wrap around her waist, pull her next to his body, and together they crouched down to the floor. She waited for the jarring impact of Sir Harlan's attack. The seconds seemed to tick by silently until a clang of metal upon stone echoed throughout the hallway.

Lord William and Lady Christine stood. Their eyes were drawn to the sword upon the floor. Sir Harlan staggered backward with the dirk protruding from the center of his chest. They watched as he bounced off the wall, fell to the floor, and gasped his last breath.

Lord William put his sword in its sheath and looked to his wife. He put his arm around her shoulders and pulled her close as she turned her face away from the bloody body and wrapped her arms around his waist. Tears pooled in her eyes. Her body began to tremble. She recalled her husband's advice and looked to his face.

"It's all a matter of timing." She replied innocently as she shrugged her shoulders.

Lord William looked upward to the ceiling and laughed. He returned his gaze to his wife and displayed a proud smile upon his face.

"Yes, it is all a matter of timing, and your timing was perfect." He complimented as he brushed a blonde curl from her face.

Lady Christine smiled in earnest as her husband kissed her on the forehead. Lord William looked down into his wife's eyes and touched the tip of his nose to her nose.

"But we are going to have to work on your listening skills." He scolded.

"I'm sure I will improve over time. After all, I have a great teacher." She assured.

"My lord, is all well?" Wilfred stepped into the hallway while holding a damp cloth to his forehead. He looked at the body on the floor.

The couple turned toward the steward.

"Yes, Wilfred, we are both fine." Lord William confirmed as he held his wife briefly. He needed to return to the village. He looked back to his wife.

"Perhaps Enid and Gilda could use your assistance while I go to the village." He suggested as he released her.

She took one last look at Sir Harlan's body and looked to her husband's face. She nodded her head in agreement, turned, and left to join the others in the Great Hall.

Lord William walked to Sir Harlan's body, pulled out his dirk, wiped it on the corpse, and replaced it in his sheath.

"I will see that this mess is taken care of while you tend to other matters," Wilfred said as Lord William approached. The steward removed the cloth and refolded it until an unsoiled portion was visible.

"Thank you." He noticed the blood trickling from the steward's forehead. "How is your head?"

"It's just a bump, my lord." Wilfred placed the cloth on the throbbing injury.

"Good. Could you see that a tailor is waiting in my old chamber when I return from the village? I need an article of clothing made for tonight."

"Yes, my lord." Wilfred turned his attention to assigning servants to remove the body and clean the hallway floor.

Lord William descended the staircase to the Great Hall. Several villagers were being treated for their injuries. He watched his wife wrap a boy's arm and approached her. He placed his palm on the small of her back and whispered into her ear.

"Christine, could you see that all within the room are made comfortable for the remainder of the night. I fear many will be homeless."

She looked into her husband's concerned face and nodded in acceptance of the responsibility.

"Thank you." He patted her back in appreciation.

As he went to the stable, Lord William passed more injured villagers who were making their way toward the Keep. He climbed atop Adair, returned to the village, and saw that much of the fire was reduced to smoldering embers. Men pulled down the last flaming rooftop. There were eight huts in all that suffered damage. Men continued to dump water on the steaming rubble to ensure the fire was extinguished.

Thomas led Sir Harlan and Sir Sheridan's horses as he approached Lord William.

"My lord, look what I found tied to a tree on the side of the road. They were acting crazy from the fire. I thought I would try to calm them down." Thomas stated proudly.

Lord William inspected the horses' saddles for weapons, but found none.

"Looks like you and Conal each own a horse, Thomas." Lord William proclaimed as he crossed his arms across his chest and grinned.

Thomas's mouth dropped open. His eyebrows arched in question.

"For me?"

Conal heard his name and went to his lord's side.

"And for me too?"

"Sure. Are the two of you willing to accept the responsibility of caring for them?"

"Yah!" The stableboys looked to one another and smiled.

"Then from now on we will no longer ride the slow little ponies!" Thomas said with a grin on his face that went from ear to ear. He placed his foot in the stirrup and tried to grab the horn, but fell short of reaching it. Lord William boosted the lad onto the top of his horse and then helped Conal atop his horse as well.

"You may have to use a bucket to help you climb atop until you grow some." Lord William advised.

"Thank you, my lord." The lads replied as they urged their horses forward and tested their steeds ability to rein and turn.

Lord William watched the young lads head toward the stable and let his eyes wander toward the Keep. *Perhaps my life as the Lord of Wildenham will be a pleasant one after all,* he thought as he recalled his wife's smiling face. He turned his attention back to the problem at hand, joined the men, and picked up a shovel to help ensure the embers had cooled.

Chapter 30

"My lady, perhaps you should return to bed. Enid and I can tend to the last few injuries," Gilda said as she continued to dress a little girl's arm.

"Yes, please go." Enid agreed.

Lady Christine looked around the Great Hall. With all of the injuries treated, those within the room seemed to be comfortable.

"Very well." She turned and made her way up the staircase to the bedchamber. She paused in the hallway and looked at the dampened spot on the floor. Her stomach fluttered. The corners of her mouth turned upward as she touched the spot on her forehead where her husband had kissed her affectionately. She opened the door to the bedchamber and discovered Jackson curled up on her side of the bed. She walked around to the feline and ran her hand along his silky body. Jackson lifted his head and looked at his mistress as she turned away and looked out the window. The sun peeking over the horizon announced the start of another day. *Could William still be in the village*, she wondered.

*   *   *

Rowena looked to the tree as she heard the flutter of wings. The owl had returned. She smiled for she knew all was as it should be. Lord William was safe. She would live the remainder of her days within her hut and administer to those who needed her remedies. Life had come full circle for the young Lord of Wildenham. She was happy for him.

*   *   *

Lord William tiptoed past their bedchamber door and made his way to his old chamber. When he opened the door and stepped into the room, several men stood and Wilfred turned to face him.

"My lord, this is our tailor, Angus. He is quite good with a needle and can design anything you wish." Wilfred introduced as the gray haired man bowed his head. "These are his assistants." The men bowed to their lord. The steward closed the door for privacy.

"It is a pleasure to meet all of you. Angus, I understand I am putting you and your men in a time constraint, but I need the tunic for tonight. I am looking for one that is appropriate for a special occasion," Lord William said as he shook the tailor's hand.

"It is our pleasure, my lord. I believe we are capable of making something that will fit your needs." The tailor replied.

"I took the liberty to have a basin, soap, and linen for you to freshen yourself." Wilfred motioned to the items on the nightstand.

"Thank you." Lord William stripped off his dirty black tunic and began to wash his face, arms, and chest.

Many of the men were surprised by the number of scars upon their lord's back. They remained respectfully silent.

Lord William rinsed the soap away from his face and picked up a cloth to dry himself.

Angus took his place in the center of the floor. Lord William stood before him. Men began measuring and rolling out material to cut.

Wilfred seemed lost in thought as he continued to stare at the scars on his lord's back. It reminded him of a child he knew many years ago, but then again, many men had scars.

"Wilfred, we must devise a wicked plan to pull this off. I am counting on you to supervise the details and above all, keep it a secret from my wife," Lord William said over his shoulder to the steward while someone lifted his arm and measured.

Hearing his name called, the steward realized he was being addressed.

"You can count on me, my lord. What do you have in mind?"

*   *   *

Lady Christine was torn between beginning her day and crawling back into bed. She turned away from the window to see Jackson on the floor arching his back and stretching. He sat and looked up to his mistress's face and tilted his head to one side.

Lady Christine gave the feline a few affectionate pats on the top of his head before picking him up.

"You had a pretty traumatic night, didn't you?"

Jackson began to purr while she continued to stroke his silky fur.

She kissed him on the head, set him on the bed, and walked to the fireplace. She picked up the poker, stoked the embers, and placed a few logs upon them to take the dampness from the air.

There was a knock upon her bedchamber door.

"Enter," Lady Christine said as she set the poker on the hook. As the door opened, Enid and Gilda entered the room.

"Happy Birthday, my lady." Gilda greeted.

"My, I have forgotten. It is my birthday," Lady Christine said as she found it difficult to believe she had lost track of the date. *How I wish father was here to celebrate it with me*, she thought.

"My goodness, anyone would forget after the night we experienced." Enid yawned and covered her mouth with her hand.

"Those poor people in the Great Hall, so many of them hurt." Gilda commented as a servant entered the bedchamber carrying her lord and lady's breakfast.

"Has Lord William returned? I hoped we would have our morning meal together," Lady Christine said as she watched the servant set the tray upon the table.

"I have yet to see him, my lady." Enid stated as she stepped toward the bed and set the lord's pillow aside.

Gilda picked up Jackson and set him on the floor. The ladies pulled the sheets toward the head of the bed and straighten out the wrinkles.

"Will you be practicing today, my lady?" Enid inquired as she fluffed a pillow.

"I doubt it. I assume my husband will need to focus his attention on the village most of the day." Lady Christine sat at the table and stared at the vacant spot across from her.

"I shall set out a dress for you to wear," Enid said as she left the bedchamber and nearly bumped into Lord William.

"Oh! Pardon me, my lord." She sidestepped Lord William as she passed through the doorway.

Hearing his name, Lady Christine looked toward the door to see her husband enter the room. He carried his black tunic in his hand and looked as if he had washed.

"Well, if you will excuse me, I shall help Enid," Gilda excused herself, left the bedchamber, and closed the door behind her.

"Breakfast has arrived." Lady Christine admired her husband's muscular chest.

"Excellent, I'm famished." He tossed his soiled tunic onto the chest at the end of the bed, sat across from her, and helped himself to a hard cooked egg.

Lady Christine watched him devour the egg in two bites before she helped herself to one as well.

"Will you be working in the village today?" She posed the question even though she anticipated the answer.

Lord William washed the dry egg down with a gulp of ale.

"Yes, there is much to do. I need to relocate those in the Great Hall and see what we can salvage from their homes." Lord William broke off a chunk of bread, smeared it with fresh butter, and took a hearty bite. He looked to his wife, whose eyes were downcast to her plate.

"Are you well?"

With her husband's voice resonating with genuine concern, Lady Christine looked up at his face.

"I am well, perhaps a little tired." She confessed.

"Rest for today. Go back to bed, read, or do needlework." Lord William suggested as he reached across the table and touched her hand.

"I have little patience for needlework." She replied numbly in reaction to the softness of his touch.

"I would imagine Enid and Gilda could demonstrate a few stitches." He removed his hand from hers and helped himself to a sweet cake.

"I will ask them to do so." She took another small bite of her egg.

Lord William emptied his tankard and rose. He donned a clean black tunic. Returning to the table, he grabbed some cheese and bread.

"My dear, I must go. I will see you at the evening meal." He bent down and kissed her cheek. "I will be eager to see your needlework creation." He raised his eyebrows teasingly and headed toward the bedchamber door.

So much for our quiet breakfast together. She sighed and ate a bit of meat. *He forgot to wish me a happy birthday.* She looked down at the floor where Jackson sat with his chubby face staring at her.

"Here you go." She tossed a chunk of meat onto the floor. Jackson sniffed it before swallowing it whole.

Lord William closed the door and was met in the hallway by Wilfred, Enid, and Gilda.

"My lord, everything is set." Wilfred assured in a whisper.

"We shall do our best," Enid said quietly. Gilda nodded her head in agreement.

"Thank you," Lord William said as he turned to leave. He had much to accomplish today, as did everyone else.

*   *   *

Lady Christine pushed the tray of food away, crossed her arms over her chest, and looked to the closed door. She sighed and wondered how she would spend her day, but soon heard a knock.

"Enter." She stated glumly.

Enid and Gilda stepped into the room.

"I see you have finished your meal. Shall we get you ready for the day?" Enid suggested.

"Very well." Lady Christine rose and went to her bedchamber. With the assistance of her ladies, she dressed in a simple forest green gown trimmed with gold.

"What are your plans for today, my lady?" Gilda inquired.

"My husband would like me to learn the fine art of needlework." She conveyed unenthusiastically.

"Oh, we would be delighted to instruct you." Enid was eager to comply with the request as she and Gilda gathered the materials. They demonstrated an easy stitch to their lady.

Lady Christine looked out the window often as she had little interest in stitching. Wanting to meet her husband's expectations, she continued to work on a simple pattern as the three women spent the day in the bedchamber.

To ensure Lady Christine remained in her room, Wilfred had the midday meal brought to her bedchamber while she stitched.

"Needlework is a slow and tedious process," Lady Christine said as she untangled a knot in her thread.

"Yes, but I also find it relaxing and creative." Enid commented as she made another stitch.

A loud metallic bang in the hallway startled the ladies.

"What is going on?" Lady Christine set aside her needlework and rose from her seat.

Enid and Gilda exchanged an alarming look, tossed their sewing projects to the floor, and ran for the door.

Lady Christine opened the bedchamber door before her ladies could stop her. She saw Wilfred supervising servants who carried a brass tub while several others hauled buckets of water.

"Who has requested a bath?" She inquired.

Wilfred turned to see Lady Christine in the doorway.

"My lady, I am sorry to disturb you. The bath is for a guest," he said.

"What guest? I was unaware we had a guest."

"I do not know his name, but I assure you, he will introduce himself to you at the evening meal." He hoped the tidbit of information would suffice her curiosity.

"My lady, let us return to our needlework." Enid suggested as she tried to coax Lady Christine back into the room.

"Yes, my lady. I think your project is coming along quite nicely. I am certain Lord William will be proud of your accomplishment," Gilda said.

Lady Christine returned to the window seat and picked up her needlework. Enid and Wilfred exchanged a look of relief before the bedchamber door was shut.

Gilda stoked the fire, returned to her chair, and watched Lady Christine pull the needle through the linen. She dared to broach the subject of her lady's evening attire.

"My lady, have you decided what gown you will wear for the evening meal?"

"I do not care what I wear. Changing my clothes for the evening meal seems so mundane." Lady Christine commented as she concentrated on her next stitch and poked the needle into the cloth.

"May I make a suggestion then?" Gilda pressed forward.

"By all means. You know I value your opinion."

"My lady, since you are already married and will never use the dress for its intention, I believe it would be appropriate for you to wear your wedding dress. It can't stay hidden away forever." Gilda suggested.

"Yes, and we shall do your hair with ribbons and flowers." Enid added as she stood next to Gilda.

"You will be so beautiful in your gown that you will take Lord William's breath away." Gilda set her sewing down and went to retrieve the dress.

Lady Christine looked up from her needlework and stared at Enid and then at Gilda, who was pulling the dress from the chest. Holding it by the shoulders, Gilda turned around, fluffed the skirt, and displayed it for her mistress.

"He thinks I'm only beautiful when I am wearing a gown?" She whispered as she stood.

Enid elbowed Gilda in the ribs.

"My lady, I did not say that. You are the most stunning of

women. It matters not what you wear. Surely, he loves you more and more each day you are together." Gilda insisted.

Lady Christine thought she and her husband had come to a mutual agreement. They had grown closer over time. They had even deepened their affection toward one another. Maybe it was her imagination, or maybe she was the only one who was in love. She recalled his kisses and how they filled her heart with happiness and his touch that was so tender and caring. Was she misreading his intentions? She was determined to find out.

"I think that is an excellent idea, Gilda. Let's take his breath away." She agreed as she joined her ladies, picked up the edge of the skirt, and admired its beauty.

*   *   *

Lord William entered the Keep. He dodged busy servants as he went to the kitchen, entered the closet, and shut the door behind him. He made his way to the tiny chamber. He picked up his father's sword where it lay upon the desk, retrieved the box containing his mother's ring, and placed it in his belt bag. Returning to the kitchen, he spotted Wilfred directing the preparations for the evening meal. Lord William stepped behind the steward.

"Wilfred, could you have someone clean and polish this?" Lord William requested.

The steward turned around to face his lord and accepted the sword shoved into his hand.

"Please have it brought to me when finished. I will be in the chamber preparing for this evening," Lord William instructed as he waited for the steward's acknowledgment.

Wilfred looked at the sword, then to Lord William's face, and then back to the sword.

"My Lord, this is the Sword of Wildenham." Wilfred looked back to his lord for an explanation.

"Yes, it is."

"Where did you get it?"

"My father hid it where he knew I would find it."

The steward recalled the scars on his lord's back.

"William, young William?" Wilfred was in disbelief. "You have returned?"

"Yes, as fate would have it."

"You have changed so over the years. Forgive me for not recognizing you." The steward apologized. "I will have this cleaned and brought to you post haste." Wilfred smiled.

"Thank you," Lord William said as he left the kitchen.

For the second time that day, Lord William tiptoed past his wife's bedchamber and returned to the chamber where he submerged into a tub of hot water and bathed. He tried to relax, but anxious thoughts of the evening forced him to leave his bath and dry off. He donned a clean pair of breeches. He sat on the bench as a knock sounded upon the door.

"Enter," Lord William said as he slipped on his boots.

"Here is your tunic, my lord." Angus announced as he presented the garment.

"Excellent." Lord William pulled it over his head.

Angus straightened the garment and scrutinized it for any last minute adjustments, but there was none. The garment fitted perfectly.

"Well done, Angus." Lord William complimented.

"Thank you, my lord."

"Do you think my wife will be surprised?"

"Yes, I believe she will be." Angus nodded and left the room.

A servant knocked upon the door, entered, and presented him with the Sword of Wildenham that sparkled anew. Lord William attached the Sword of Wildenham upon his belt and Wilfred entered the room.

"We are ready, my lord." The steward announced.

Lord William exhaled and straightened his tunic one last time.

"Thank you, Wilfred, for all that you have done."

"You are more than welcome, my lord."

They walked down the hallway and passed Lady Christine's bedchamber. Wilfred stopped at the top of the staircase. He waited for Lord William to descend and take his place at the bottom. Lord William nodded his head indicating he was ready. Wilfred went to Lady Christine's bedchamber and knocked.

"My lady, the evening meal is ready." He announced.

Enid opened the bedchamber door. Lady Christine stood before the steward in the most beautiful gown he had ever seen.

"My lady, you look lovely."

Lady Christine blushed as she placed both hands to her sides and lifted the full ivory skirt with pride. Enid and Gilda had taken special care to braid her long blonde hair into a soft, dainty, sophisticated pattern and added ivory ribbon and flowers as embellishments. The bodice fit tightly to her petite body with its dipping neckline trimmed with delicate lace that also draped over each shoulder. Beading and pearls embellished the entire dress.

"Thank you, Wilfred."

Lady Christine stepped into the hallway and walked toward the Great Hall. With the room usually filled with people for an evening meal, she thought it strange to hear quiet whispers echoing from below. As she came to the balcony, she stopped and caught her breath, for as she looked down into the hall, everyone was standing and looking at her. The room was decorated with flowers and greenery. Table cloths adorned every table. The candles were aglow. She looked over the railing and saw her husband at the bottom of the stairs. She walked to the top of the staircase and paused. He was looking up at her and smiling. Lady Christine descended and stopped before her husband. She stared at his clothing.

"Your tunic is blue." She touched the fine fabric. "You're wearing blue." She smiled before looking up to her husband's eyes.

"I thought you would like it." He replied, looking down at her. "Happy Birthday." He wiped his hands along his tunic in order to take away the clammy perspiration. "My darling wife, you are beautiful, simply stunning."

"Thank you." Lady Christine looked to the floor as her face reddened and she realized those in attendance could hear her husband's every word.

Lord William took her right hand within his and lifted it to his lips. He placed a gentle kiss upon the back of her hand and looked into her eyes.

"I know when we wed that neither of us did so by choice.

We married because it was necessary. Fate brought us together. Tonight, I am reaffirming fate's decision. I would like to give you the opportunity to do the same, for I believe both husband and wife should be willing partners in a marriage."

Lady Christine looked at her husband a little puzzled.

"What are you trying to say?" Her voice cracked and quivered.

Lord William took a step backward and knelt down upon one knee.

"Will you marry me, again?"

Everyone in the hall remained silent as they waited for their lady's reply.

Lady Christine looked into his hazel eyes with the sparkling gold flecks. Perhaps fate had thrown them together, but the man who knelt before her, asking for her heart, was a man worthy of her love. Above all, he was man she could trust. He was giving her a choice to be his partner in life, a partner she always hoped to find. He was giving her the wedding she had dreamed of since she was a little girl. She stood before him in her beautiful gown with the Great Hall decorated in celebration and received a proper proposal from a handsome man who was strong, kind, thoughtful, and above all, trustworthy. She knew his heart to be true. Her eyes began to well with tears.

"Yes." She said as a tear escaped her eye and rolled down her cheek.

Lord William stood and placed her right hand on the top of his left. He took his right thumb and brushed a tear away from her cheek. The couple turned and walked down the aisle between the tables toward Father Frederick, who had entered from the hallway and took his place before the High Table. Corvus sat perched upon his master's chair. Jackson sat rudely upon the table near his mistress's chair. They watched as their lord and lady walked toward them.

Chapter 31

As the Lord and Lady of Wildenham stood before Father Frederick, their guests sat on the benches. The kitchen staff stepped into the room and stood along the back wall to observe the ceremony.

"Friends, we gather here today to honor our lord and lady and celebrate their commitment to each other. I would normally ask if there is anyone who is against this couple joining, to speak now. However, these two have already been joined." Father Frederick jested.

Those within the Great Hall chuckled.

"So we shall go directly to the vows. Lord William, do you promise to love and honor your wife all the days of your life?"

Lord William turned to his wife and held both of her hands within his.

"I do," he said with confidence. He tried to remain serious, but a smile grew upon his face.

"Lady Christine, do you promise to love and honor your husband all the days of your life?"

Lady Christine smiled. The man standing before her was truly worthy of her heart. He was the companion she had hoped to find and one she could trust. She was happy and in love.

"I do."

Lord William released her hands, reached into his belt bag, and withdrew his mother's ring.

Lady Christine looked down as he slipped the ring onto her finger. She recognized it instantly. It was the very same ring his mother was wearing in the portrait. She met his questioning eyes with a smile of approval.

"By the power invested in me by the Lord our God, I now pronounce you husband and wife, again." Father Frederick announced.

Lord William turned to his wife, gently cupped her face within his right hand, looked into her eyes as he bent down toward her lips, and kissed her.

Lady Christine put her arms around her husband's neck, pulled him close, and kissed him deeply. Surprised by her passion, Lord William wrapped his arms around her waist, picked her up, and spun around in several circles.

Many onlookers laughed and applauded as they watched their lord stop and set his wife gently upon the floor. Father Frederick escorted the couple to their chairs at the High Table. Lord William pulled out his wife's chair and helped her to sit, and then took his rightful place to her left.

In honor of the couple, Sir Gunther, Sir Farrell, Enid, Gilda, Father Frederick, and Wilfred seated themselves with the guests on the benches. Servants carried trays of meat, vegetables, breads, and fruit to each table. Several pitchers of ale and spiced wine dotted each table as well. When all held a full tankard, the servers sat at an empty table at the back of the room, filled their mugs, and joined the celebration. Sir Farrell stood and those in attendance did the same. They raised their tankards toward the Lord and Lady of Wildenham.

"My lord, my lady, may your lives be long, your hearts stay true, and your reign be grand!" Sir Farrell toasted for all to hear.

Good wishes and cheers came from the crowd.

"Hear! Hear!"

"Huzzah!"

All returned to their seats, and Lord William rose.

"I would like to thank all of those who were involved in making our celebration special." He lifted his tankard toward several in the crowd and made sure to seek out Wilfred and salute him. "To my dear wife, happy birthday." He lifted his tankard in her direction as well.

Cheers and good wishes echoed within the hall.

As Lord William returned to his seat, he looked to the balcony and saw his father leaning on the railing with a smile upon his face. The Lord of Wildenham raised his tankard as if toasting to the apparition. The image broke into many miniscule pieces and dissipated. The air became lighter and easier to breathe. *Perhaps my father's spirit is finally at rest,* he thought.

Lady Christine turned to her husband.

"This was your idea?" She recalled the deliberate isolation within her bedchamber throughout the day and looked toward Enid, Gilda, and Wilfred.

"Yes. Many helped with the preparations," he said as he lifted her left hand toward his mouth and kissed it. "I care for you deeply, Christine, and I want you to be happy. Perhaps we needed to start over, from the beginning, and what better way to do that than to get married properly?"

"I am honored by your gift," she said as she held her hand out with her fingers fanned to admire the ring. The amethyst and diamonds sparkled in the candlelight.

"It belonged to my mother." He replied.

"I recognized it from the portrait. It is lovely, and I shall treasure it always." She looked into his eyes to convey her gratitude. "Thank you for the wedding, William. It was very thoughtful of you."

"You're welcome."

"But what would you have done if I would have said 'no'?" She arched a devilish eyebrow.

"Well, that would have put a damper on the celebration. However, since we are legally husband and wife, your answer would have been moot. I thank you for becoming my wife, again, and saving me the embarrassment." He brushed the knuckle of his index finger on the side of her cheek. "I think you and I are going to do just fine."

She looked into his eyes.

"I think so too." She held her tankard up toward her husband. He touched his tankard to hers. They smiled and drank a toast to themselves as the merriment within the Great Hall resonated throughout the kingdom of Wildenham.